Tolstoy's Beard

Susana Cory-Wright

ISBN: 9798848554212

ACKNOWLEDGMENTS

As ever, *Tolstoy's Beard* is for my children, Emma, James and Maximilian

For Jonathan, whose love and support is unfailing

And in memory of my father Alfonso Torrents dels Prats, who, even when dying, would ask 'qué tal la barba de Tolstoy?'

Well, here it is.

Author's Note

While one of Russia's greatest writers Lev Tolstoy and the equally famous Ukrainian artist Ilya Repin really existed, the story that unfolds in this novel did not. I have taken considerable poetic license in suggesting any kind of violence in the Tolstoy household or impropriety in the Repin one. Repin and Tolstoy enjoyed a long, close friendship that endured despite an age difference of sixteen years and severe ideological differences. Repin would paint over twenty portraits of the writer and it is due to these portraits that his iconic image has survived today.

As is so often the case, great men subsume the characters of even greater women. Sophia Tolstaya was a cultured, intelligent woman who longed for the very society her husband shunned, but her life was dedicated to the literary genius she had married. It is thanks to her diaries that her interior life is known to posterity. She remains, to my mind, one of the greatest unsung heroines of all time.

The character of Arkady is pure fantasy.

Tatyana Tolstaya, Lev and Sophia's eldest daughter, was a painter and memoirist. She was director of the Tolstoy museum in Moscow before emigrating to Paris. She was painted (and taught) by Repin but the romantic relationship described here is completely imagined.

I am grateful to Leah Bendavid-Val's superb book *Song Without Words The photographs & Diaries of Countess Sophia Tolstoy* from which I have drawn endless inspiration.

And finally, since writing this, we have entered into a bleak time with the invasion of Ukraine. However, it would be even more bleak if we refrained from reading the great Russian writers, listening to their music or viewing their art. Or anything pertaining to that country and culture.

Ultimately, this is a story of marital strife, of family life, of young love and the age-long conundrum voiced as far back as Diderot-namely how to balance good parenting with a chosen career. These questions transcend political discord or military aggression.

It might be said that I have chosen the very worst of times to publish this book. Or the very best.

'All happy families resemble one another; every unhappy family is unhappy in its own way.'

Lev Tolstoy, *Anna Karenina*

Tolstoy's Beard

1

Playing ball with an orange sun as it dipped behind skinny birch trees, our troika flew through the snow. "Faster!" we shrieked as if the Cossack could possibly outrun a star. His whip cackled through the air, a live dangerous thing. Already, all memory of the arduous train journey, the soot that lay as a second skin on our faces and clothes, the watery tea and inadequate dried pelmeni, was being eroded by the excitement of arriving in a new place. Even Sergei who would never admit to enjoying anything as mundane as a simple sleigh ride, took quick, jerky puffs on a cigarette. Mother, who normally scolds him for smoking in front of Masha (I don't seem to count being sixteen), was too busy directing the driver to pay attention. Too busy and too animated. I looked at her closely. She could scarcely keep still, bobbing up and down, those famous agate eyes of hers bright in her flushed face.

Yes, there was definitely a change. Even the day before, as we set out on our adventure, she had displayed none of her usual impatience. With exquisite stoicism she had waited for Masha (a slow eater) to finish breakfast while all the time listening to Olga Feodova's litany of woes. Mostly to do with the horrors of a big city. That old witch had been our father's nanny when he was a child and was the most pessimistic person I had ever met, which was saying something given the nature of the Slavic soul. The fact that we eventually left some two hours after our mother had said that we must a-b-s-olutley be ready, seemed only to add to her good humour. It was a humour however, that was not without limit. While indulging Sergei's request to stop off in the village to say goodbye to his lady friend, despite the horses stomping the ground impatiently, it did not extend to lending me her new sable hood.

Twenty years ago, our father had promised our mother that one day they would return to Moscow. But it was not a promise lightly made, and Mother knew what a sacrifice it would be to leave his beloved country home. Yasnaya Polyana was ours too, of course, but it was also isolated and far from the cultural delights of a city. And so, to find us a suitable place to live, Papa had gone on ahead of us and we hadn't seen him in several months. The journey, therefore, elicited various degrees of apprehension in us all. Together with the sharp slicing of sledge runners, bells tinkled delicately as if announcing our arrival to the world, to this new beginning. The horses snorted, pounding their feet along the crusty snow, their breath leaving a trail behind them. Masha and I huddled together under fur rugs, whispering stories to each other.

"Just imagine!" Mama was saying dreamily. She had calmed down a little and was now happily ensconced against a velvet bolster, seemingly oblivious of the icy wind. "Ballet at the Bolshoi, concertos at the Conservatoire, not to mention Art! Do you know we might even have a chance to view Pavel Tretyakov's collection? Rumour has it that this M. Pavel is progressive. He's not intent on keeping his acquisitions for friends and family alone but wants to build a gallery so that the general public might have a chance to see them too. He must be the kindest of men! And books of course!"

Sergei raised an eyebrow at that. He didn't have to say that for obvious reasons, the gift of books (or anything to do with them) was like 'taking a samovar to Tula.' If we had lived in Newcastle, taking coals there would have meant the same thing. Tula–the closest town to our estate–being where samovars were produced.

But Mother wasn't finished. "The glorious convent at Novdevichy," she breathed. "And oh, how could I forget! The church of Christ the Saviour!"

"It doesn't look like Moscow," said Sergei throwing his cigarette butt over the side of the sledge as the horses slowed to a trot. I followed the glow of ash as it spun through the air before fizzing on the snow. He was right, the driver had veered into a wood that looked for all the world exactly like the one we'd just left. The sprawling wooden house glimpsed through the trees was ablaze with light (candles and lanterns we soon discovered, not electricity) and very like the peasant dwellings on our country estate. I had to agree with my brother. Was this really what all the fuss had been about?

Our mother leapt to her feet. "Doesn't it?" she said shrilly. "What do you mean, it doesn't?"

"For God's sake Mama, sit down! We haven't stopped."

Our mother lurched forward steadying herself on Sergei's shoulder as her long cloak became entangled with our feet. Masha yanked the rug to her side. I pulled it back.

"Oh, I can see better now," she said, her relief palpable. "It's *completely* different! He's done it! I can't believe he's actually done it! Just look at the trouble he's taken!"

Her voice continued to rise joyfully, buoyed by the incredulous notion that our father had listened at last. *I* found it incredulous that she appeared not to notice the similarity with home. Actually, our new house was not just similar to the peasant houses at Yasnaya Polyana it *was* the peasant house. Or houses. And I could tell because the balustrade around the verandah had the same, distinctive lattice effect. The paper chain relief of horses and doll-like figures had delighted us as children. I tried to catch mother's eye, but she was transfixed. Later, we learned that Papa had simply transported three suitable peasant cottages from Yasnaya, complete with potted plants and outside railings. They had been rebuilt in the city and knocked together to form a single dwelling. As far as I understood it, we would live in the exact same house, in an exact same wood, just in another district.

But Mama's smile split her face. It was a moment before I registered its importance. Perhaps now, our parents would be happy. I reached for Masha's hand as her chubby little fingers laced themselves through mine. The horses slowed to a walk as we approached an avenue of widely spaced trees. Their coats were shiny with sweat as they tossed their heads, emitting loud snorts and puffs of foul-smelling breath. Above them, snow crystals cartwheeled through the air, a miniature milky way before sticking to the trees, twisting round the bark like giant peppermint sticks.

The sledge came to an abrupt stop in the open courtyard around which the cottages from Yasnaya had been reconstructed. Along one side was the pretty verandah now sporting a new green roof supported by oak pillars. Stone steps led up to the main entrance which had a pink door, and a heart fashioned from corn husks was attached to the knocker. Garden lights flickering in the distance lit the way to a small pavilion. In the spring, there would be an abundance of fruit trees (just like at Yasnaya) but now the orchard doubled as a skating rink.

"He's thought of everything," said our mother in wonder.

"Except that you couldn't really call this the city," complained Sergei grumpily. He wiped snow from his boot. "It's Khamovniki. I don't see much night life going on here."

"Khamovniki is still Moscow," insisted Mama dreamily. "You'll soon see that it's not far. And if your father…" her voice trailed.

The driver having tied the horses to a metal ring on one of the wooden stumps by the gate, unhooked a lantern. Swinging it high over the sledge, he helped Mama extricate herself from the heap of furs. Behind him, a black shadow momentarily plunged us into darkness. I squinted but the man's figure was still hidden and only his palm held skyward, pale and luminescent gradually became visible. It was as if the house was the favour to be found in a Fabergé egg, and he was presenting it to her.

"Countess," said Papa emerging into the light.

I thought he sounded nervous. I held my breath willing Mama to smile the way she had done only minutes before. I looked from one to the other. Do it! I wanted to say! Just smile! But she couldn't or wouldn't. Instead, she nodded tersely and whatever precious moment that had spun precariously between them dissipated in her eagerness to explore.

14

She dropped gracefully onto the snow and we tumbled out behind her, squabbling as we pushed against her, fighting for the lower step. Squatting on the snow beneath the lanterns were peasants I recognised from the estate. To the right of the front door and through the windows, the dining room shimmered in a light of its own. Mirrors reflected sparkling cut glass, mother's porcelain with its embossed coat of arms and confectionary in rainbow colours, dusted with icing sugar–all designed to be as inviting as possible and welcoming us to an early supper. But what I hoped Mama hadn't noticed, was that wooden utensils replaced her precious silver. Fluttering cobwebs of unease quivered in my stomach.

"Happy Saint's Day Tanya," Papa whispered in my ear and I whirled round to see a bearded man I hardly recognized. He wore a peasant's smock and odd-shaped boots. I flung my arms around him as much out of relief as love and he hugged me tightly, the new beard tickling my cheek.

"Lyovushka!" Mama said as though at last remembering why we were here. I didn't mind at all when my father pushed me gently aside.

"Sonyetka," he smiled tenderly, touching her face.

"You are well?" he asked in Russian.

"*Très bien,*" she replied and for a moment that all too familiar cloud passed over his face but happily did not stay there.

I let out my breath not realizing that until then I had been holding it in. Just for once, let us be happy, I prayed. On my name day, let us be happy.

For a moment, Papa gripped our mother's arms tightly, his fingers disappearing completely in the rich velvet of her sleeves, under her cloak. There was a flash of inner struggle and then Sergei, stubbing out another hastily smoked cigarette caught his attention. His lips lingered for a moment on Mama's cheek which had flushed under his touch.

"But *this* is a *seigneur* if I ever saw one!" he said picking at the exquisite fabric of Sergei's coat. His gaze flickered to the highly polished boots, the silk cravat, the beautiful cashmere trousers. Colour shot through Sergei's face as my brother pushed away Papa's hands. But Papa only pressed Sergei's shoulder all the harder.

"I am dressed like a peasant and live in the city, but you–*you* my boy are dressed like a gentleman and come from the country!"

His face was animated, crinkling all over with amusement. It was a long time since I'd seen him so at ease and my own mouth twitched in response. He scanned our faces, his usually hooded eyes bright with curiosity while he searched for some appreciation of his wit. After a few seconds however, the lids closed over and seeing no reaction, he shook his head, held up his hands in mock horror and chuckled to himself all the way indoors. I hoped it was time to go in ourselves. The bright sun had long sunk behind the birches and Masha's breath was coming out in balloons of white air. I could no longer feel the tips of my toes.

"Bastard!" Sergei muttered after him, immediately delving into his pockets for another cigarette. Mama put her hand in the same pocket and for a second or two they wrestled until my brother withdrew his in frustration together with the striped silk lining.

"Not now, Seryozha, let it be."

Sergei ran his hand over his head. He looked faintly ridiculous with his pockets inside out and his typically smooth hair now kinked and sprinkled with snow.

"That's what you always say! Why do you defend him? There's always some excuse. He–" Sergei spat the words. "He's always too busy, too tired, too awake, too God only knows, too *disturbed*!"

Mama tried to catch hold of his sleeve, but he threw up his arm in a wide upwards circle almost cuffing a passing servant. It was bitterly cold and the initial excitement that had kept us warm had worn off. It was also surprisingly quiet–as quiet as Yasnaya Polyana and just as dark. I had expected the city to be somehow more alive, to hear other horses and sledges and carriages. The shadows filling the space between the trees and the house were dense and mysterious. I began to imagine all sorts of strange creatures and when an owl hooted, I took a step closer beside my brother.

"Do you think there are wolves in Moscow?" I said daring to touch his arm.

"*What* are you talking about?"

Sergei brushed me off him as if I were a flee. I looked longingly towards the house, but no one seemed in the least hurry to go inside. Masha buried her face in the delicious fur of Mama's cloak much as I longed to. Mama held my sister close to her, fondling her head absent-mindedly. Slowly, they began to walk as though roped together in a three-legged race. Sergei began to pace, his hands behind his back.

"That's simply not true Seryozha. You know what a great man your father is."

"I know what a first-class fool looks like."

Mama sighed. "We wouldn't be here if it weren't for your father."

"Exactly." Sergei pulled up his coat collar so that it dwarfed his chin. His eyes flashed defiantly as he sucked in his cheeks.

"Given the choice I'd be tucked up with Kitty. And I'd be warm. You remember what that's like Mama, do you? That particular warmth?"

He smacked one beautifully crafted riding boot against the other and snorted noisily just as the horses had done earlier. Our mother's face drained of the colour Papa had put there and her eyes ignited with that flash of anger we were especially alert to.

"Given a choice, we'd be in Moscow. I mean properly in Moscow. Who has even heard of Khamovniki? What on earth was the point of moving if it's just to another Yasnaya?"

"I think your father has chosen very well and I'm glad it's familiar," said our mother somewhat primly. "I think it's particularly touching. He must have worried so much that we'd be homesick."

"Homesick!" Sergei spat tobacco from his tongue. "I've never seen a place more identical to home in my life! I thought the whole idea was to be in a city. You've been going on about it long enough. Christ, it's just as freezing too."

17

"Well, we're not," snapped our mother. "We're here and we're together." She uttered the words through thin lips, and I wondered why she didn't pretend just a little, to mean them. I willed Masha to look up so that I could communicate with her, however silently, but my sister wasn't budging.

"I've waited a long time for this. We all have. Don't spoil it now. Look, I know you're disappointed."

Our mother tried a different approach although I knew from experience, that just one more complaint from our brother and she would storm off. Her eyes brimmed. No one could ever resist our mother's tears.

"I know my darling, how keenly you feel Papa's sarcasm. It can sting like strips of flesh being torn away."

Sergei looked at her. "Don't be melodramatic. It's not that bad."

"There!" Instantly her eyes cleared and the lilt in Mama's voice was enchanting. "You see how really it isn't!"

Mama moved closer to our brother with the limpet Masha still clinging to her leg. This time Sergei did not recoil from her but bowed his head sheepishly. My stomach began to rumble in earnest and my fingers were prickly with cold. I wanted to reach through the windows, into the dining room and grab fistfuls of cake.

"Let's go into the house then, Seryozha."

At last! Mama's admiration for our father's work seemed to have made her impervious to the inclement weather. I fluttered my eyelashes frantically in agreement.

"We haven't been inside yet. You might even like it." She smiled at her first born and best beloved. "I will speak to your father. You will have more freedom here, I promise, and you may have a horse immediately. And..." I could see her take an emotional deep breath before promising rashly, "you may have my sleigh when I'm not using it." Another shaky intake. "You might even take the train to... Tula."

Their eyes met. She didn't have to add, "to see Kitty." Sergei drew back his shoulders, straightening his back so that he towered over her. Once again, he was every inch the young lover, not the errant schoolboy.

18

"I apologize Mama," he said flashing his charismatic simile.

Sergei was always good at apologizing. Our mother considered this to be evidence of an inherent good nature, our father, that practice made perfect.

"I didn't know what to expect. I–I just had a different picture in my head."

"We all have different pictures," said our mother. "The trick is not to let one image become too fixed. You have to be able to reshape them occasionally."

Masha emerged from the folds of Mama's fur, her face flushed and warm. Mine felt even more pinched and numb. She stuck out her tongue. I was too cold to retaliate.

"Is that what you do?" Sergei held out his arm to our mother who accepted graciously pulling the limpet alongside. I followed behind making faces at their backs.

Mama's voice was low and modulated–the voice of a woman at the height of her beauty, well aware of her allure, the aura of mystery that would always follow her.

"All the time," she said.

2

Exploring the house, we did delight in what we found–Sergei too–I hoped. The wide, carpeted staircase led to first-floor reception rooms which were light and airy. Papa had made every effort to furnish that shared living area as comfortably as possible. In contrast, his study was tucked away in one of the many attics. The ceiling there was so low that I could touch it without standing on tiptoe. Papa had two desks: an enormous bureau with its border of tiny chiselled columns, placed in the middle of the room and a tall, narrow writing table by the window. At night, he allowed himself a single candle. He worked incessantly and when he had pins and needles in his legs, he moved to the table to write standing up.

Making every effort to disguise the fact that we might have been in his study, Masha and I chased each other through the interconnecting rooms to the floor below. We tried to sneak into Sergei's bedroom for a peak, but he kept his door bolted and when we knocked, he shouted at us to go away. Giggling, we crept from room to room, marvelling at the opulence of their decor. Papa, we knew, would have preferred to live modestly. As with our country house, there was no electricity or plumbing.

In high spirits and ravenous with hunger, Masha and I slid down the gleaming banisters, our skirts tucked into our knickers. Here at least, there would be no Olga Feodova to wag her bony finger at us, logging our every misdemeanour like a Russian Madame Defarge. Laughing, we careered into the large but cosy dining room where unusually, everyone seemed to be talking at once.

We all tried our very best to make this first supper in our new home as jolly as possible. And to my relief, Mama didn't comment on the wooden utensils nor at the news that Papa, in our absence, had renounced eating meat to become a vegetarian. There was borscht (an obvious choice) for those wishing to follow his example. Masha immediately launched twenty questions on the subject. Mama's jaw clenched as if masticating a reply into tiny pieces before it choked her. And she did almost choke; afterwards she said it was because candlelight made it almost impossible to see what we were eating, but at the time, the shrill and tiny bird that shot out from the newly purchased cuckoo clock made us all jump.

"Come Tanya," said Papa when our mother had retired to her new bedroom and the limpet was asleep and he and I had been playing chess, a game that he loved but later repudiated as being too aggressive. "I have something for you. Something for your name day."

I followed him up the same stairs Masha and I had spent the earlier part of the evening running down, past Masha's nursery, mother's apartments (later when our parents no longer shared anything let alone a bedroom, he was to call it her 'bloody bonbonnière') to the vast salon, where once in one day, he would receive a record eight hundred visitors, to the end of a long corridor and stopped in front of a door I had dismissed as a cupboard.

"This is for you Tanya," said Papa. "Because you are the only one who like me, understands the creative process–the only one not blinded by so much bourgeois frivolity. The only one."

I wanted to ask him if 'bourgeois frivolity' included eating with knives and forks but thought better of it not wishing to spoil the moment's closeness.

He opened the door onto a spacious room surrounded on three sides by long wide windows. Tubes of oil paint, pastels, bundles of pencils and chalks all still in their wrapping paper were piled on a table in the centre. Blank canvases stood in readiness against one wall and two tripods had been erected, one to face the west, the other east.

"The light is good here. It will be quiet, and I am not too far away." He motioned shyly to the floor above. "Um…

and I know how you like to be warm." He pointed to the small grate where a fire had been prepared.

I swallowed. I knew how *he* preferred to work in the cold, always up early and never to lie abed as we girls did, precisely because of the very cold he so desired. He always maintained that his brain had to be freezing. Warmth by contrast, suffused my being now. I felt as if the house and I were one, as if I had been waiting all my life to come here. Blindly, I held out my hand to his and he grasped it.

"Tell me we can stay," I said. "Tell me we won't go back."

Papa dropped my hand. "I can't promise that."

I thought of my brother's beautiful city clothes and of their waste if they weren't put to good use.

"Because of Sergei?"

"No, of course not because of your brother!" he said irritably.

"Well then, just not yet," I said quickly and in Russian for effect. He smiled placated that I had used his language.

"All right," he agreed gruffly.

"When your beard is down to here." I spread my fingers across the space in front of his heart. "Then we can go back."

3

That night, I lay awake too excited to sleep. The journey from Yasnaya Polyana had been a long one and it was very late by the time we finally settled down after supper. I was overwhelmed by the change in our father which had manifested itself in so many ways beginning with the decoration of our 'city' house. Everywhere were thoughtful little details designed to make the transition from the country all the easier. Books of course, abounded, lining bedroom walls and living spaces alike, but there were also hot house flowers and huge bowls I recognised from Yasnaya, filled with dried fruit. With our mother in mind, Papa had set up an enormous samovar in the scullery, even though by then he had given up drinking both tea and coffee– a gesture that especially pleased her. She smiled constantly, flitting from room to room, her hands trailing along the surface of the furniture, hugging plump cushions to an equally plump bosom. And if she secretly wondered why our father had taken to wearing a peasant smock, or how it was that he managed to reconcile the furnishing of our little nest with the austerity I knew he craved, she kept that little conundrum to herself.

If Mama was happy with the house, the gift of my studio had simply astounded me. I didn't think Papa had taken my wish to be an artist seriously. Sergei called it a 'past-time' while Mama said the smell of paint always made her nauseous. Olga Feodova said her sickness had nothing to do with paint, but breeding, and that the number of children she'd had was indecent. Sergei said it wasn't the number so much as the intervals between, was what the old witch inferred. When I, in turn asked him to explain, given that there appeared to be (even by my sketchy grasp of arithmetic) a decent decade between his birth and mine, and yet another between mine and Masha's, his expression darkened. Which left me none the wiser. It was only when I was older that I discovered that Mama had had five other children all of whom died in infancy. I didn't remember these ghost infants who continued to haunt her until the time when they became more real than we, her live ones. But Sergei did. I wondered if he was sincere though with the tears he shed. For someone who purported to miss his siblings as much as he claimed he did, he didn't seem overly fond of Masha or me. I knew he found the limpet just as annoying as I did on occasion. I thought of the way Masha was forever disrupting my peace, seeking me out no matter where I tried to hide, forever coming in and messing up all my paints or insisting on drawing cats on fresh canvases.

But now, my head was full of images: colour and contour, all jumbled up together with memories of the country, of the things we'd seen along the way here and of this new, happy place. My 'city' bedroom was much warmer than the one I was used to sharing with Masha. I was used to cuddling up to her plump little body and feeling her cold little toes occasionally jab my ankles. Here I was told I should feel all grown up with a room to myself, but I missed Masha to talk to at bedtime.

Moonlight seeped through the shutters etching unintelligible shapes on unfamiliar furniture. I lay on my back in my new flannel nightgown flapping my arms and legs to make an angel on the mattress. Soon I was too hot, kicking off the blankets with my feet but I still couldn't sleep. I listened to the sound of the cuckoo clock whose irritating chirp fluttered up through the floorboards and the occasional soft thud as snow fell through the trees to land on the already thick blanket enveloping the house. I tried to make sense of the new sounds, the strange creaks that one day would be as familiar and welcome, I hoped, as those at Yasnaya Polyana but now were vaguely unnerving and alien. I heard the house shudder and groan as though its ingeniously devised heating–large floor-to-ceiling stoves–was too much for it to cope with. And from time to time, I heard my parents, their murmurs harmonious in the dark.

At Yasnaya Polyana I had made many sketches of the house and surrounding landscape, many more of our pet animals, some of the family, and now that I thought about it, one or two of Papa. As I lay awake, I became totally preoccupied with trying to remember where I had packed the drawings of my father. By dawn, I could wait no longer and I crept to Sergei's room (the door to my surprise wasn't locked) anticipating the first signs of life. When they came, they were considerable. He grunted, groaned, scratched, scratched some more and in such places that I had to look away, turned over, turned back, shook a foot, snorted and fell back onto the pillows hurling himself once more into sleep. He didn't look quite the *seigneur* now, I thought. The room smelled of stale tobacco and drink.

"How fast does hair grow?" I whispered kneeling beside the bed on the soft thick carpet. At Yasnaya there were bare, draughty floorboards where the wind whistled up your nightgown and you shivered through your teeth.

Sergei didn't so much blink as grimace–the green, yellow-flecked eyes rolling in their sockets–so that for one terrifying moment I believed they really had turned back on themselves. He stared at me, as if he had never seen me before in his life. He made a strange, guttural sound that resounded in his throat. Not for the first time, I wondered if my brother even liked me.

"It's important."

"Please tell me this is a dream," he said when he could speak. "I'm with Lisa? That I don't live here."

"Lisa? I thought you were in love with Kitty!" I was momentarily deflected.

"I am." Sergei sat up slowly. "I'm confused."

I was beginning to be as well. He pulled the sheet around his shoulders. I think he was naked. I certainly couldn't see his nightshirt and with his tousled hair he looked much younger than his twenty-six years. I averted my eyes as he reached for a cigarette from the bedside table.

"I don't think Papa would like you smoking," I said in a Mama-like tone. Sergei's response was to blow a smoke ring in my face.

"I don't care what Papa thinks but I do care about being woken up. What the devil's the time and what are you doing here? I'm sure I locked the door."

"Maybe you only *thought* you had," I said looking knowingly at a tray on which there was a half empty vodka bottle and a broken tumbler.

Like mine, Sergei's bedroom was lavishly furnished but as befitted a young gentleman's, his was significantly more grown up. The walls were covered in emerald green taffeta and the huge four poster was swathed in crimson raw silk. Nestling amidst the sumptuous fabric was an oil painting of Denisov, the hussar officer our father had immortalized in *War and Peace*. A beautiful walnut tallboy became tawney–orange and gold–in a sudden shaft of dawn light. Books lined one wall and dying embers sparked upwards in the enormous fireplace. Like mine it was as warm as sitting atop a mud and brick oven. Or sleeping there as Olga Feodova (or cats) sometimes did at Yasnaya.

I leaned forward so my chin touched his arm. He recoiled as if I'd touched him with a hot poker. "I really do need to know. How fast does hair grow?"

"You *are* joking?" he said testily. "You've woken me up for this?"

Sergei inhaled deeply, pummelling a pillow with his free hand.

"I like your room," I said amiably. "Mine's good too, though I'd rather be sharing with Masha. Papa certainly seems to have changed his ideas here. It's all so…so luxurious. You were already waking up," I added.

"How would you know?"

"Well, I was watching you, of course."

Sergei's eyes narrowed into slits, boring into mine. His hand paused halfway to his mouth; his head cocked to one side as if all the better to hear me. My illustrious brother had never paid me such close attention before and for the first time in my life I felt (however briefly) what it was to be empowered.

"Did I say anything?"

"What? As in sleep talk?"

He nodded rapidly.

So *that's* what he's afraid of …

"Um…"

Sergei grabbed my wrist. "Well did I?"

"I–"

His grip tightened. His eyes were completely closed, the lashes forming a straight black line.

"I can't remember," I said breathlessly. "No, I don't think so."

My brother released my arm and I moved away from him as quickly as possible to perch on the end of the bed. He made a few attempts to kick me off, but I wedged myself firmly in the gap between mattress and bed post.

"Don't ever do it again," he said darkly. "Ever. Do you understand Tatyana Lvovna Tolstaya?"

He *must* be cross I thought, to call me by my full name and I was just on the point of retorting from the safety of my new position, when a scream made us both freeze. Or rather I did. Sergei finished his cigarette.

"That didn't take long," he said reaching for his dressing gown which, like all the clothes my brother possessed, was of a gorgeous rich brocade with thick velvet cuffs and sable lapels. "Not even a night together and they're already at each other's throats."

But, as accustomed as I was to the battles that raged between our headstrong parents, nothing prepared me for the sight that awaited us in the dining room. Some dozen or so pails of water were placed haphazardly on the floor. Beside each pail was also a chair and in what surely must have been an eccentric game of hopscotch, our mother appeared to have been leaping from one to the other. She cowered, nightdress pulled up, her plaits swinging, ready to jump.

"You promised, *deroghoe*, you promised!" she pleaded although the use of the endearment struck me as odd given the destruction of the room. She gave a sudden yelp leaping

27

in the air as our father aimed a fresh bucket of water at her feet. Her pretty bedroom slippers were wet through, colour from the dyed silk staining her ankles.

"I did *not!*" he raged his face flushed, his soaked tunic sleeves hanging to his knees. He was misguided but magnificent in his fury and for a moment I glimpsed the dashing cavalry officer that he had once been.

"But nothing has changed!" wailed our mother. "You've got rid of the servants, there's no electricity, no plumbing and now the only running water is this filth that you've thrown on the floor!"

"It is NOT filth! It comes from the well! It's purer than the water from Mytischi. Besides, the house is warm isn't it? That's what you complained of at Yasnaya Polyana–that the cold would kill you one day! If you don't make me do it first!"

"But why are you living like this Lev Nikolaevich? Why? You are dressed like a peasant. You *smell* like a peasant! This is still, despite your attempts to make it appear otherwise, a peasant's house!"

An exaggeration we all knew but it caused Papa to stumble. He was unbalanced as it was by the weight of the bucket he was preparing to hurl at our mother and by his drenched clothes.

"What do you see?" he asked suddenly meek, setting down the bucket. "What do you *really* see?"

Our mother closed her eyes as Papa continued softly.

"Open your eyes, Sonya. Open your eyes and I'll tell you."

Mother's eyes remained firmly shut.

Papa persevered. "What stands before you is a Russian," he said so quietly we held our breath, all the better to hear. "No count, no landowner, just a Russian."

Mother's eyes flew open. "I see a man playing at something he doesn't understand."

"No," said Papa with genuine feeling, "it's *you* who don't understand! How can we possibly hope to attain goodness when we are burdened by our possessions, by decorum, fashion and fussy manners?"

Mama sighed, standing tall, allowing her nightdress to fall but still not daring to move from the chair. "I'm not trying to attain goodness," she said. "I'm merely hoping to stay dry!"

Sergei supressed a smile while not daring to meet my eye.

"Sonya, Sonya." Papa shook his head. "Why can't you have faith in me? We don't need these luxuries! We don't need servants. Don't you see that only a peasant can be truly happy leading a simple, unadorned life?"

I was beginning to see his point but perhaps I had missed Mama's.

"Don't be ridiculous," she snapped. "I've never known a happy peasant, certainly not one that wouldn't swap their life with yours given half a chance. You're already living with more than any peasant I've ever seen. This conflict of yours Lev, is just that. But it isn't ours. I understand that you are fighting something all the time, trying for something more. You are a wonderful man, you write wonderful, wonderful books but you make my life very, very difficult. There are certain things that I must have, *deroghoe*, that the *children* must have."

We looked from one parent to the other.

"There are indeed many things to have in this world, Sonya, but how to live is the only thing that really matters."

"Christ," muttered Sergei.

Our mother took a deep breath and stepped down from her chair holding the hem of her nightdress away from the flooded floor. "You're right," she said shrugging. "Maybe it doesn't matter whether water comes from a tap or out of one of these buckets, but I tell you solemnly, I am not going to the well."

Papa moved swiftly towards her enfolding her in sodden arms. "Oh, Sonya, *lubimy*, I didn't mean that *you* should carry all these buckets! *I* will go out every morning to fetch water. I like to work hard when I first get up so that my brain is fresh when I sit down to work."

"But you have, you *own* hundreds of serfs, Lev. Why not get just one of them to help?"

29

Papa stared wildly. "That is not what I meant by this. Not at all."

"Neither did I." Our mother pulled away from him. "I want the children to go to school."

Sergei prodded me. "That means *you!*" he hissed.

Papa grunted. "What? Like petit bourgeois?"

"Like *children*," insisted our mother.

"No. I won't allow it. You've been here one day. Not even. Mere hours. I thought you—that *we* were happy last night. Why suddenly all these demands? Did you have this all planned just to hurt me? You'll be taking them to expensive tailors next. They'll be poisoned by too much rich food and bad theatre! Haven't you heard anything I've said? I want us to live a simple life. Is that too much to ask?"

Our father slumped onto an upturned bucket. His face was edged with despair. Our mother drew herself to her full height, tightening the cord of her dressing gown.

"Lev Nikolaevich, I shall tell you what is simple. Very simple in fact. If you want to chop wood every morning for the fire as a true peasant, then bring it to the house, build the fire, go to the garden well and fill it with eleven buckets of water, and bring those to the house, if you want to cook three meals a day, clean the house, do the laundry, teach the children, *clothe* the children, amuse the children, put them to bed, nurse them when they're ill staying up half the night and, if after all that, you have time, let alone *inspiration* to write, then go ahead! This morning," she gestured to the destroyed dining room, "this is all too much. I am going out."

"Out?" If our mother had suddenly spoken in Georgian, Papa could not have seemed more baffled. "Out where?" he boomed. Despite his obvious bewilderment, he seemed suddenly entranced by the fine bone of her clavicle.

"I'm going to Moscow, to proper Moscow," she said defiantly. "Right this minute. In fact, just as soon as I can dress myself—no mean feat seeing as you've dismissed my maid. But then, no doubt I shall find some obliging *seigneur* to help me. It wouldn't do now, would it, for the Countess Tolstaya to be seen half naked in the street? I hear Pushkin was thrown out of the English Club for appearing with a neck button undone and you know better than anyone what Moscow gossips can be like! We shall have breakfast in Trebeskaya and then I shall take the children to see, and I quote you on this, *deroghoe*, the place referred to by your very own Napoleon, as '*la fortresse kremline*'."

I think that even if she hadn't hurled a napkin at the cuckoo that popped untimely from its Tyrolean house, Sergei would have.

4

We had a wonderful day. Like so many before us we entered the Kitai-Gorod by way of Resurrection gate, that 'miraculous shrine' as my father wrote in *War and Peace*, of the Iberian Madonna. There was so much to remember about that day. Tripping across the uneven cobblestones of the Beautiful Square (Red Square as it would come to be known later; the adjectives in Russian being one and the same) we were aware of people looking at us. People did indeed stop and stare at our mother but not because she was inappropriately dressed, or that buttons weren't done up correctly or not at all. They stopped because of who she was, because of her beauty, because it was known that she alone managed a huge estate, money settlements with printers and the upbringing of her children. She was the only one capable of interpreting Papa's writing and had painstakingly copied every word of Papa's great novel, not once, but many times. Not that Papa was particularly grateful. She used to complain that he began re-writing on purpose, the very moment she had a final copy ready for the publisher.

By the green and white painted house in Arbat where Pushkin lived as a young man, we consumed hot bowls of chocolate so thick you could slice it with a knife. Fortified by the hot beverages, we went on to skate in Gorky Park. If people ogled our mother in the Square, it was nothing to what they did as she glided effortlessly, her cloak and skirts billowing in the wind and her children falling in like chicks (or in Sergei's case like a bad-tempered cockerel) behind her.

Someone else was staring too and it was as we were making our way along the path through the trees, that we first saw him. In the failing light, he seemed to appear from nowhere, a tall broad-shouldered man in a long, cloth coat edged in sable.

"The Countess Tolstaya," said the man smiling. He pulled off a glove to hold her tiny hand, his lips skimming the air above it. Even to my objective mind, this Countess Tolstaya seemed unusually flustered.

"Prince!" she said her voice rising excitedly. She was flushed. Had I been painting with pastels, I'd have chosen a true carmine to smudge across those high cheekbones. She blew away a loose strand of hair that had escaped from under her mink cap, mouth pursing prettily and at the same time pushed Masha and me forward to meet this stranger. Sergei who had been skating on ahead turned back abruptly, wary and alert.

"This is a friend of–of ours," announced our mother gaily.

The 'friend' looked first at Mama raising a slight eyebrow and then from Masha to me. His gaze lingered on Sergei as though assessing the extent of his hostility. Instinctively, I moved closer to him and for once Sergei did not elbow me out of the way. The man called Prince Demidov (given name Arkady) inclined his head before removing his tall astrakhan hat in a wide gesture, so wide in fact, that I followed its trajectory half expecting it to soar up and away all by itself. As he straightened, I gasped because unlike Papa who was intent on growing as much as possible, this man hadn't a single hair on his head. Without his hat, the man's appearance changed dramatically–his face appeared longer, the eyes under arched eyebrows were of an arresting blue not unlike our mother's. Above a cleft chin, the lips were wide and generous. His gaze held mine so long, I blushed.

"Your mother has spoken a great deal about you all," he said.

So, he sees our mother I thought immediately. His gaze turned back to me. His whole face was smiling, his eyes hooded and his mouth twisting with amusement at my obvious embarrassment. Masha began to do a slow, backwards skate which I knew meant she liked him. I felt an irresistible urge to put out my foot and trip her. I was sure that this man could see through her too, but on the contrary, he seemed enchanted by her as he pushed off on one skate to grab her hands and twirl her around. He was surprisingly graceful for one so tall and heavy and I felt that both Mama and I wished he were doing the same with us. When Masha suddenly caught an edge and would have fallen, he held her as lightly as if she'd been a doll. Her fur cap had fallen onto the ice and her blonde hair was a fetching tangle of curls. He laughed and bowing exaggeratedly performing a neat camel spin before scooping it up. Masha clapped her hands at this acrobatic display while our mother gazed at him in wonder. In a perfect complexion, her cheeks were rosy, her lips full and parted. She was the happiest I had ever seen her. She too began to laugh, holding her large sable muff to her chest and closing her eyes. Sergei looked from one to the other and then to me with a faintly disgusted expression on his usually bored features.

"Prince, has our mother told you about our father?" said Sergei acidly. The smile vanished from Mama's face and the sharpness returned to the narrowing eyes. The man called Arkady seemed unfazed by my brother's hostility.

"Indeed, yes," he said pleasantly. "But she needn't have. Who hasn't heard of the great Tolstoy?" Again, he inclined his head with mock respect.

"Well, the great Tolstoy," said our brother executing small figures of eight and puffing out warm air, "doesn't like to be kept waiting at dinner time."

"Nor should he be." Arkady raised an eyebrow again. He was good at that. Our mother glowered at Sergei. "You'd better be getting home then, children." He raised his hat an inch or two in the air. "Countess," he said so sweetly that he might just as well have said 'lubimy' before gliding away towards the darkening trees.

Mama smiled although her eyes did not as she grabbed Masha none too gently by the hand. "How *dare* you be so rude!" she said her voice staccato. She skated to a bench where our coachman waited with our boots. We stumbled behind her holding on to each other for support while we unlaced our skates.

"What was *he* doing here?" Sergei jerked his head in Arkady's direction. Skaters swept past us and Sergei narrowly avoided being knocked over. Our mother shoved her feet into her boots leaving the coachman to collect our skates and telling him that we would walk home.

"Skating?" said Masha brightly.

Sergei rolled his eyes.

"He's a friend," said our mother. "Just a friend."

She began walking briskly. It was strange without skates and my feet felt wooden and clumsy. Streaking past the gold onion domes of Christ the Saviour, the air had become frosty and thin. No one spoke much after that. Sergei smoked; the smell of his tobacco oddly comforting. My stomach began to rumble. When it was cold like this, I was always hungry, and I licked my lips for traces of the hot chocolate we'd had earlier. The walk seemed to do us all good because by the time we got home Mama was smiling, her body supple again, not all rigid and sharp and Sergei hummed a tune under his breath–a tune that soon came to an abrupt end.

Even before we entered the house, I could tell something was wrong. Mama seemed not to notice but the silence was thundering, the dimly lit hall static with foreboding. Worse, the gut-clenching dread I thought gone forever, seemed to have stalked us all the way from Yasnaya.

"I've written a story," our father announced vaulting sideways down the stairs to greet us, or menace us, God only knew which. It was as if he'd been sitting on the landing, ready to pounce the very moment we entered the house. Our mother continued hanging up our cloaks, calmly shaking snow from the fur. In the strange half-light the glistening pelts were as flayed animals suspended from a meat hook. I shuddered involuntarily.

"It's my best ever," he taunted. And when none of us replied, continued, "Thank you for asking but I've called it, *The Kreutzer Sonata.*"

"When do you want me to copy?" asked Mama still intent on smoothing our furs.

She didn't look at him. But I did. I was amazed at how casually she could offer her services, when we'd hardly arrived, when she should still be angry with him. Papa's manuscripts were famously a mess of criss-crosses, added paragraphs, deleted paragraphs, ink splodges (Mama was somehow supposed to know what lay under the stains), geometric lines, undecipherable codes and the whole written in the tiniest, spider-like writing.

"Don't you want to know what it's about?" Papa's eyes were positively burning and holding a candle in front of him so that the flame flickered upwards, he looked like a demented village fool. But before she had time to reply, he jumped the last step falling against her. He didn't steady her though. Instead, his large hands encircled her throat.

"It's about a husband who strangles his wife," he went on, in that tight, furious voice that always made my heart lurch. Sergei on his way past them, hesitated and Masha felt for my hand.

"He knows *exactly* what he's doing and he's not sorry. You see he has interrupted his wife and her lover in the drawing room of his very own house. *His very own house.*" Papa hissed the last words with deadly intent, repeating them for good measure. "Their children are asleep in adjoining rooms. He cannot believe that she can behave in this way."

I don't think *we* could believe that Papa was. Except that we could. This was very much the way our father behaved towards our mother. A marionette in his hands, she was completely frozen, completely still, as we all were, rigid with fear. His hands were tight around her throat, so tight that a vein stood proud and blue, but she said nothing. Not a word, not a murmur, and not because I suspected she couldn't, but out of defiance, out of hatred. Her eyes shone in the orange, blue light of the candle. I concentrated on the black crinkly wick, the burning tip twinkling like a jewel and then the fat grey and yellow flame as it melted upwards. Above it, Papa's eyes were no less brilliant, boring into Mama's and I saw mischief, provocation and sheer delight at Mama's undisguised repugnance.

"And here's the thing, Sonyetka," he said his tone distorting the endearment into one of loathing. "The wife wants only to be happy, for her happiness to continue and for nothing to stop it. The lover wonders only if it will be possible to lie. When the lover sees what the husband intends to do, he of course runs away."

"Why of course?"

Had *I* spoken? Was that *my* voice? I shrank against the wall, appalled at my foolish bravery. But if I had hoped to deflect our father, it was an empty gesture. He appeared not to have heard me, at least not to have identified a voice outside his head, outside the conversation he imagined he was having with our mother. He neither lessened nor relinquished his hold.

"Yes, can you imagine that?" he continued undaunted. "The coward actually *hides* behind the piano as if waiting to see the drama unfold…It is the *wife* who shows courage. She lunges at her husband. At this point it must be said that the husband is almost deflected from his mission." And at his next words my stomach plummeted, my heart felt near to bursting and I thought I would fall face first to the hard wood floor. "But she makes the mistake of speaking," said Papa. "She begins swearing repeatedly that nothing has happened and this irritating, hysterical lie, only infuriates the husband. Naturally he concludes just the opposite. With one hand he grips his wife's throat. He's amazed at how hard it is to actually…"

Papa's fingers pressed downwards so suddenly that Mama finally was able to cry out and blue smudges sprang from under his thumbs on her fine white throat. Masha tried to scream but no sound came while I emitted one long wildcat shriek, as though all the furs so neatly lined up on their hooks had been given life and were leaping towards us…

"You crazy bastard!" Sergei lunged, knocking Papa sideways.

Masha began to cry and all at once the room was spinning in that all too familiar vacuum that makes everything go black. And suddenly I was on the ground and while they fussed above me and Mama blamed Papa and Sergei blamed them both, I kept my eyes firmly shut. I wanted more than anything to wake up alone, not there, but in some other place where our mother would be safe and where our father behaved like a sane man. Where I would forget everything that had happened, except for when I was sliding through the trees, the ice slicing under my skates.

5

Most days now, the sickly smell of Papa's brew–a chemical substitute for coffee that had taken him some time to perfect–woke me. He had long given up eating and drinking anything a peasant might not be able to afford. I longed for the smell of fresh coffee and sweet rolls to waft up to my studio. But the time that had gone into making coffee was now better deployed, so he told us, in making shoes. Papa had found some poor, unsuspecting cobbler in the Steppes and persuaded him to come and live with us and teach our father the craft. Already the peasant had been in the house some weeks. Mama complained that she didn't know what was worse, the stink of my paints or the hammering of nails or the smoke form Sergei's tobacco.

One morning, not long after my faint, I rose quietly and made my way to Papa's study. I found him hunched over his desk in his extraordinary chair. He had grown short-sighted but as he didn't believe a peasant would have worn glasses, he had sewn off the legs of his chair (not very expertly) so that his head was closer to his papers. He was sobbing, and ink had spilled everywhere. He had been reading Diderot's *Le Neveu de Rameau*, but the book was carelessly splayed, its spine wrinkled. I moved it gently aside, away from the ink well.

"How can I preach about Truth and living a certain way when I treat HER so abominably?" How indeed. His eyes were rimmed and puffy. "I have tried so hard. I have dressed simply, lived simply, sat up all night with a drunk I've never met, made these pairs of shoes. Every day I have tried to do good, to be better, to be kind."

I nodded with feeling. I could think of many examples of Papa's 'kindness.' To this day, I am haunted by the fact that he was unable to offer the sensitive, self-doubting Chekov the slightest word of encouragement. Believing that he was doing the man a favour, he was an unnecessarily harsh and unforgiving critic. But when Chekov died, my father was moved to write a truly memorable eulogy. And no one in our family would ever forget when the great Tchaikovsky came to tea having composed a piece of music specially for Papa. In the end, Tchaikovsky didn't stay long enough for tea and Mama was furious, having spent days baking poppy seed cakes. The fact was, that even though this great musician had written remarkable pieces, he had only begun composing as an adult and couldn't play the piano. At least, not well enough in Papa's opinion. Papa, on the other hand, having been subjected to an aristocrat's education, had played since he was four years old. Papa insisted Tchaikovsky sit at the piano and pick out a tune which he did willingly enough but clumsily. The melody sounded tinny and unconvincing until Papa sat down and added crashing chords and archipelagos that may or may not have existed in the original score. Tchaikovsky never came to see us again.

"There are greater things at stake here Tanya," said Papa shaking his head. "I am fighting for my soul! And this man confirms everything I have ever thought." My father jabbed the book. For someone who loved literature he was not always gentle with books. "I hate to admit to a French bourgeois being right, Tanya, but you see, even a hundred years ago, writers found themselves in the same terrible predicament that I have experienced ever since I married your mother."

I sank onto a low chair beside him.

"And what is that Papa?" I asked touching his sleeve.

"Well, isn't it obvious?" Papa said looking at me as though I were an imbecile. "It's impossible to write *and* be a good husband."

"'Good husband?'" I echoed almost choking. "I see."

"I don't think you do." Papa ran his hands through his beard. "I can't go on. It would be wrong to continue as we are. She has done everything to thwart me. Everything. She insists on French when she knows a peasant knows only

Russian. She must have flowers, which in the bedroom is such a vulgar custom; all that knitting and sewing and quilting in that absurd room that she tries to entice me into! She thinks I don't realize what she's doing. I have a single night's peace on the sofa and there she is with, '*Deroghoe*, come and see the soft, cosy blanket I've made you, come and lie down. I know how you hate the cold. You don't have to sleep here but just lie down beside me!' Lie down? Bones of the saints! *All* you children are the result of quilting! If only she knew how it disgusts me! She has even taken to writing silly novellas just to spite me! The miracle is that they are published at all! Ugh! And the money! How can she not see that every smallest kopek she spends and more importantly, *wastes*, is my pain and torment!"

I wanted to ask him what he thought our mother did with their money other than to clothe and feed us. The thought of food reminded me that I had not yet had breakfast and I didn't want to hear another word said against Mama. I half rose to get up when something else caught my attention. By his shoes, the ones he had so proudly made for himself, was a small basket crammed with paper and pens, linen blouses and the rustic felt boots he changed into in winter. A different kind of panic entered my brain. My heart quickened with treacherous elation.

"Yes, I am going Tanya, but not because I'm angry with anyone. I don't accuse you of anything! On the contrary, I look back with love and gratitude to our life as a family, but our ways are running in different directions. I can't blame myself because I know that my change was not meant for myself or for the people around me: it was simply bound to come. I know that none of you can ever really follow me."

"Masha–" I stuttered. "Masha will. I know she's only a child, but she wants so much to be like you. Even last night she told me that she has decided to renounce meat."

Papa held up his long thin hand, the fingers of the left weighed down by the heavy gold signet ring.

"Child, child," he said. "Don't you understand? It has to come from the heart. You have to live it." A moment before I had felt excitement at the thought that he was leaving but that we would stay. Now, I wracked my brain to think of ways to keep him. He wasn't listening. Already he had disappeared into that world of his from which we were always excluded.

"But where will you go?"

"Go? Go?" Papa waved a hand impatiently. "It is not important. The destination hardly matters. The fact remains that my life in a family is useless. The conventionality paralyses me. It's all too sweet. There's too much excess in everything. Too much food, too much music, too much dressing up."

Not in Papa's case I thought, looking at his unshaven face and baggy trousers. There were holes in his stockinged feet. He leant on his desk holding his head in his hands. For a moment, I thought he was about to start crying again, something even more alarming than the prospect of his departure. I hovered uncertainly, my mind swarming with questions. How to make him stay? Did Mama know about his plans? What had I done wrong? Had I displeased him in some way? And most pertinent of all, could I have made a difference?

The clatter of hooves beneath his window distracted us both. My father sat bolt upright and I sprang to open the shutters.

"It's Sergei!" I said in astonishment. My brother never went out so early, but he looked magnificent on his black stallion, his riding coat fanned out across the horse's flanks, his fur cap tilted at an angle. As usual, he was smoking, the reins held carelessly in one hand.

"That's something else," Papa said gloomily sitting back down. "They must all go."

I turned from the window, somewhat revived by the blast of fresh air, but just as hungry as ever.

"What must Papa?"

"Why the horses of course! It's a complete indulgence to have a stable full of horses. What was I thinking? Allowing myself such a luxury?"

So there goes Mama's transport, I thought to myself and that was one quarrel I had no wish to witness. "But you love your horses!" I exclaimed. This was true, but I was also motivated by the notion that Mama would never forgive me if she knew I'd had the opportunity to influence Papa's decision.

"At Yasnaya…" my voice trailed. I remembered a very different Papa setting off on a morning such as this and much as Sergei was doing now, clean shaven and lean, sitting tall in the saddle in his sable hat, as happy and comfortable on his horse as he was now in his peasant's smock. By the end of his life, Papa concluded that he must have spent seven years in the saddle. At least. I chased away the vision of Papa, the cavalry officer and the many portraits that hung of him across our vast nation. And beyond. We had heard that as far as the Americas, our father was revered. I found it increasingly difficult to reconcile the image of the old man before me with the fit and virile parent who had hunted most days in winter and danced the evenings away afterwards, in the company of beautiful women.

"I know what I must do," declared Papa pulling out blotting paper from a little cubby hole in his desk. Laying a fresh sheet of paper on top of it, he dipped his pen in ink. "I shall write an ode to the horse. I wasn't at all sure what I'd write next, but now, God and to some extent your brother, have given me inspiration. Do you realise that horses are like humans? They are such sociable creatures too. They have friendships just as we do, and they scream if they're separated from their friends. And just as spawning salmon and bees and even misplaced cats…"

"Cats?" I dreaded to think what he might come out with next.

"*Horses*," continued my father firmly, "have an incredible homing instinct. I've known a horse slide open a stable door with his teeth and make his way in the dark, back to the farm where he was raised over three versts away." He smoothed the paper and then peered at me as if I'd just interrupted him from an important task. "Well?"

"So, you're not leaving? I mean not immediately?"

Papa's eyes blazed. "Bones of the saints Tanya, can't you see I'm busy? All this prattle is such a distraction! Pure agony! I don't know how I survive as I do. I don't see how *anyone* survives!" He stroked his beard suddenly thoughtful. "Are we any better than those beasts?" He jerked his head in Sergei's direction. "I think not. Look how superior that animal is to us–how graceful and strong! Look how its eyes blaze with passion and purpose. See how its ears are pricked back, its tail stands erect. Hadrian knew what it was to love a horse. Do you know he said that his horse obeyed him as if he were his own brain."

"*Hadrian*?" Brains? What on earth was my father talking about?

"Yes, yes. The Emperor Hadrian," said Papa impatiently. He always forgot that not everyone was as well read as he was. Or as familiar with the ancient world. "Hadrian loved his horse more than any living creature. Well perhaps not *exactly* more than…"

Papa suddenly got to his feet and grabbing my hand drew me back to the window. He heaved the sash window as far as it would go and this time the gust of cold air took my breath away. His hand was at the nape of my neck underneath my hair, forcing me to follow his line of vision. Sergei was prancing up and down, his horse momentarily poised in an extended trot. Papa's hands continued to move through my hair, kneading my scalp. A warm, smooth feeling extended over me so that I was no longer hungry. But then the pressure changed and his fingers were no longer gentle. They pressed down and across, holding my head in a vice-like grip. My heart began to beat in my mouth. I could taste its pulse as it coursed from the roof of my mouth to my tongue, the familiar shivers of anxiety corralling the nerves in my stomach.

"Look Tatyana, just look. Is he not magnificent? He hasn't an ounce of spare flesh! See how the veins throb under the skin, see how the smooth flanks are perfectly extended. It is true that your brother rides him wonderfully and that he shouldn't be smoking. But even so, Sergei is skilled enough. The reins are caught in his left hand, beautifully taught. See the exquisite loop they make and how the horse's head is held proud by them. Look at how he anticipates the gallop, how excited he is! Can you not see that this animal is so much better than the rest of our human race put together! We are the creatures that do not fit into the beauty of God's creation, not the other way round!"

This creature began to sway with dizziness and the pressure point of pain made by my father's fingers. All at once Papa let go of me.

"Ride then!" he shouted down to my brother. "Can't you see the horse is desperate to get going? What are you waiting for?"

Sergei, hearing my father's voice, threw away his cigarette. He doffed his cap shooting me a look that said, 'Siding with the enemy, eh?' and cantered off.

I steadied myself on Papa's desk.

"Tatyana," said my father dropping down into his low chair. He began to make long scratches on the paper, the same sort of sound I remembered the rats making as they skittered through the eaves at Yasnaya. It made me want to snatch it away from him and sweep away the contents of his desk. "I've engaged a teacher for you." Papa paused his writing. "I'm going to call the horse in my story Stryder. What do you think?"

I was nonplussed. "I don't know. Is it well known? Is it...?" I took a breath about to mention the unmentionable. "Is it German?"

Papa raised his eyes. "Bones of the saints! Not of the name, child! What do you think of having a teacher?"

Oh...

"I thought," I said in a quiet voice, "that mother wanted us to go to school."

Papa folded the top section of the paper with exquisite precision just as he did when we played the writing game–the one where you wrote a couple of lines of a story, covered them up before passing them onto the next player.

"He's called Ilya Yefimovich–"

I started. Repin. Ilya Yefimovich Repin. I knew the rest. Who *didn't* know of the famous Repin? At the age of sixteen (my age exactly), Repin had begun his career painting icons but was soon winning prestigious art prizes. But I could still feel the imprint of my father's fingers on my temples. I wasn't about to be effusive.

"You mean the Ukrainian?" I knew my tone was less than respectful.

"I mean Ilya Repin. He was born in Chuguev, yes. But his greatest wish is to enhance the reputation of *Russian* painters so that one day they will be as well-known as the French. Which is something I support wholeheartedly." Papa's bushy eyebrows knitted together. "What is this?"

I shrugged.

"Ah, you're uncertain? Don't be. I've been to his studio in Bolshoi Trubny. I want him to paint me, actually. I think we can even be friends."

When I was still silent, my father shook his head.

"This is exactly what I feared." And then, when my small victory shrank even further, he added, "Oh, don't stand there like a frightened goose, Tanya! Have some breakfast, if you must. You people have no stamina! How will I make decent Russians from such feeble stock?" Papa held his head again in despair. "I thought it would be possible, that by my example you would learn to do without, but I can see the predisposition towards gentility is strong, stronger than I could have imagined."

The only strong feeling I was experiencing at that moment was one of hunger and as if on cue, my stomach began to rumble loudly. Papa heard it too.

"Go, go!" he said waving a hand dismissively. "But Repin will be here mid-morning. Make sure you have something to show him. And he's not coming here because he needs the work, you understand. Do not disappoint me!"

I'd forgotten I was at all hungry by the time I entered the dining room. Earlier, I would have drooled at the sight and smell of sweet cheese pastries, but Papa's news instead made me want to slide down banisters, and dance through the house. Plate in hand, I stood stupefied before silver dishes overflowing with eggs, bread, curd cheese and thick cream. Small pottery bowls from Yasnaya were over filled with berry preserve.

Repin! If Metropolitan Niarchos were coming to see us or even the Czar himself I could not have been more surprised. Or more terrified. What on earth would I show him? How could he possibly be interested in me, when the greatest artists in Russia begged a conversation, let alone a tutorial with the man?

"So, is he leaving or not?"

I hadn't noticed my sister calmly eating all by herself at one end of the table. Masha was such a painfully slow eater that no one could bear to sit with her. She didn't seem to have made much progress. In front of her was a plate loaded with brioche and cake. Even so, her cheeks bulged. Like a pelican, she kept her mouth full of food without necessarily swallowing it. There was a messy spread of jam on her fingers and on the edge of her cup.

"Not."

Masha nodded agreeably, satisfied with the reply. I poured myself a cup of Papa's nasty coffee hardly aware of its taste.

"You know, Masha, becoming a vegetarian doesn't mean you have to eat continuously. It just means you eat differently."

"I'm hungry."

I shrugged. "Maybe you should go back to eating meat then."

She glared at me.

"It'll be lunchtime soon anyway," I added helpfully.

"I know and I'm storing up."

She took an excruciatingly small sip of milk. "Sergei's gone riding with that girl," she said slyly. "And I saw them kissing."

"You never did! I don't believe you!"

Masha nodded triumphantly, systematically building another sandwich of cake, cheese and jam. "They were here, just outside the window. I was eating ever so quietly," she said. Crumbs sprinkled her bottom lip. "No one knew I was here."

"I'm sure they didn't."

Along with being a famously slow eater, Masha was known for tiptoeing around the place and surprising people unawares, but only after she'd overheard most of their conversation. For a long time, she was thought too young to make sense of what she'd heard, but she had stored enough secrets to keep the family nervously guessing one way or another.

"And?"

Masha chewed slowly.

"And?" I repeated impatiently. "Which girl was it? Kitty?"

Masha shook her head so that the enormous bow pinned to the side of her head wobbled furiously.

"Couldn't see," she said between mouthfuls. "They were playing with Sergei's hat. She was trying it on, and it covered most of her face and then they leant together and *ick*…" Masha wiped the back of her mouth with her hand. "They started sucking each other, just as if they were eating an ice cream, lick, lick, lick…slurp, slurp…"

"Yes, all right." I held up my hand, dipping a roll into Masha's hot chocolate. Her sing-song voice was beginning to grate. "Does Mama know?"

Masha shook her head vigorously.

"Well, don't tell her. Do you know where they went? What they were talking about?"

Masha shrugged. She chased a bit of bun around her plate with her thumb. "Oh, the usual. Where to catch the hunt, whose horse is faster. I liked hers actually. It has pretty eyes and a white star on its forelock and long ears. Sergei's is just like him. Big and ugly and black. I don't like Sergei anymore. He's too bossy. And…"

"Yes?"

"Babies."

"Babies!" I slipped into a chair beside her. "Tell me *exactly* what you heard."

Masha turned saucer round, innocent eyes. "That was all."

"I don't believe you."

Masha shook her head. "I couldn't hear anything else. A sweet little bird popped out of the cuckoo clock. You didn't see it last night, Tanyushka, not really. It's got a painted yellow neck and it really tweets."

"No, it doesn't Masha, it's only meant to *look* as if it does."

Masha seemed unconvinced.

"Never mind," I said briskly. "Just tell me exactly what you heard. Everything. Try and remember. It's important."

"But why do you want to know. Why is it important?"

"It just is."

"Tell me why then," Masha popped another piece of bread in her mouth.

I shrugged. "Because she's not very nice. Kitty I mean. We need to look after Sergei."

Masha looked at me in astonishment. "But he's not a baby!"

"No of course not," I replied patiently. "Sometimes the wrong kind of women fall in love with him and want to come and live with us. Look, I don't know, just tell me!"

Masha regarded me calmly. "I really didn't hear. Sergei looked cross and galloped off even though the girl was wearing his hat and when she tried to follow, the hat fell off and then he had to come back, and he was swearing a lot and then he stopped and lit a cigarette and then I heard Papa shouting so I shut the shutters. Will you come and skate Tanya?"

I shook my head scooping out another bit of chocolate from her cup and rising from my seat. "Sorry, I've got a lesson. You can come find me later though."

My easel with its rough sketch of Papa was just as I had left it, but paper and chalk were strewn over the table and still-life arrangements were grouped together over most surfaces. I cleared a way to the window. If only I had painted something truly wonderful! I put on my artist's smock and decided to continue with what I was doing, just as though I were not expecting a visitor. Methodically, I began to mix paint, oblivious of the smell that so bothered my mother. Gradually, as I became absorbed in my work, my mind once again took flight with the contentment that I only ever felt when painting.

When the knock at the door came, I had completed the tiny row of columns on Papa's desk. I intended to paint him leaning over his work, pen in hand, his beard clearly visible. I had already sketched the suggestion of a door frame behind him and the darkening shadows would highlight his slumped figure but illuminate his face. One shoulder would hint at the royal blue of his smock, the other would be almost indigo. His right hand, the smooth bone white hand of a gentleman, with its wedding and signet rings, would be clearly visible while the other would be tucked in a sleeve. An edge of white would reveal the coarse linen of his undershirt and a strip of naked neck would, I hoped, convey vulnerability.

I wanted to show a strong face frowning in concentration, a face still manly and virile and of course, for my own purposes, I wanted to chart its beard's growth. I also needed to convey something deeper. Just as Holbein had famously painted Anne of Cleves, not as a princess, but as the woman he loved, my portrait of Papa would be the most important work of my life. Everything hinged on my revealing the man I believed still existed beneath the peasant disguise. I wanted Mama to see my picture and fall in love with Papa all over again.

6

It was already dark when I opened the door to my future; to Repin the man and Repin the teacher. The fire had long died down though happily my little studio was still warm. The apricot light that had earlier wrapped itself round my pictures in an all-forgiving glow had also faded. Probably therefore, erroneously, I was pleased with my day's work. The hesitant tap was followed by a cough and when I flung open the door, I thought it was Masha playing games. The corridor was in darkness–the servants had not yet come upstairs with lanterns–and I was sightless in the gloom.

"I'm sorry, I'm so late. You–"

I could hear the voice but not see the speaker. I stepped out of my studio bumping straight into Repin and... a pair of shoes.

Giggling, we both took a step back, Repin banging his head on the door jamb for good measure. I still couldn't see him until a watery moon suddenly appearing above one of the skylights, brought him sharply into focus. He was very tall and thin with broad sloping shoulders and a shock of black, badly cut hair. As he turned to me, I was also aware of a cast in one eye. I blushed. I wasn't sure what I'd been expecting–perhaps a man of my father's age but not a man not much older than Sergei. I blushed even deeper when I saw that he was clutching a pair of Papa's hand-made shoes.

"Your father requested I visit," said Repin. "I mean before our appointment."

"I can see that," I said curtly, furious with Papa. "Or should I say *smell*?" Because the odour of pigskin was overwhelming. "And they're obviously too small!"

Repin shrugged. "I have huge feet." He held out his right foot. He wasn't exaggerating.

Papa's latest hobby was one I found extremely embarrassing, but then no doubt, so too did the recipients of his endeavour. Quickly bored with our resident cobbler, Papa had declared himself, in his words, 'sufficiently proficient.' Having assembled the necessary tools and materials, he had then set about making shoes at the (uneven) workbench which he had also constructed. Papa took his hobby very seriously, grunting and groaning and cursing with the effort. The result was quite charming if you liked the one-size-fits-all sort of thing, mis-matched, untanned (therefore stinking leather)–a peasant's clog to be worn over normal shoes. Mama for one, didn't at all and not everyone appreciated having their own shoes taken off them to be replaced with Papa's either. In fact, the poet Afanasi Fet had stormed out of the house insulted to the core, taking Papa's gift to mean that he thought Fet too poor to be able to afford his own shoes.

To my relief, Repin didn't seem so much annoyed as bewildered. He kept glancing down at his feet as if to reassure himself that it was Papa's boots and not his own that smelled so strangely.

"I'm surprised Papa allowed you to keep your own shoes," I said. "He usually keeps them to try and copy them."

"Successfully?"

I shrugged not wanting to show disloyalty to this stranger and touched the boots. "As you see."

"As I said, it's only that my feet are so big. I think even your father was surprised. These were made for a poet who must have accidentally left them behind."

"Indeed, he must have."

"I really don't think that even these are going to fit," he said regretfully. "I would love to wear them, I would." He looked as uncertain as Masha did when deciding on which pastry to have for tea. We exchanged glances and I smiled at his little boy expression. I took the boots from him.

"It really doesn't matter. For Papa it's a sort of test anyway."

Repin looked alarmed.

"The fact that you're still here is a good sign," I reassured him hastily. "You'd be amazed at how some people react."

"How do...?"

"Some people never talk to Papa again. I mean Rachmaninoff told Papa that in his opinion, Papa was obsessed with bestiality. He said it was very clear to him that while he was doing everything possible to behave to the contrary, Papa should really remember that he was still a man and a count. And Pasternak–"

Repin rubbed his head on the spot where he must have bumped it.

"Good heavens," he said nervously. "I don't want to displease him. He's a great man. He strikes me as a completely honest soul. I loved his voice. I could have listened to him forever."

As we have to...

"He's a known writer, yes." I touched his arm. "*You* are also a great man." And then it was my turn to be embarrassed. Luckily, in the dim light I didn't think he could see my pink cheeks and so I rattled on. "I mean everyone has heard of you! Mama says Pavel Tretyakov plans to exhibit some of your pictures when he sets up a gallery. Mama loves galleries. We went to one only the other day and then we went skating. That's when we bumped into Arkady."

"Arkady?"

"I thought you might know him."

"There are many Arkadys in Moscow," Repin pointed out gently. "Do you know his patronymic?"

"Well, he's bald," I said helpfully.

Repin smiled. "Anything else?"

"He has very blue eyes."

"I see." Repin's smile vanished. "Well, that might be our first exercise. I was going to suggest we paint these boots maybe in pastels but perhaps painting this Arkady might engage you more."

His manner had changed from being indulgent and amused to brusque and business-like. I stood back to let him pass. Only embers were left in the grate and the room was cast in shadow with the only light coming from the outdoor lantern. I felt my way in the dark and lit a candle. Repin's face was illuminated, divorced from the rest of his body in an uncanny fashion. It was as if it floated with a life of its own, moving this way and that. Our eyes met again and although I looked away first, I felt him still examining me as I knew the artist in him would, dispassionately, objectively looking for the planes and shadows, the luminescence and suppleness.

"It is you who have beautiful eyes," he said almost accusingly. "I propose something. You will paint Arkady, or what you remember of him. That should prove a good exercise in itself–seeing what it is you recall from memory– and I will paint you."

"Oh no–" I protested taking a step back.

"It would give me great pleasure," Repin said sternly. "Besides, anything is better than painting these boots!" Repin touched my wrist lightly to pull the candle away from my body. His touch shot through me as hot chocolate, as cold vodka on a freezing sleigh ride, as–

"Sit here." Repin guided me to a chair by the window hardly glancing at the drawing that sat expectantly on the easel. He covered it carelessly with a fresh canvas and felt for the charcoal that nestled along the easel's edge. "Light is not always what we make of it," he said beginning to draw. "It's not the obvious contrast between night and day. It's more important to see in the dark, to feel it, to notice the shapes around the form, rather than the form itself. To paint, to paint with the soul, one must learn to reuse one's sight, to really look on darkness…"

Never mind seeing–it was the sense of touch, *his* touch, that was foremost on my mind. It was a different feeling too from when Papa held my hand or took my arm to draw my attention to something. On those occasions, I felt warm and close to him but not churned up as I did now when Repin touched my shoulder. I could still feel his fingers through my linen smock. I shivered with a mixture of cold and inexplicable excitement. Had he meant to touch me? Had his hand stayed longer than he intended? Did it touch me at all? And I was beginning to grasp what he meant. I could hardly make out his form, but I was intensely aware of the dense mass around him.

"'...looking on darkness which the blind do see,'" I murmured.

He looked at me strangely. "'...save that my soul's imaginary sight, presents thy shadow to my sightless view...'" He held my gaze a moment longer before turning back to the canvas. "That is what we must work on," he said crisply. "The imaginary sight."

I looked at an imaginary spot on my skirt. Swiftly he swooped down to turn my face in profile, lifting my chin, his thumb and forefinger brushing against my cheekbone. I felt my stomach turn to liquid and not the liquid of fear that I felt if Sergei caught Masha and me eavesdropping or when our parents were quarrelling, this was a delicious fluid sensation I'd never felt before and one that I wanted to continue to feel, to go on feeling.

"So, you can begin when you like," he said.

"But I really can't see!" I protested. As we'd been talking, what little moonlight there was, receded behind steely clouds. I was aware of his hands moving deftly in front of me and his voice above me in the shadows.

"You can feel the canvas, you can smell the paint, the rough edges as it dries, the bristles on the poor bristles that are left behind. Use every sensory device other than your sight. Come Tanya, we're not going down to tea until you show me what you can do!"

His hand clamped over mine, placing a piece of charcoal between my fingers. I closed my eyes internally shivering with the pleasure of his touch while at the same time trying to remember the sensation of skating, of struggling to tow a tired Masha and how her dead weight had become a pressure on the small of my back. I felt again the cold, my breath and hers as we puffed behind the graceful moving form of our mother and how I loved the way her skirt fantailed behind her. I saw Sergei spin round to light a cigarette, as graceful on skates as he was astride a horse and once again, I remembered how the bald man called Arkady had seemed to spring from nowhere. But again, it was not his baldness that one noticed. In fact, it was the last detail to strike the newcomer. It was his eyes, deeply set and of such a vivid, startling blue that they commanded your attention, they shook you awake, they fixed you to him so that you could not squirm free, they bore through your soul demanding a response. I began to draw. I would make a small sketch of what the larger canvas would later envelop and for which, despite what this new teacher said, I would need light.

I do not know how long we painted together in the dark, in silence with only the scratch of charcoal on paper and the odd call from servants directing one another with lanterns. My stomach began to rumble as I remembered that apart from breakfast, I hadn't eaten all day. And then suddenly something occurred to me.

"We've been speaking in Russian," I said. I heard the scrape against paper suddenly cease and a sigh.

"You're not concentrating," he said.

I too put down my brush. "Oh, but I am!" I leaned my head against the back of my chair. "I was thinking of Prince Demidov."

"You know the Prince?" Repin seemed surprised.

"Well, yes. That's Arkady. I told you. But you know him too?"

Repin shrugged. "I may have painted his portrait. So, you *did* know his patronymic."

"Yes. No. I'd forgotten," I said confused. "But that's not important. You see he spoke French. That's what made Sergei turn round. I thought it was because he seemed to appear out of nowhere, but it wasn't. It was because he was talking to our mother in French."

"And your father prefers…?"

"Russian of course. A lot of their arguments are about language and which one we should be speaking at home. He says it's ridiculous how many of his friends still speak it so badly, some of them not at all. He says that some of our greatest writers only learned Russian from their servants. He wants Russians, rich or poor to speak the same language."

"And you can see why." Repin moved to sit on the window seat beside me. His profile was outlined against the darker mass of the window, in varying tones of grey. Devoid of colour, and without knowing much about the person, he was still more vibrant and rich than the patchwork kaleidoscope that was my brother Sergei or even what I suspected to be the pigment base that formed Arkady. "In Pushkin's time, which is not so long ago, words had to be invented, borrowed from French, German, English–from any language, really. We simply didn't have the mechanism to express complicated thought."

I thought about the idea of not having tools with which to speak, in a household where expression, whether it was through my medium or my father's, was the only reason for existing at all.

"Maybe there should only be one language, maybe there is...a–a sort of universal, inborn language." Inadvertently, I touched his knee. His hand moved swiftly to cover mine.

"What, as in a tower of Babylon?"

I shook my head. "More in the way that animals communicate, the way that apes do."

I could feel him smiling in the dark.

"I'm not sure about an inherent language," said Repin leaning back in his chair, the wool cloth of his coat chafing against the linen stuffing of his seat. "In fact, there's a case in the thirteenth century, of a Holy Roman Emperor, unintentionally, carrying out an experiment of human bonding."

"Really?" Not Hadrian again I hoped. But then I would have done anything at that point to keep Repin talking. It was getting darker by the minute and any moment now, Masha or a servant would stomp up the attic stairs to say that supper was ready. "How did he do that?" I asked encouragingly.

Repin paused, his arm making a movement in front of my face. Perhaps he was running a hand through his hair or touching his chin. I couldn't tell.

"Well, this emperor was determined to discover a common, inborn language so he determined to bring up a group of children who would never hear speech. A group of babies were to be clothed and suckled and washed but never spoken to."

Now, he had my attention. I sat up leaning towards him, sitting on my hands.

"So, what happened? Did they learn to speak a new language?"

"No, no they didn't," said Repin clearing his voice. "They all died without uttering a word."

"Oh."

And then as if to counterbalance the effect of his words, not knowing the degree of my sensitivity, Repin rushed on, "but I do think there's a universal language of emotion. In fact, Darwin considered emotions to be as evolutionary as other bodily alterations. He went as far as to say that animals with an advanced somatic structure have a competitive edge over other organisms."

"Is that what you believe?"

"I believe that children cannot survive without human interaction, they need to be petted and cooed and talked to. Without love, quite simply, they die." Repin's voice was gruff. "Without love–"

"Yes?"

His breath was on my cheek as my heart began to pound in my chest. For a moment his head was so close, his hair tickled my forehead and then suddenly he pulled away. He stood up quickly, banging into my easel. In the dark, my hand shot out to steady it and as we lunged in the same direction, I fell against him. His hands held my upper arms and for a moment I thought he would hug me to him, but he didn't. After a few seconds he held me firmly away from him as if willing me to stay rooted to my spot.

"If we think about language influencing character though, Russian is an interesting case," said my teacher softly. "It's a passive, rather than an active language. Things are done *to* one–you are not responsible for your actions. You aren't cold for example, the way you are in English say or

French. In Russian, cold is inflicted *on* you. What I often wonder, is which came first, the character or the language. Did the language form this negation of responsibility of the Russian psyche or was language a result?"

"Neither," I said firmly. "The weather caused both."

Repin laughed.

"It's true," I continued archly. "The peasant in Siberia knows full well that if it snows in June his crop and therefore his livelihood will be destroyed and there's nothing whatsoever, he can do about it. No optimism, no amount of wishful thinking, or poetry, is going to alter the topographical fact. It makes the Russian soul fatalistic and mournful. In Italy they can afford to sing and be warm and bask in the sun. They have all the time in the world to talk of love."

"So, Russians don't love?" said Repin in his funnily accented Russian but I again I could hear the smile in his voice.

"Only passively," I said returning a smile.

"And love just happens? One's not responsible?"

"It depends on what one does with it," I said moving closer towards him, my hand touching his. "Besides, Papa says that Russian is the language of sincerity."

"Tanya–Tatyana," he began. "You are very sweet. You are very young. We have much work to do. I'm sorry." His fingers felt for my lips, briefly tracing their outline. As if from a long way away, I heard the exquisite song of a nightingale and by the speed from which it was cut short, realised too that it came not from outside, but from the dining room clock. "I'm sorry," he repeated and before I could respond, my teacher rushed from the room.

7

"How are the lessons going?" asked Papa some weeks later.

I was bending down to tie the laces of my outdoor boots, my skates slung around my neck. In my desire to get out of the house as quickly as possible, I'd put on all my heavy clothes in the bedroom and I was now panting with exertion and overheating from the fur around my neck. I stood up breathless to see my father hovering at the top of the stairs. I hesitated. He appeared calm enough standing as he was in characteristic pose: right hand wedged behind the leather belt that cinched his voluminous smock, the other ever ready for combat. But a frown flirted with his forehead. In the brief ensuing silence, we were both uncertain as to which way his mood would turn.

For my part, I was surprised to see him at all and wondered vaguely if Mama knew he was home. He had been visiting his sister Maria in the Crimea. Tetya Maria had also gone native–I'd seen pictures of her dressed all in black like a female metropolitan. Routinely, he rotated visits to the defunct estates he still owned in the Steppes. He said he was still responsible for these places where often a ramshackle pigs' shed was the only evidence of former habitation. I think the truth was that he was on the lookout for some poor unsuspecting artisan with the intention of kidnapping him and bringing him back to the city. The shoemaking fetish was coming to an end and I knew it was only a matter of weeks before my father would be restless once again, in search of something, or someone, new.

"What, going out?" Already another question when I hadn't even answered the first! I felt the familiar mixture of apprehension and impatience.

I nodded. "But I've been painting all morning," I said quickly in lieu of an explanation.

Papa shook his head. "Yes, but Tanya, Tanya, the light..." he jerked his head to the landing window. "Should you be wasting...?"

"I'm meeting Repin," I said hastily. "And I'm late. Oh, it's all to do with work."

"I see." Now Papa was frowning in earnest. "Outdoors?"

"Yes."

"Now? Right this minute?"

"Yes." I turned, my hand already on the door handle, reticent affection giving way to active dislike. I wanted to blow him apart like a dandelion top, off the landing and out of the window to be scooped out of the sky by Baba Yaga as in the fairy tale of *The Magic Swan Geese*.

"I've heard about my Stryder story," said my father.

I wracked my brains. Stryder? Stryder? For once however, Papa's razor-sharp brain didn't pick up on my vagueness, for in his sudden need to hold my attention he rambled on quickly.

"Turgenev has replied at last. He read my little effort in one sitting and says he's certain that I must have been a horse myself in another lifetime."

And when I didn't reply, Papa added stiffly as though I were simple. "Because he found the portrayal of Stryder so convincing."

"How... gratifying." I would have added a high-pitched whiney of my own but felt that somehow Papa's mood might not appreciate my attempt at humour. However, lame.

"He says that I have managed to show the suffering of humanity within a mirror social structure, in the different stages of a stallion's life. For example, he starts proud and strong, confident of his future-"

"Really?" Never mind Stryder's suffering–I was having the vapours at the thought of Repin waiting for me on the ice in the snatched half hour we anticipated before school broke up and Masha and her friends descended on the pond.

My heart pounded in my chest and my palms were clammy in my fur mittens. Every inch of my back rebelled against the rough wool vest I had thought vital for today's outing. I had wanted to appear pleasantly flushed as I walked down the narrow path through the trees. Composed, yet ready for a gentle skate. Perspiration-soaked fur stuck to a damp forehead with powder quickly drying in rounds, was not the intended effect.

"…and ends with a broken beast, humbled by life, a miserable creature–"

"You believe in reincarnation then, Papa?" I interrupted. Hoping this might bring the conversation to a close, I prized the door open with my toe.

"Bones of the saints Tanya!" my father exploded. "You live in this house and eat our food, have you learned nothing? I believe in–"

"What *do* you believe in Papa?" I asked tightly, every muscle in my face set with resentment, my entire body stiffening as I flattened my back against the warm wood. Removing my mittens, I cooled my palms on my skates. Like it or not, I was going to have to listen. Worse. Look at him. I realised with a start that his beard had grown. And not just his beard. Hair everywhere. The hair around his ears was particularly bushy, his moustache and beard rolling into one, all but masking his mouth. Even the eyes that habitually glowered in all Mama's black and white photographs to date, were now hidden under thick eyebrows that formed a continuous hirsute line.

It was Papa's turn to view me with a reciprocated and new aversion. He rocked on his feet before placing both hands behind his belt which further dragged the blouse out of shape, accentuating his thin hips. The knees of his britches too were baggy, falling well below the natural indentation of bone. When he looked up again there was no mistaking the depth of passion that reverberated through his body.

"Faith," he said deceptively gentle, enunciating every word. "Truth. I believe in simplicity. Not all this… this garishness…!" His hands relinquished his belt, shooting upwards like birds suddenly released from captivity. "I suffer so much from these visible signs of greed. I can't bear it! I must know, I must discover how to live… but without being crushed by suffering either. That's the issue. It's not about coming back in a different form of life Tanya." He began to pull at his beard until to my alarm I noticed actual handfuls of hair coming away just as easily as cotton from a spool. "My position couldn't be further away from reincarnation! You mustn't dream of paradise somewhere else, doing some heroic deed far into the future! The paradise is here!"

My father punched the fist of one hand into the palm of the other. The impact of his words and obvious genuine feeling behind them reduced only momentarily by the alarming reality that this time his britches might actually fall down. He hooked his fingers once more behind his belt. "The challenge we all face is to suppress carnal desire." My father tossed back his head and stared directly at me. In spite of myself I felt my cheeks blaze. "Suppress it. Better still, eradicate it completely and spend every day working to change this life and turn from evil to good." He raised his head. "Can't you see how tormented I am?"

I could yes, but at this point these tirades were tormenting me too. Every second spent listening to Papa talk deprived me of time with Repin. He would be wondering what I was doing, why I hadn't come. Would he doubt my feeling for him? Would he wonder if everything was beginning to be, as I sometimes did, just a little too difficult?

"The thing is Tanyushka," said my father oblivious of my disinterest. "I have given this much thought." He was suddenly calm again. "Apart from the Stryder story I have been thinking of little else. In fact, I will no longer write fiction of any description. I shall devout the rest of my literary life to solving the religious and philosophical questions that haunt me."

"Papa–"

"Oh, don't be alarmed Tanya, they aren't difficult! Not at all–in fact everything can be condensed into a single, central endeavour. How to live a better life. Really nothing else matters and the sooner I can open your eyes to this and those of everyone around you, the better."

Panic was now rising in my stomach along with the familiar blackness that came when I felt cornered. Under my cloak, my lace jabot felt like a noose.

"Papa really I–"

My father snorted and at that moment I completely understood how Turgenev might have imagined him to be a horse in another life. With his mane of unruly hair, his puffed-up chest in its shapeless shirt, he was decidedly equine-like. Only I wasn't exactly certain as to what stage in evolution he had reached. He held up a hand to indicate any further interruption would not go unpunished.

"There are four human abilities," Papa said dogmatically. "These four kinds of good necessary to man, need to be alternated with daily tasks. For example, one part of the day and preferably the first, should be given to manual labour, another to thinking, a third to creating with your hands and the last to communication in whatever form you chose. Yours, for instance Tanya, is clearly art. However, as we continue to see and in such a depressing fashion, communication and art together can be explosive. It can result…" Once more his eyes blazed into mine. "In too much quilting."

Quilting? A million miles away, I'd forgotten Papa's quaint term for lovemaking. His eyes stubbornly refused to leave my face.

"And that is where celibacy is a welcome intermediary. It is a vital tool to keep the mind from idle and pointless pleasure."

Ah, that again. I wondered if my mother had had any right to veto this ruling and if that was why after Masha, we'd had no more brothers or sisters. And then just to provoke him and because I'd had enough of being held captive to the dogma of the moment *and* in an attempt to shut him up, I began to edge once again towards the front door. I pulled on my mittens.

"But art is pleasure," I said over my shoulder. "It gives, reflects, imitates pleasure. Isn't it the ultimate titillation of the senses? Would you have it that art is pointless? That what *I* am doing is pointless?"

"Bones of the saints! Do you really understand so little? You know that the only art for me is one that represents truth."

I hadn't exactly forgotten. How could any of us. Papa had written an article *On Art* and had an ongoing discussion about this very subject with Chekov our neighbour (well neighbour of one hundred and fifty versts away) whose writing he dismissed outright. Part of Papa's disdain was due to the doctor's admiration for the Italian masters. Papa thought this risible. Needless to say, Mama thought Papa's opinion risible especially when, in the name of 'Art', Papa plastered the walls of his study at Yasnaya with 'realistic' pictures of peasants going about their daily chores. It was only when Chekov died, that Papa grudgingly admitted that he might have been wrong. In an unexpected act of humility, he even put up a copy of Chekov's favourite picture: Rafael's Madonna. Chekov had always upheld it to be the finest example of female beauty and Papa (naturally), the ugliest.

"Why can't it do both? Papa?"

There was a sudden cry followed by the sound of splintered glass. I spun round. In a burst of temper, my father had smashed the windowpane of the landing casement with his fist. Blood spurted from his wrist faster than any outdoor spring in Yalta and was quickly drenching his linen shirt.

"Papa!" I called more out of annoyance than concern. The man would do absolutely anything to hold your attention when he wanted something. Dropping my skates and clutching my skirts I sprinted up the stairs. Hunkering down beside him I used the bottom part of his own capacious shirt to stem the bleeding. Slumped on the ground, with his arm folded against his chest, he resembled a defeated Napoleon. I sat back on my heels.

"This isn't enough," I said. "I'll have to get something else. Shouldn't I find Mama?"

"None of you understands anything, especially not Sonya," my father grunted. "Not even you, Tanya." But reminded of my mother, he grabbed my arm with his other hand. "No, don't tell your mother. She doesn't know I'm back. Call one of the girls and get along with you. Weren't you supposed to be meeting Repin? So, what's keeping you? I hope you haven't kept him waiting. You know how he's only giving you lessons as a favour to me. It would be embarrassing if he thought you weren't serious. Go!"

This was all said through short, angry bursts. For a moment I grappled between filial duty and a strong urge to simply step over him and walk away. Suppressing an even greater temptation to scream with frustration, I began to climb the second flight of stairs to the servants' attic rooms.

"I'll fetch Kasha," I said calling down. "Don't move Papa–someone will be down in a minute.

I had no idea how many hours had passed when I eventually let myself out of the house, in my third attempt of the day to meet Repin. It was twilight at any rate, and a strange grey light I had so often tried to replicate in pictures of Yasnaya, ran a thick brushstroke between birch tree and snow. Perched on ladders, house servants shovelled snow from the roof, pushing it sideways with large wooden paddles. Great ball-shaped lanterns helped them work in the encroaching dark. It was very quiet. Perhaps it wasn't as late as I thought as there was no sign of Masha and her friends.

I had almost boiled alive inside the house but once outside, I was instantly frozen. I tried wriggling the end of my nose but it felt numb. Skirting the house and taking a short cut by clambering over a snowbank, I soon made my way to the central courtyard. Groups of serfs stood talking amongst themselves. I smiled but they didn't respond and the new surliness in their attitude niggled me. It couldn't be that they thought us in any way lazy. No one was more industrious than our father (albeit in the pursuit of sometimes questionable hobbies) and our mother never stopped in her own endeavours, drawing, writing stories for children, knitting, sewing and in the upbringing of her remaining offspring. No, it wasn't for lack of example. It was something more insidious, but I was in too much of a hurry to find Repin, to analyse my unease any further, if indeed it warranted so much attention.

I ran the last part of the way propelled only by the thought of Repin and my longing for him, and so desperate to see him that nothing else mattered. I chided myself for not being stronger with Papa. I ought to have simply walked away before he became too worked up. I prayed fervently that Repin would be waiting, making every pact with God and all the saints and the bones of the saints, that if he were still there when I rounded the last bend through the trees, I would... I would... what?

My breath was coming in short rasps as I gulped the cold air. I covered my mouth with my hands to warm my face and shut my eyes, making my pact. Snowbanks formed a tunnel to the opening onto the ice which was crisscrossed with figures of eight. Only when–*if* I saw Repin–would I put on my skates. I didn't want to be out on the pond when it got dark. I stopped short, my heart pounding, closing my eyes in a childish way, to make a wish. One more second, I prayed. Just one more and when I open them I will ... I will...

...lose my balance rather dramatically and skid the remaining few feet on my bottom. More surprised than bruised, I was winded, half-hidden by the snowbank. A movement caught my eye as still on my bottom, yet gaining purchase, I shuffled forward on the ice. Anxiously I scanned the rink for Repin. And there he was! He'd waited after all! I let out a muffled cry, struggling to my knees but with my cloak bunched underneath me, I felt as grounded as a capsized sailing boat, my skirts as tightly bound as any unfurled sail.

I waved just as the figure, mirrored my gesture. I sank back on my heels There was no point in struggling further, I would wait for Repin to hoist me to my feet. Happily, I hugged myself, knowing that any minute strong hands would reach down to me. I closed my eyes anticipating the wonderful moment when... But the figure though certainly gliding smoothly across the ice was moving away, not towards me. I frowned. The figure wore long skirts and held a sable muff. And unless Repin had suddenly become a woman ...

It suddenly dawned on me that I hadn't been seen at all. I leant sideways, my cheek pressed against compressed snow breathing slowly as the woman who was my mother waved again, joyfully, and not to me of course, but to the man I recognised as Arkady. My heartbeat slowed painfully, sank painfully, because as on the first occasion of our meeting, he was sashaying perfectly across the ice to greet her.

8

I sat deflated on the snow, my skirts not only tight around me, but wet through now too. Repin no doubt had tired of waiting and had gone home. It was growing darker by the minute. My mother still hadn't seen me, and I felt suddenly awkward as though I were intruding. Why that should be I had no idea but the happiness on her face when she turned to Arkady was somehow shocking and private. She certainly never looked at us with that same softness of expression. Once again, I peered around the corner from the safety of my snowbank. Part of me knew I should creep away as quickly and quietly as possible, while the other, the shameful one that was unused to such grown up things, felt compelled to stay. And the longer I remained in place, the more difficult it was to get up and go. I no longer felt the cold; on the contrary, I was enlivened, electrified by the risk of discovery. Masha was usually the eavesdropper in the family, well this time I'd have something to tell her!

I removed my skates from where I had been carrying them around my neck and pressed myself deeper into the snow. In the encroaching darkness, it wasn't easy to see Mama's face but her whole body inclined towards Arkady. She was fiddling with the buttons on his coat in the charming way Papa must have known once and now she applied only to Sergei and even then, only if he was in a good mood. In profile, her face tilted prettily and then was covered completely when Arkady's bent down, his large sable fur cap brushing the top of hers. I held my breath, not daring to move. They stood on their skates, their bodies folded into one another, his arms holding hers. Her hands were clasped against his chest as if in prayer. I saw her nod slowly and then to my surprise and I'm sure hers, he sprang away so quickly she almost lost her balance. But it was Arkady who looked winded, not my mother. He thumped his chest several times as if in an attempt to re-start his heart and then began coughing, clouds of white air spiralling upwards. He bent double, hands on his knees inhaling deeply.

"Another?" Is what I think he said, when he could at last speak and in French, but then it could have been any word that rhymed. I wracked my brain: a lover? A brother? Cover? *Suffer*? No, 'another' was the only one that made sense because Mama nodded smiling. Arkady wasn't smiling though. He had skated backwards and away from her so that she was forced to skate too, to keep up. To my alarm, they changed tack, heading in my direction. I ducked down.

"But you said this couldn't happen!" Arkady's voice was angry and absolutely clear. I could hear every word as it sliced through the cold air. "You assured me it wasn't a possibility. You promised. Or you lied to me."

"I didn't lie!" Mama's voice had switched from one of elation to that small, anaemic tone I knew only too well. "I didn't think–not at my age–not for a minute." I could hear the suspended tears–far more disturbing than the joyfulness with which she'd greeted Arkady only moments before. I heard the scratch of blades when to my relief they moved away, but I didn't dare hazard a look. "Arkady, please," she pleaded. "I'm sorry. I never meant for this to happen!"

"But it has," Arkady said coldly. "I don't know whether it's incompetence or duplicity but either way it's disappointing, Sonya, very disappointing."

"So, what are we going to do?" More sniffs. A cough, clearing of throat. A warble. There was more scraping. They must have been talking at a distance from each other because the heavier tread was Arkady's as he covered the space between them.

"*Do?*" he said loudly, so loudly that I turned away from the rink altogether. Pressing my back against the snowbank, I tried to make myself as invisible as possible. My palms were sweating inside their mittens, my heart hammered in my chest. He sounded so close, I wondered he couldn't hear it.

"Do?" he repeated crisply. "Why, you're going to get rid of it, of course."

There was a gasp and then immediate, hollow sobs.

"How *did* you think it would work?" said Arkady impatiently. "How on earth can it? It would destroy everything! My God, you can see that, can't you? I mean your position, your family, your children."

"*Don't* bring my children into this, Prince!" said Mama fiercely between sobs. "*Don't* pretend you care about them or my family! You know perfectly well that you're only thinking of yourself and what it would do to *your* reputation! It's not quite the image is it? It's not the way you imagined things would be."

Mama was sobbing hysterically. More scratching of blades.

"No, it's not," said Arkady more calmly this time. "But you didn't either, did you?"

There were more sobs. I was becoming irritated by how much she was crying. And bored. I wanted to go back to the house. Forget this silly conversation. I had no idea what they were talking about. My experience of men was limited to Papa (sometimes, if not most of the time certifiable) and Sergei (morose and private). Neither one, entirely reliable. More recently, I had come to know Repin, but even he (especially he) was a mystery of manhood.

"Tell me how it can work then," said Arkady quietly. "Tell me."

There was a long pause.

"I don't know," Mama said again through tears. "I don't know. You're right I wasn't thinking but I really didn't believe–it's been so difficult for so long. When I met you, I forgot about everything. It was complete joy. So much joy! I haven't had so much fun in ages, not since I was a girl. And all because of you! You made me want to live again, to do better, to be everything I'd forgotten how to be. You have no idea. You can't imagine." There was a jumble of words some of them incoherent. Mama seemed to be talking incessantly, panicked into a confession of sorts. I was horrified but also morbidly fascinated, intent on listening. "I was so young when I met Lev," Mama was saying. "I'd never lived in the country and when we arrived at Yasnaya–well it was awful. It was cold, there wasn't any furniture, not even beds! The servants slept where they fell asleep, sometimes standing in corners and Lev with them. There wasn't any privacy, and I was so lonely. On our wedding night, Lev showed me his diary."

"Oh, *zaika*," murmured Arkady. I made a face at the snowbank. *Golden one*? I'd never heard anyone call my mother that before. Either way, I hoped he was taking her in his arms. It had begun to snow again, snow flurries floating in every direction. I raised my face, sticking out my tongue to catch the thick fat flakes as they fell.

"Don't say any more," he said.

"But I *want* to tell you," said my mother. "On our wedding night, Lev showed me his diary," she repeated. "He said he wanted us to have complete trust in one another, that from that moment on we should show each other everything we wrote, that we should have no secrets." Mama swallowed. "In the diary, he had written in extraordinary detail about every woman he had ever had…relations with." Mama's voice was flat. "They were mostly serfs still working at Yasnaya–they were women I would see on a daily basis. There were already several children."

"Sonyetka," said Arkady, his tone dull.

"Can you imagine what that did to me? The love that I had for Lev was gobbled up on my wedding night and by morning there was nothing left. I was trapped on a godforsaken estate with no friends and nothing to do. And then all those children! All those dead–well I didn't think I'd ever feel again–" Another sob. "Not until you."

"We've had a wonderful time," interrupted Arkady. "And we can, once more, but not like this."

"Then you're asking too much."

"I'm being realistic."

Mama must have skated away because Arkady called out, "Sonya!" and then there was a quick slice of blade as he made to follow. Mama was a wonderful skater, but I knew Arkady was an even better athlete. If she gave chase, he would catch her. For a few moments I heard the even, rapid swish of skirts and ice as the sounds became faster, sharper and closer together.

"Sonya!" he called again, and the skating stopped. There was the soft sound of skin against skin, material rubbing fur and slow rhythmic crying.

"It's just so sad," Mama was saying. "Not once, in the past has this *ever* brought joy. Not once. I thought this time it might be different. I see it as the ultimate bond with someone you really love but you're right I must have been insane, completely and totally insane. I should have been more careful. I never ever thought-"

"No, you didn't," Arkady said strongly. "On the other hand, I've never known someone of your age to be so, so *innocent*. I don't know what happened. There's...untidiness here somewhere, but we can...correct it."

"I've always been more fatalistic myself," said Mama with the faintest hint of humour.

"How very Russian," said Arkady in Russian.

"No, neither French nor Russian, Arkasha, just human."

It was very dark now. I wriggled uncomfortably on a numb bottom. With fresh snow fall, night had suddenly descended. Emboldened, I moved slightly so that I could see the rink again. A slither of moonlight turned the ice and birch trees silver. Against paler snowbanks, the silhouettes of Arkady and my mother stood as one. Her head rested on his shoulder. With one hand, Arkady caressed her hair which had come undone from its chignon, the other held her fur cap by his side. An owl hooted long and persistently and ahead, the house ablaze with light, was inviting and warm.

"There *is* a way," he said at length. "A way to save face, to preserve the status quo so that no one need ever know. Your life remains intact. You save your reputation and your children."

My mother raised a tear-stained face, her blonde hair falling loose down her back. I had never seen Mama with her hair in anything but a braid or piled high on her head and I could see why Arkady might call her 'golden,' after all. She was certainly so tonight, despite her obvious distress. In a childlike gesture, Mama wiped her face roughly with the back of her hand. Arkady reaching for the nape of her neck pulled her head towards his. I thought he was about to kiss her and was prepared to look away in disgust but instead he suddenly swooped on her ear whispering.

For what seemed a long time after he'd finished speaking, my mother stayed in that position. Slowly she withdrew.

"But Lev won't have anything more to do with quilting," she said at last in a tight, controlled voice. "I admit I wish he'd taken that decision years ago at Yasnaya but there it is. He's adamant."

"Then persuade him."

My mother blinked. "Is that what you want?"

Arkady nodded. My mother continued to stare at him as if memorising his face, as if condensing it, as I might have in order to recreate it in oil at a later stage. But I knew her better than this man she professed to care so much about. Something distasteful had been revealed to her. Something she would rather not have known and yet it was there, being registered, recorded too, in her heart. Snatching her hat from him, she suddenly twirled away in a billow of fur and skirts, her hair flying out behind her like a girl's. Arkady called after her but she was swallowed up by the trees and the snow-covered fields.

"Sonya! Sonyetka!" He called after her. "Is it still all right if I stay to supper?"

9

I sat rooted like an icicle to a Siberian pine seemingly easily dislodged yet in reality, tenacious and not quite ready to melt away. Mama had left the rink, but I couldn't be certain that Arkady had followed her. I hadn't heard the tell-tale scrape of his skates as they scissored through the orchard. There was every chance he would soon be making his way up this very path to where I was hiding. There was no time to lose but getting up wasn't as easy as sitting down had been. Snow virtually covered the lower half of my body and the weight of my wet clothing kept me pinioned. I kicked as hard as I could hearing the rip of undergarments as I did so. But I was now able to wriggle free and crouch on all fours. It was just as I was finally heaving myself to my feet, that a falling branch or something with incredible force slammed into me. Caught completely off guard, I was knocked backwards, my head cracking on the icy ground. Whatever it was, let out a long woosh of air. Wolves! I thought in horror, my entire body rigid with fear. Sergei wouldn't be nearly so dismissive now, when my blood-stained rags were found as the ice melted…

Gingerly I moved my limbs, my head, my frozen fingers. Well, I was still alive. I hadn't been torn to pieces. There was heavy breathing but it didn't appear to be coming from an animal after all. Perhaps it was *my* breathing. I lay still a moment longer before opening my eyes to a slate-coloured sky that seemed to be falling on top of me too. And that was because it was, or at least if not sky, then what felt like a barrel load of snow as it dislodged itself from the branches above to land directly on my face. I spluttered as snow filled my mouth, nostrils and eyelashes. Quickly melting, it slid off my face mingling with my tears. I was crying now in earnest. I was weeping snow. The more I cried, the sorrier I felt for myself, until I was sobbing in loud abandon. And then a voice I recognised called to me and arms I knew gathered me in his.

"Tanya, Tanya!" said Repin so that we were lying alongside each other in the snow. "I didn't mean to hurt you! I've been looking for you all afternoon!" And when my cries only grew louder, he pressed my head against his warm coat. "There, there little one. I'm sorry I tripped. I thought you were a log–I mean not that you could be mistaken–" he finished hastily.

I shook my head already comforted by his soothing tone and strong arms and the feeling that though I'd been lost, I was somehow found.

"So, it was you! Not a wolf!" I said after a while and my sobs had subsided.

"Wolf?" echoed Repin. "No wolf. But there might be a bear or two."

"What?" I squealed struggling against him.

"Sh!" he quietened. "It's all right. Be still. Just a little longer."

And I was. Quiet and still. For the first time in weeks.

"I'm just a bit stunned," I said lamely. "Confused." Which didn't even begin to convey what I was feeling. There was so much I could have said and yet was unable to communicate what it was I really felt–if there was anything to feel at all and whether I was right to interpret what I thought I'd understood from Mama and Arkady's conversation, and yet again, how on earth to recount such a thing? I continued to cry quietly at the revelation that the familiar, intelligible world of my childhood, through which I had comfortably negotiated my way up until now, was evidently something quite different. What was most shocking, was that the adult world upon whose threshold I so eagerly awaited, seemed somehow more sinister and duplicitous than I could ever have imagined.

"Not about us I hope," said Repin anxiously.

I shook my head vigorously allowing myself to relax against him. Mimicking the rhythmic motion of his hands on my back, my breathing resumed an even pace. In the same instance that I raised my face to his, he lowered his lips to mine, pressing gently.

"I've been waiting all week for this," he said.

"I've never spent so much time in the snow," said I and he laughed leaping to his feet and pulling me to mine in a slightly clumsy move. We fell against each other in exactly the way I'd hoped (and dreamt) we would earlier. I continued to lean against him, as warmth emanated from his body. He didn't seem to mind at all, that my sodden clothes had made his wet too. And as much as I began to feel safe again in his embrace, I was suddenly homesick for Yasnaya Polyana and even for Olga Feodova. Perhaps, especially for Olga Feodova who was ugly and old and unchanging and who could never ever surprise me by kissing a stranger with hooded eyes on an ice rink.

"Would you do something for me?" I said suddenly. We had begun to walk with difficulty through the heavy snow. My toes felt webbed together and I started to shiver uncontrollably. Repin stopped and scooped me up easily in his arms.

"You know I would."

"I want to go home," I said, hooking my hands around his neck. I knew he understood that by 'home' I didn't mean the house ahead of us. "And I would very much like you to come with me. I want to paint there. I–"

Repin covered my mouth again with his. "I know what you want," he said.

*

The house was noisy and full of people in only the way it ever was if Mama knew our father was away. I had almost forgotten Papa's earlier accident with the window or at least I found it difficult to remember it taking place that same day. There was no sign of him, and I wondered if he'd slipped away again. At any rate, I was still too preoccupied with what I'd overheard at the rink to dwell too much on Papa.

Servants bustled from kitchen to dining room setting the table for supper. Logs of ash and birch blazed merrily in the enormous hall fireplace and hundreds of candles gave the whole house a golden, rosy glow. I couldn't help thinking that Papa might have approved the quasi-spiritual effect. What he may not have, was that there wasn't a wooden utensil in sight. Mama's silver, china and crystal shimmered and shone, reflected many times over in long mirrors. Bowls of flowers gave off an exotic scent.

It was almost as if Mama had cause for celebration or was simply affording herself of every available weapon. I wasn't sure which. Masha sat by the fire binding all four of her kitten's paws in fine linen bandages. Sergei smoked moodily, something he wasn't allowed to do when Papa was home, his elegant, beautifully shod foot resting on the fender. From time to time, he cast nervous glances at the watch that he pulled from his waistcoat. He must have an appointment with someone somewhere, I thought. That is, if he could escape the house. There was no sign of our mother.

Repin removed my hat, as though I were a child. I smiled my fingers hovering over his.

"I can manage now," I said.

Repin nodded and spoke in Russian with that peculiar intonation I found amusing. As with other Ukrainians he commonly pronounced a 'g' as an 'h'. "Go (ho) and change little one, you've caught cold and had a shock. I shall talk to your brother."

"Good luck," I said wryly. "I'm not sure how talkative you'll find him."

I hung up my cloak and stepped out of my outdoor boots. Repin touched my back.

"But don't be long," he said. "Otherwise, I shall think it a re-run of this afternoon and be persuaded that you no longer care."

I climbed the stairs to the first floor noticing how the broken glass on the landing had been tidied up and the window itself boarded with strips of wood. I hesitated outside my mother's room, the room Papa said was done up like a chocolate box but to us was mysterious and beautiful. I sniffed the air for that delicious perfume that was her own and which seemed to follow her wherever she went. I wanted to see her, to remind myself that she was still my mother not some foolish woman in love with a man who was not my father. Was she foolish? I found it difficult to see her as anyone other than my mother and it was unthinkable to imagine she had a secret life which didn't involve us. Overhearing her on the ice was like seeing an actress on the stage–only as Mama drew closer, did she became familiar and beloved. About to knock, I heard voices within and stopped.

"But you've said repeatedly that you weren't happy." Arkady sounded weary.

"Yes, Arkasha," said Mama in that humouring tone I knew very well. The playing for time tone, the one that that meant she had made up her mind. "But I have a structure here, a structure worth preserving. It took me years to get Lev to move to the city and allow the children to go to school. You know how he is about education."

"You mean that he doesn't believe in any."

"No, he does, just in a different way," replied Mama loftily. "He hopes that one day, as we all do, they will follow his example and fight social and economic injustice."

"You mean by toiling all day with the two hundred and fifty serfs he inherited and then coming home to a table waited upon by white-gloved servants?"

Mama sighed. This was an argument I had heard a hundred times over but mostly between my parents. Papa complained all the time that owning so much depressed him, that he longed to give it all away. It was this very attitude however, that so distressed and frustrated our mother.

"I admit there are contradictions. He finds aristocratic life empty and meaningless, but you can't fault a person for trying."

"You sound just like him," said Arkady sulkily.

"Well, I've lived with him long enough," said Mama. "It's hardly surprising."

There was a silence before Mama spoke again. "The point is," she said firmly. "The children are finally happy. They have a stability that I have given them, that I have fought for. Lev can be as eccentric as he likes but nothing will change here. I have protected them from so much."

"That may be, but they won't be children for much longer. Masha is young, I grant you, but Tatyana is on the brink…" There was a muffled word I didn't hear. I took a step closer feeling my heart in my mouth and so loud I was sure they could hear it thumping through the door. There were a few more garbled sentences before a clear, "… and Sergei's a man, Sonya."

"Don't I know it! Sergei's far too selfish to think of anything but his love affairs and his horses." Mama's tone was caustic. There was a pause and then an anguished cry. "Don't you understand? You're asking me to destroy something I love already or destroy my family!"

And because my heart did a flip and a floorboard creaked as I shifted my weight, I knocked on the door. I was trapped between wanting to hear more and having had enough of these adults and their strange secrets. I wanted my mother all to myself and immediately. Now. This instance. I wanted to tell her about Papa's accident. I wanted to tell her not to worry about us. That perhaps the Prince was right, we weren't children (except of course I couldn't say that last bit without admitting to eavesdropping), and finally that perhaps it was already time to leave Moscow, that the 'city' experiment hadn't quite worked as she had hoped it would. I didn't want to have to wait one more second for her attention and I certainly didn't want to have to share her at supper with everyone else, especially Arkady. Above all, I wanted Mama to look into my face in the adoring, if soppy way she looked into his.

At first though, they just continued talking so I thumped even louder, this time with the flat of my hand and not just my knuckles.

There was a warbly, "Y-yes?" Then the sound of a chair or similar small piece of furniture being knocked over.

"It's only me, Mamushka."

"Is supper ready?"

"I don't know." I rattled her door handle, but it was locked. "I need to ask you something."

"Oh darling, can't it (muffled sounds) wait?"

"No, no it can't. I really have to see you."

There was more scraping across floorboards (perhaps Arkady had tripped over a rug), a pause and then the door appeared to open as if by magic. My mother was seated at her dressing table, for all intents and purposes as though getting ready for dinner. She wore a revealing peignoir with cascades of lace at the elbows and elaborate bows at the waist. I'd never seen it before, and I wasn't entirely convinced it suited her. It made her look decidedly un-motherly. You certainly didn't feel you could throw yourself on a lap as delicate as that. I wondered vaguely if I could ever create such a gossamer effect in paint. Mama was pinning up her hair without the help of her maid and not very successfully. She had overdone the rouge too and her eyes were strangely bright. But there was no trace of tears and her hands fluttered inexpertly across her dressing table, touching the silver-topped bottles, dabbing her wrists with scent (spilling the scent), and dispersing powder so that everything–including her jewels and hair pins–was covered in a fine white dust.

Lowering my eyes, feigning shyness, I scanned the candlelit room. There was no sign at all of Arkady, and I wondered where on earth he'd got to. Had he slipped into a cupboard or under the bed? But he was heavy enough to make the latter suggestion improbable. I wished I could have discussed it with Sergei; having not inconsiderable practice in making hasty retreats, he would have known where to look.

The mere fact of being in Mama's boudoir, distracted me briefly from my purpose. Like the Czarina's famous mauve bedroom, it was entirely one colour and the effect was soothing and soporific. And cleverly achieved. Although at first sight the colours appeared monotone, in reality every shade and texture of the sea was represented. Voluminous silk curtains as wide as any ball gown, sprang from a gilt corona. The feather-stuffed mattress was the plumpest I had ever seen. Oversize linen pillows, fine lawn sheets and a sable blanket the size of a small carpet completed such an enticing invitation to repose, I had a hard job resisting the urge to dive under the covers. The rest of the furniture was delicate, painted French Louis XV. There was a sweet little slipper chair by the fire, a small side table scattered with books and a vase of lily of the valley.

My gaze stayed longer on the flowers than on any other object in the room. I could well understand why Papa worked himself up so. Flowers were imported from the South of France and kept on ice to preserve their freshness during the long train journey to Russia. As a result, only the imperial family or the very rich could afford such a luxury. Perhaps they were a gift from Arkady? Either way, I was intoxicated by their scent, by the warmth, by the pure comfort of the room. With the shadows of the flames licking the silk-covered walls and the gentle candlelight creating a bewitching glow, I was drawn into this other world, this haven from the starkness of Papa's austere one. He wasn't exaggerating when he nick-named it the bonbonnière.

"Well, what is it, little Kotchka? What is so urgent if it's not to do with supper?" Mama addressed me in French but used the Russian word for kitten which was her nickname for me. And then, when I still didn't speak, wondering myself why I was there and wrestling the delicious dilemma of whether or not I'd rather be curled up in that chair by the fire or drowning under the sable fur on a mattress, she added, "You're staring at me as though you've never seen me in your whole life!"

I blinked, noticing how her gown fell from her shoulders and the smooth whiteness of a full, round breast was exposed. I looked at her again. It certainly seemed as though I were seeing her for the first time, at least I'd never seen her looking like this before. In here, in her bedroom, she was someone entirely different–someone altogether more flirtatious, more youthful than the sometimes stern, vague woman who was always too busy, too distracted by her chores to pay us the attention we would have liked. I wondered at her composure, her ability to act normal and now that she was there before me, all I wanted was for her to take me in her arms and kiss me and tell me everything would be all right. But she turned back to the mirror, shaking out her hair which fell easily from its inexpert knot and picked up her silver, monogrammed hairbrush.

"Kotchka?"

"I–" my eyes swivelled back to the reflection in the mirror and behind her head to the capacious bed hangings … that swelled like a woman's wedding dress…that… so *that's* where Arkady must be hiding!

Mama's eyes narrowed in the way they did when she was irritated.

"I want to go to Yasnaya," I blurted out clumsily, nervously in the way I used to when I needed to ask Mama for something but was pretty confident that she'd say no. Mama set down her brush carefully so that the huge embossed crest appeared like a butterfly hovering above the surface. It was precisely this display of privilege Papa hated even if the coat of arms was in fact his.

"Why?" asked Mama her playful humour evaporating with the word. Anything to do with the old place was a betrayal in her eyes of what she was endeavouring to create for us in Moscow. It showed an allegiance to Papa and his way of life as opposed to hers. Already Masha, in her decision to renounce meat, was displaying a rebelliousness that alarmed her and although Sergei had taken to city life with gusto, his laziness and debauchery didn't exactly prove her point to Papa either.

I shrugged. "I want to paint."

Mama's eyes met mine in the mirror. "But you have a studio here. And a teacher."

I took a breath hoping I wasn't blushing. "I'd like him to come too."

"I see." Mama arched an eyebrow. "So, you'd travel alone with this man. Have you any idea how that would look?" Her expression was no longer gentle.

I shifted my weight, actually balancing on one foot. Concentrating on this balletic move, for some reason helped me to compose myself. "No, I mean yes, but Olga Feodova would be there–"

"Olga?" At the mention of our nanny, Mama's eyes began to vibrate in the highly revealing way they did when she was thinking (or scheming). She turned on her little dressing table stool to face me and took my hand. "You could bring her back with you, couldn't you Kotchka? She has never been to Moscow and the change would...do her good."

I must have expressed surprise at this. I didn't think Olga Feodova had ever set foot outside Yasnaya in her entire life. She'd been born on the estate as had her mother and her mother before her, and even if technically she now had her freedom, she knew no other home. I couldn't think of a more shocking trip for an old woman to make. Besides which, Olga had made her thoughts on the city perfectly clear before we left. Mama dropped my hand.

"I miss her," she said unconvincingly.

"So do I." Which was true.

Mama rose and I realised, I was expected to leave.

I also knew that if I had any hope of winning Mama's support, I had less than ten seconds in which to do so.

"We could visit Chekov on the way," I suggested helpfully.

Mama snorted. "What, that funny doctor?"

"I thought then he could visit us here and you could make your poppy seed cakes. It might cheer Papa up."

"Or depress him." Mama's eyes were once again darting back and forth as she eased me to the door. "The one thing that can be said about Chekov is that he knows how to live. It's curious Kotchka, there's your father who was born a count doing everything in his power to appear a peasant and there's Chekov whose father was a serf, doing the best he can to live like a count!" It was certainly true that while Papa seemed intent on growing a Confucius-type beard, Chekov's goatee was always neatly trimmed. "You should see his house!" she enthused. "He has the very finest china and now that he's friends with Lubonov, the walls are hung with the most wonderful pictures, maybe with yours too one day if you play your cards right. You have me thinking... little Kot. Perhaps, it wouldn't be such a bad thing for him to see how a normal family lives!"

What was normal? I loved that each of us believed the other to be less than. Papa revelled in Chekhov family exploits. In particular, I recalled one story concerning Chekov's father who still lived with him and whose every second was governed by a rigid timetable. Chekov, at vast expense, had transported an aquarium full of exotic fish from Moscow for his pond. The event was inaugurated with a special ceremony to which Chekov's father would not attend because, according to his 'timetable' he was out cutting grass at that precise moment. Later during the day, when he had an allocated hour's leisure time he went fishing. That evening two exquisite carp were served at dinner...

I nodded and suddenly threw my arms around my mother's waist.

"Kotchka!" she exclaimed not displeased and then ushering me out of the door, out of her world, added, "I'll think about what you propose, but I'm not promising anything."

10

It was a barn owl this time, that shot out of the Tyrolean clock as I entered the dining room. For a moment, there was a cacophony of bird song, the artificial competing with the real fowl out of doors. Mama with the help of one of the abler, if rather ancient valets, was offering guests glasses of champagne.

"No nasty Hungarian stuff either, Tanya," said Sergei sipping his appreciatively.

There was a steady din of voices, the tinkle of crystal, the hiss as candles were snuffed out only to be replaced by fresh ones. Like Mama's boudoir, this room came to life when Papa was away. As with Yasnaya Polyana, she had transformed an unloved dwelling into a beautiful home. The room was awash with colour, the spicy aromas emanating from the kitchen mingling with the sweetness of wood from fruit trees crackling in the fire. And Mama was the centre of it all, pirouetting from one family member to the next, happier and more vivacious than I had seen her in a long time. She was glowing and exotic in a bilberry blue velvet gown slashed with silver and gold sleeves. Jewels caught the light at her throat, waist and wrists and she had opted for the traditional Muscovite kokoshnik to cover her hair. The one-time earthiness that had once attracted Papa in his quest for simplicity, was no more. Mama was nothing less than imperial. With all the excitement, no one noticed that Masha was happily drinking champagne as though it were barley water.

"To my favourite pupil," said Repin in my ear, folding my fingers around the cold stem of a champagne flute.

"To my favourite teacher," I replied somewhat stiffly. Was that how he saw me? And then it occurred to me that perhaps he liked me more for my supposed talent, than for myself as a woman. Woman? I wasn't sure I was even quite that, but he made me feel like one, even though I knew I was still a girl.

"Do you–do you have many pupils?" I asked scanning his face and taking nervous little sips of my drink. The warm feeling that we had shared when we lay in the snow earlier was quickly replaced by something more unsettling.

I realised with a pang, that I really didn't know very much about Ilya Yefimovich Repin. I called him by his patronymic. Even that was strange and yet he was my teacher. It seemed respectful and only right to address a friend of my father's in such a way. But then of course he hadn't always been held in such esteem. It was heartening to think that he was only my age when he first started painting. He had failed on his first time attempt to enter the Imperial Academy of Fine Arts in St. Petersburg (also heartening) but it appeared to have made little difference as shortly after he had won a gold medal for his painting 'Job and His Brothers'. What I appreciated most about him was that he loved his country and many of his sketches were representative of Ukrainian life and culture which he called 'sweet and joyful.'

But Repin the man? What of him? What did he ever really allow me to know? It was a question I would ask myself throughout our time together. I still ask it. But, in the wonder and cocoon of our affair, I hadn't given his life when we weren't together, any thought at all. I took a step back, observing him as though I were to paint him, forcing myself to examine him as dispassionately as possible. He was a little stooped because of his extreme height and perhaps too thin. If it weren't for powerful shoulders, he might even be considered gawky. His hands were slender, tapered, the thumbs bending upwards and over sensitive I knew, to extremes of temperature. And yet they could weald strength. I'd seen it. One side of his face appealed to me more than the other. The one with the slightly drooping eye was vigorous and manly, whilst the other by contrast, was effeminate, foolish even. There were creases at his eyes and broad mouth and grey was beginning to lighten his dark hair. Did he look so much older than me? Would people comment if…would it matter if they did?

I turned away, then instantly back as Arkady catching my eye, crossed the room with the agility of a cat.

"You're not jealous, are you?" said Repin in genuine surprise.

"Of course not!" I hissed as Arkady sensing the tension between us raised an eyebrow, his cheeks sucked in making his extraordinary cheekbones more pronounced. He looked like a Tartar–in fact he called to mind Repin's own portrait 'Ivan the Terrible'–a picture my teacher would later defend as 'avoiding the acrobatics of the brush.' It had been vandalized many times.

"So, Kotchka," said Arkady and I bristled at the use of Mama's nickname for me. "Your mother tells me that you are planning a trip to Tula."

"I'm thinking of going home, yes."

"And you're to go with him?" Arkady inclined his head to Repin as though he were no more than a wayward schoolboy. He did not mention that Repin had ever painted him.

"Tatyana is my pupil," said Repin rather formally. And when Arkady merely smiled added, "she will be a great painter, you will see."

"I'm sure she will succeed in whatever she sets her heart on," and again he smiled in that all knowing, all seeing manner that made me want to slap him. He set down his glass on the mantelpiece and took out a cigar which he placed carefully between his lips and which Mama, covering the distance between them as though she were gliding on ice, removed just as deftly.

"We're about to sit down," she said. "Come, finish your drinks."

Mama, keeping her eyes fixed on Arkady's face held his gaze until his features had once more settled into that cool aloofness, I was beginning to associate with him. Calmly he tucked his cigar into his jacket pocket but ignored the rest of his champagne. He bowed elegantly first to Repin and then to me, clicking his heels in the way cavalry officers of the time did and for a moment, as occasionally happened with my father, I caught a glimpse of the man he had once been at another stage of his life. I felt a funny lurch in the pit of my stomach affected by the sudden, old world charm of his gesture which lay at odds with his animal-like magnetism.

Servants began to serve large platters of zakusi and caviar to work up a thirst. There was the sound of popping corks, another log being tossed on the fire, the swish of doors being opened and closed and a then a loud unmistakable hiccup. I started. It was almost immediately accompanied by the staccato, chirping trill of a skylark as the doors of the clock sprang open and the plaster bird revealed its painted head. Had an hour already passed in the dining room? The hiccup came again. It seemed, improbably, to be coming from under the table. The sound grew louder. As discretely as I could, I edged towards the table and on the pretext of adjusting my petticoat, sank down to raise the cloth. At first glance, I couldn't see anything. But with the next hiccup, a grinning, stupid-looking Masha, sitting with her legs apart came into view. There was a half-drunk bottle of champagne by her side. I let the cloth drop back into place and sidled towards the other end of the table.

"Come out!" I hissed.

Masha shook her head, shuffling away from me on her bottom.

Again, I ducked down, reaching blindly, only to be met with a smart kick. As I stood up red-faced, nursing my hand from where Masha had lashed out, Sergei pushed roughly past. Planting his feet firmly apart, as if to examine a horse's hoof, he leant down half-pulling, half-lifting Masha from her hiding place.

Between hiccups, she began imitating the cuckoo clock.

"Very clever," I said.

"Oh, no you don't!" said Sergei intercepting her as she made to dive under the table again.

"Out of curiosity," I said. "How many birds *do* you know?"

Masha cupped her hands to her mouth perfectly imitating a bullfinch. So perfectly that Mama glanced at the Tyrolean clock frowning. "Then there's a moorhen and a woodpecker and a pipit. I like the kestrel. Oh, I can do a swallow too. And willow warbler and–"

"I'll willow warbler you, if you don't shut up," said Sergei keeping tight hold of Masha's arm. "There's a good case for children being kept in the nursery. Olga Feodova would never allow you to stay up if she was here."

"Well, she's not," said Masha crossly. "I like the kingfisher, the peregrine–"

"My God you're tipsy!" said Sergei genuinely surprised and sniffing her breath. "Mam-" he began but I stopped him.

"Oh, let her be Seryozha," I said seeing Mama whisper something in Arkady's ear.

"Then keep an eye on her," said my brother. "I've got other things on my mind without having to worry about *it*." He jerked his head to indicate he meant our sister. I wanted to say that there were a lot of other people too with 'things' on their mind but didn't.

We moved to the table; our mother at the head, Arkady on her right and Repin on her left. Sergei sat opposite and Masha and her kitten took up two places. I slipped in beside Repin touching his knee under the cloth. He flashed me a quick, relieved smile and the warmth between us returned. Masha began to chirrup, and I kicked her under the table.

Arkady was telling Mama an anecdote about some deeply religious courtier at the time of Catherine the Great who refused to eat meat during one of her famous banquets. 'Maybe it was to do with Papa's renunciation of the flesh– both kinds' Arkady joked and Sergei smiled weakly torn between a desire to appear adult enough and yet not entirely in his absence, disloyal to Papa. I clearly didn't understand it though, as the punch line came and went as did the laughter before I realised the joke had ended. Mama smiled incessantly, her long agate earbobs mirroring the colour of her eyes, her cheeks flushed, her skin glowing in the candlelight. Her low-cut gown revealed the soft curve of her breasts and repeatedly my eyes, like Repin's were drawn to her laughing, luminous image. I found it almost impossible to marry this confident, happy woman with the distressed, tormented creature on the ice.

Champagne flowed, and supper was a feast. There was kulebyaka, one of my favourite dishes–a pie stuffed with different layers of fish–and shchi soup which Masha hadn't even begun, when the carp and peasant-baked khleb arrived. Dishes were whisked away the moment the last crumb was consumed, so that you had to virtually hang on to your plate if you hadn't quite finished. I noticed Repin huddled over his, having left a particularly scrumptious bit of pastry to smother in pickle, only to find it had gone when his attention was diverted. There was blintchik too, large square pancakes made from wheat flour, not the usual buckwheat, so fragile and thin I wondered how they could have been removed from the pan without breaking and more immaculate dollops of soured cream.

Arkady expertly folded his, eating with feline delicacy. Mama could hardly tear her eyes off him, savouring him as though he were more delicious than the feast laid out before us. She leant towards him, every word directed to the rest of the table when in reality, they were intended for him alone. From time to time, he would whisper something so quietly that try as I might, I couldn't hear, and she would toss back her head so that I trembled for her kokoshnik.

Arkady was as effervescent as she and his steady flow of conversation was as amusing as it was trivial. There was never a second's silence. While we waited for ice-cream and the salted peaches, I'd seen piled on vast silver platters, he told us how the great Potemkin, whose obsession with food rivalled that of his love of women, had whole pigs de-boned, stuffed with sausage and then cooked in pastry marinated in wine. Then there was the story of the poet Derzhavin who had sent a huge pie as a gift to a princess he was in love with. When she opened the pie, a dwarf had stepped out clutching a bunch of flowers.

"You asked me what I wanted for my birthday," said my mother prettily. "Well, something along those lines would do.

"So, it's originality you're after," said Arkady.

My mother turned her entire bosom towards him.

"You're always that, Arkasha."

"I feel sick," Masha announced suddenly before nose-diving with a significant splash, into her soup.

So did I at the turn in the conversation but Sergei's "Get her out of here!" propelled me from my seat.

I glanced around the room. Mama was oblivious to anything but Arkady and only Repin expressed concern. He pulled back my chair as I moved to help my sister. She flopped against me, shivering.

"I feel howid," she said.

"Don't you *dare* be sick on me!" I hissed as we made our way out of the dining room. "I've got on my best blue serge." And as she made a dubious choking sound, I gripped her arm. "I'm warning you!"

"I've forgotten kitty," she said suddenly when we were half-way up the stairs, turning on her heel so quickly that we both almost fell. One of the servants passing us on the landing, made clucking sounds and set down the basket of laundry she was carrying. She scooped Masha up in arms that were stronger, more capable and certainly more sympathetic, than mine.

"I'll get kitty," I said testily wanting only to be back beside Repin. "If I can find her. You'll be fine." As an afterthought, I added generously. "You can be sick now, if you like."

I ran down the stairs jumping the last two. I slowed my pace pausing by the hall mirror to pinch my cheeks. Licking my index finger, I smoothed my eyebrows into shape and retied my ponytail. I drew myself to my full height. By the way I'd noticed Repin watching my mother, it was clear that the mature woman was more appealing than the schoolgirl and I resolved to make myself as alluring and grown up as possible. Something would have to be done about my hair, but without Mama's lady's maid who was still at Yasnaya, there wasn't much hope of addressing that particular problem. If Mama's hairdo was anything to go by, I wasn't convinced she'd be much help either.

With renewed determination, I pushed open the dining room doors expecting to slip into my seat beside Repin and to enjoy the rest of the evening without being distracted by Masha. I was determined too, to have another glass of champagne. But at the very moment that I opened the dining room doors at my end, so too did Papa coming through the doors that led to the kitchen, at the other. There was a stunned, horrified silence. I stood frozen as if caught stark naked. Papa, unperturbed, smiled delightedly. He was barefoot, one hand dramatically bandaged, the other clutched a mug of his homebrewed kvass.

"Well, well, well. Like uncut dogs!" he said in Russian using the idiom to denote chaos and mayhem.

Mama's expression was unreadable. Only her magnificent breasts quivered while Arkady's languid, hooded eyes blinked once to convey only the very slightest annoyance at having been interrupted. Sergei taking a mouthful of ice-cream, grimaced as the cold sent needles of pain through his head. Repin faced with his idol, gazed at Papa in awe.

For a moment, the dinner table might have been a carefully construed still life. For a moment, I pondered how to emulate the quality of light seeping through the cracks of the door frame and the pallid areas above the diners' heads. How too, to perfectly capture the brilliance of Mama's skin and that metallic shot of silver around her hair? For a moment. After that, everyone leapt from their seats. Servants brought re-heated dishes and Papa settled himself in Masha's chair. He never placed himself at the head, declaring such a position to be one of dominance. I could see him taking in the remains of our banquet and the lavish display of linen and cutlery. But surprisingly, he didn't seem unduly disturbed by the presence of a stranger. Here, as at Yasnaya Polyana, visitors were always welcomed with exquisite ease and grace. Arkady rising to his feet, executed the same elegant bow of earlier in the evening and Papa acknowledged it with a formal, "Prince." To which my mother's lover hardly needed to have murmured, "Count, I know who you are…"

Mama began to heap far too much food on a family-crested plate and pass it down the table. To my utter amazement she then said, "So, *deroghoe*, what is your *strany*?" A common Russian greeting whose apparent banality is never to be underestimated and woe betide the person who cannot wait for an answer! A Russian is always prepared to recount several days' worth of emotional upset. In Papa's case, his countless moods were as immediate and demanding of attention, as a baby's. Now, his bushy eyebrows virtually covered his lowered lids. "If we'd known you were coming-" she added uselessly.

Papa's head shot up faster than the bird popping out of the cuckoo clock at that precise moment.

"Goodness, I wasn't expecting…" he said softly to himself and to my alarm I knew he was quoting from his own book, *The Kreutzer Sonata*.

I reached for Repin's hand under the table, gripping it tightly. By now we were both familiar with the dreadful story especially as it had provoked such a strong reaction in Papa when he first told us about it and after he had all but throttled Mama. We certainly didn't need reminding of its ending. I felt a cold, uncanny sense of recognition, of déjà vu even. In his book, the author interrupts his wife having a cosy evening with her friend. I needed no reminding that the casualness with which he is greeted so incenses the author's already heightened paranoia, that he kills his wife. I thought about the whole question of art imitating life and vice versa–of violence and regret. I thought of Repin's picture, said to be his most psychologically intense of Ivan the Terrible killing his son in a fit of passion. There is the realization, that Repin so brilliantly depicted, by the son of the father's madness before the act, and the father's awareness of his own insanity after, when he realizes just what he has done.

Despite the roaring fires and the stodgy winter fare, I felt cold to the bone. Mama feigned ignorance and I could sense her wondering whether or not she should lie and what it was exactly that she would lie about. But Papa seemed merely amused at Mama's obvious discomfort if rather more perplexed by Arkady himself. Neither person appeared to cause him much concern and I began to wonder if I hadn't imagined tension where none existed and to read meanings into my mother's conversations that simply didn't exist. As if to ward off any further, insignificant dialogue, Papa held up his bandaged hand. Mama's eyes settled upon it as her voice dwindled. To my relief, however, Papa set off on an altogether different tangent.

"I've just come from Melikhovo," said Papa referring to Chekov's estate. This was a journey that was achievable in a day–a long day. Papa had an excellent troika and horses. On the other hand, when Chekov had come to visit us, he had ridden his favourite nag called Maria, a wretched beast unable to cover more than a verst an hour. Chekov had been forced to stay a week to recover from his exhausting journey.

"Oh, yes?" I looked up. Mama's voice was a little too loud, a little too eager.

Papa took a sip of kvass and ignoring the silver utensils, picked up a blin with the thumb and index finger of his good hand.

"The good doctor has written a play," he said. "A rather good one as it so happens. The interesting thing is that it's really about Pelageya." Papa mentioned Chekov's mistress. I reached for my champagne and Repin visibly relaxed in his chair. Sergei uncorked another bottle, not waiting for the valet whose hands were already trembling so much I'm not sure he could have managed it anyway.

"Sounds as entertaining as *The Three Sisters*," said Mama tossing back her head and fiddling with an earbob, the strain easing from her tone. I sometimes wondered if Chekov had based his heroine and her longing to return to Moscow, on Mama. I wondered even more why the play didn't resonate with her.

"Oh, it's entertaining," said Papa popping another blin loaded with carp and sour cream into his mouth. I didn't dare comment on the fact that I thought he was supposed to be a vegetarian. Perhaps he was just especially fond of blini because in pre-Christian times they were considered symbols of the sun. "Did you know that Pelageya was having an affair with Chekov's best friend?"

Nothing sunny about that comment. Sergei all but choked on his food.

"I thought *you* were his best friend, Papa," I murmured under my breath. Repin pinched my arm.

"How extraordinary," said Mama uncomfortably.

"And that she was having a baby?"

Papa looked around the table enjoying the collective intake of breath. Mama turned a paler shade and Arkady's eyes emerging from their hoods, widened with interest.

"He's thrown her out, of course. I mean he's not unsympathetic and the really great thing is, that it hasn't affected his friendship with Nicolai. Not at all. His response to all difficult events, is to write about them. I'm beginning to admire this."

"It's one thing to write from the imagination," protested Mama hotly. "It's quite another, to write about things that have really happened, things as personal as this! It betrays a trust!"

Papa looked at her coldly. "A *trust*?"

"It's stealing her dignity, her privacy, her *soul*!" she finished dramatically.

"Her 'soul' seems to have existed in one place only," said Papa.

"Poor Pelageya," said Mama sadly.

Papa shrugged. "She'll survive. She's an actress."

Mama's eyes blazed.

"It's what he does though, isn't it?" said Sergei pushing his dessert bowl away in disgust. "It's the way he writes–borrowing shamelessly from the lives of those around him. I hear he lifts entire conversations, hangs around parties eavesdropping, follows lovers home just in order to listen as they say good night. I wonder he has any friends left at all!"

Papa smiled revealing gaps between his teeth. I couldn't remember the last time I'd seen him smile.

"A few."

"But then, you do that too," said Mama challengingly. "I mean in *War and Peace* sometimes you've only changed the

names of real-life characters by a single letter! All Moscow
knows *exactly* who they are. I'm surprised you haven't been
sued."

"I expect I will be, some day."

Papa wiped his mouth and beard with his napkin.
Did peasants even have napkins, I wondered. Now wasn't the
time to bring up such a detail.

"Come, come Sonya," said Papa smoothly. "Don't tell
me that in your little novellas you don't write about mothers
and their children, the snow, skating–oh I don't know, catty
Muscovite seamstresses? You write about what you know.
Isn't that right Seryozha?" Papa peered at my brother with
anything but affection, despite the endearment. "You listen to
music, you read–everything goes into the melting pot and
comes out as your own creation." He was thoughtful. "But as
interesting as this all is, it's not what brings me home."

It was Repin's turn to reach for the champagne.

"I hear there's to be a new addition," said Papa
enunciating every. "I mean in the quilting sense, not to the
stables or to this wretched clock which appears to have more
birds than I have words in my head."

Both Mama and Sergei leapt to their feet.

"I–I can explain," stammered Mama, knocking over a
glass.

Sergei looked at our mother in astonishment. "You
can?" he said.

Arkady placed a hand on Mama's wrist, a gesture that
did not go unnoticed by our father.

"Just wait," he said firmly.

Mama sat back in her chair so that only Sergei was left
standing, his face turning the colour of borscht.

"You must marry her," pronounced Papa.

Mama blinked. "I don't understand," she said.

"Don't you?" Papa's tone was like a pistol shot. He
waved to my brother. "Then *he* will explain."

11

The motion of the carriage as we hurtled towards Tula, together with the sound of the steam engine merely echoed the volley of conversational pings that ricocheted round my head. 'Does he love her?' Mama had asked. 'Do you love her?' Papa had asked Sergei and then answering the question himself, 'Bones of the saints Sonya, love has nothing to do with this! The girl is pregnant; Sergei must marry her!' 'No, he mustn't, not if he doesn't love her.' 'Yes, he must.' 'No, he must not! *You* didn't marry that–that peasant girl!' 'That was different.' 'How.' It wasn't a question.

Papa had slammed down his fist, forgetting it was his bad hand and blood had rapidly soaked the tablecloth even seeping into the wood beneath. I saw pink and red and crimson: the same pure, unadulterated colours Repin used to depict the Czarevitch's dying. I blinked. It wasn't a portrait I was examining but a very real scene unfolding before my very eyes. A distressed Masha had appeared at that point with an even more distressed cat–a drunk cat to be precise– and almost everyone in the room, with the exception of Repin, had shouted at her to go away.

No, he mustn't, yes, he must, no he mustn't–there was the long whistle as the train approaching a level crossing, slowed dramatically.

"Wolves, I expect," Repin whispered.

I shivered as we left the familiarity of Moscow for the vast expanses of flat, frozen landscape with its skeletal birches and endless sky–the real Russia and real cold. Despite the comfortable, button backed seats, I huddled into the sable cloak Mama had leant me, wrapping it around me like a blanket. I flexed my boots against the steam heater that pushed out tepid heat into the compartment. Repin drew my head onto his shoulder and I shut my eyes too weary to talk, yet unable to blot out the voices from the night before.

The debate as to whether or not Sergei should marry Kitty had disintegrated almost immediately into a bitter argument between our parents over some peasant girl with whom Papa had once been in love.

'But you wrote in your diary…!' Mama had cried accusingly. 'You *said* you cared for her like a husband, that your feelings were worse than lust, no longer those of a stag. You said you wanted to live with her in a hut in the village, that you felt like a beast!'

'I *did* care for her, but then who wouldn't?' Papa retorted testily. 'She was–*is* everything that is admirable in the Russian peasant. She's proud and strong and…' Papa's eyes had risen from their calamitous eyebrows to settle briefly on Mama's flushed cheeks and heaving bosom. 'Calm.'

I stole a glance at Arkady. I suspected he rather thought the same.

'So is it your opinion that they should marry or not?' My parents had rounded on him in equal fury.

'Kitty's a peasant! No better than a washer woman!' And they were off again.

'Precisely why they *should* be married,' Papa had said rising from the table. 'I can't think of anything more perfect. I'd marry her myself if I were free. Every time, I look on my children and see how much they will inherit, frankly it depresses me. At least the boy will be happy.'

The oil lamps had long dimmed and only the Lenten moon gave off any kind of light as we hurtled south. Throughout the night, the off-key cry of wolves imagined or otherwise, woke me from my slumber and I would start, twitching against Repin. Reaching for him and feeling his reciprocated squeeze, I revelled in being with him. There had been one positive outcome from Sergei's drama. Repin and I had been able to slip away virtually unnoticed. Mama, touching her forehead with a jewelled hand, had waved a dramatic, 'Go, then go!' Arkady in the background made a shooing motion that would have been comical had we not been so desperate to escape. Now, leaning against Repin, I could feel the firmness of his thigh against mine and the strength of his arms through the thickness of my fur.

"Why are you called Tatyana?" he whispered during the night when he saw that I was awake. Frost covered the windowpanes and outside, the Steppes were still enveloped in an eerie mist of grey light.

I moved my head, my hair snagging under his shoulder.

"I'm named after Pushkin's heroine," I said used to giving this reply. "It is a name given to the common people, something you can imagine, when he discovered it, that delighted my father. But also, because the Tatyana in *Eugene Onegin*, represents all that is natural and unaffected in the Russian nation. But surely you know this?"

"You forget, I am a man of humble beginnings." Repin had begun absent-mindedly tracing the contours of my face, his thumb smoothing my cheekbone, dabbing the corners of my mouth. "My education has come from pictures and listening. I only came to Moscow to study icons."

"And what did you learn from them?"

"I learned that you can indeed find simplicity in the most unexpected places," he whispered, his breath on mine.

"And that pleases you?"

Repin's lips skimmed my skin. "Oh, yes," he said. "Very much."

I had only just fallen asleep when, in a final explosion of steam, the train pulled into Tula. Porters sprang from the running boards like clockwork toys. Repin took my arm helping me alight. I rubbed my eyes sleepily, allowing him to take control of our luggage, following like a child. A piercing wind shot up my skirts as I huddled in my cloak. Even at such an early hour the station was a bustling hive of activity. It was as though some colossal giant had pulled apart several matryoshka dolls scattering them randomly. And like matryoshka dolls, peasant women of all sizes in bright scarves squatted on wooden stools, selling pirog and kumis. The smell of the hot pastry triggered an immediate response in my stomach, and I longed to be tucked up in bed with a belly full of food, fussed over by Olga Feodova.

Travellers pushed past us as we made our way along the platform. And then I saw him, the coachman from Yasnaya Polyana, who seemed as old as the house itself and whose bowed knees were as distinctive as the white stone entrance gates to the estate.

"Seven Asses!" I shrieked, relieved to see a familiar face amongst so many strange ones and then again so loudly that Repin winced. "Seven Asses!"

"Am I hearing correctly?" he asked as our servant lumbered towards us pulling a luggage trolley behind him.

"Oh, Papa christened him that when he inherited him along with other serfs from one of his villages," I said lightly. "He was born in the Samara Steppes."

Repin shook his head. "You own property as far as the Steppes?" His tone was incredulous. "The peasant count, eh? How many serfs did he inherit?"

I'd rather not have answered. "Two hundred and fifty."

"*How* many?"

"Yes, but with their emancipation," I said hurrying on before we argued the inconsistencies in my father's ideology. "When serfs who formerly had no last names, were told to adopt them, Seven Asses petitioned the Czar to be allowed to change his."

I sensed hesitation in Repin as he took hold of my hand. "So, what happened? The Czar ignored him?"

I grinned sheepishly. "Almost. He said he could change his name to *Five* Asses."

Repin looked at the coachman's curved back. "Good for Seven Asses."

Seven Asses brought the troika to the station entrance, the horses snorting and stamping snow that had set harder than concrete. Soon we were snug, swaddled in furs. I covered my face with my muff, pulling my hood as far as it would go to protect my skin from the searing wind. I had no intention of ending up like the babushkas who worked in the kitchens. The accepted norm of beauty at the time was the face that shone from oil paintings, the kind that even Repin might paint, flawless skin with bright spots of high colour.

But I knew that in reality, these beautiful complexions were simply broken blood capillaries the result of over exposure to the elements.

With a crack of the whip, Seven Asses drove the horses into a gallop. And soon the arguments of the past few days, the twinges of apprehension that I had felt concerning Repin and my own frustration at not painting in the way I wanted to, all went as we left the town for the familiar and vast terrain. We spoke little, bending our bodies to the melodic rhythm of the troika. The three horses threw back their heads in unison, the Valdai bells, chains and leather tassels around their necks rising to a steady singing cadence. Were the horses listening for something specific? Another troika perhaps? I knew that the many bells each with a specific tone, were used to communicate a sleigh's approach. In the cold air their breath hung in small clouds before dispersing into crystals. As we flew along, soaring above the ground as a three-headed bird, snowflakes dancing, the wind whistling along the horizon, we seemed bound for the Steppes and Siberia.

I must have fallen asleep for I woke with a start, cold air fanning my cheeks. Repin's head lolled on his chest, his hair falling over his eyes. I lowered my hood peering in the darkness. The trace horses continued to gallop smoothly, their heads bowed, while the shaft horse moved at a canter, its head proud and erect. We had passed the small arched bridge that marked the entrance to the plantation. I sat up, gripped with the excitement that always accompanied any visit home. No matter how many times I returned to Yasnaya, my heart leapt with joy as we passed boskets thick with maple and conifer, ornamental pavilions and the Gothic gateway that led nowhere.

Without turning my head, I was aware that Repin too was awake and running stiff fingers through straggly snow-encrusted hair. His skin was chapped and raw and the wool from his muffler had meshed together into a solid, frozen mass. Tears had iced on his cheeks, pulling away skin. He was silent and I was grateful that he was not overawed as most first-time visitors to Yasnaya were, either by the

vastness and beauty of Papa's estate or the fact that it was
Papa's in the first place. I hadn't wanted to talk about him
and was relieved that apart from a correct respect for Papa as
my father, Repin showed rather less enthusiasm for Papa the
man, or indeed even Papa the writer. Moreover, he seemed
wholly unconvinced by Papa's attempts to emulate the
peasant, derisive of the blatant contradictions in his life, his
inability to tolerate differences in others.

And yet, in spite of a resolution not to, I felt words
spill out of me in a desire to share the markers of my
childhood, the tree-like rings that shaped Yasnaya's history.
As we trotted along the avenue, everything was startling
white as if some artist had deliberately omitted colour from
his palette. The stone entrance gates were white; white too
was the snow-enveloped parkland, the sky, trees and when it
came into view, in a sudden and startling deviation from the
arrow-straight drive, the house itself. Everything in this
petrifying cold was white, tinged with the grey-blue of a
human vein, of a seagull, of a streak left by caviar on a marble
surface.

I told Repin, even if he knew it already, how Papa
had lost the original house in a two-day game of shtoss, how
even up until the last moment he had believed that the timber
merchant to whom he had lost the house, would not claim his
debt. Papa had hoped to appease him by giving him all
eleven (eleven!) of his other villages together with their serfs,
timber stocks and horses and when all of that had been
accepted, Papa had counted on the house itself, which he
believed to be made of stone, being unmovable. The house,
however, though covered with a convincing enough plaster
face, was in fact made of wood and the timber merchant had
quite successfully removed every single door frame and
supporting beam. Papa had been left with six hundred versts
and the one remaining wing which was where we lived now.
When he was asked where he was born, Papa would point to
the third branch of an arboretum of poplars that he had
planted to commemorate his youthful stupidity, 'There!' he
would say to mystified visitors. 'Somewhere along that
branch, but on a black leather sofa, is where I was born.'

I turned to look in the direction of the pond where at the first sign of spring, Papa swam naked like a peasant. In winter, the pond became a skating rink and there we all skated or tobogganed together–governesses, tutors and nursemaids alike. I swept a hand across the sloping hills as though with brush strokes, to show Repin the place that had inspired the setting for Bald Hills, Nicolai Bolkonsky's home in *War and Peace*, and the trees that Mama had Papa had planted to commemorate their marriage; one a birch, the other an ash to grow side by side.

I showed him as we slid past, the spot deep, deep in the wood that my uncle (Papa's oldest brother) had told my father was magical and where a green wand with extraordinary powers was hidden. Papa's parents had both died when he was a child and to cheer up his younger siblings my uncle Pavel had told the smallest children, that a magic wand was buried in a secret place, that this wand could make even the saddest child happy. Despite the obvious melancholy of that memorable summer, Papa always said that he had spent many a blissful day combing the woods for angels' wings and broken nests in the vein hope that any one of these findings might represent the mystical stick.

And as we raced towards the last turn and the troika's blades skidded on ice and then became stuck, I realised that in my attempt to paint my father, I had been looking for him in the wrong place. The tortured, unhappy man in Moscow whose moral crisis affected us all, whose renunciation of family life and artistic creation was the cornerstone of his personal calvary, was not the father we should know. His complete spirit, his soul stripped of nationality and politics could only ever thrive here at Yasnaya. If my portrait of him set in his Moscow study had grown stultified and lifeless, it was because the ghost of his former self continued to flourish here. More than that–it was as if the house continued to co-exist independently and that a bustling, happy family with our father, young and virile at its head, moved and breathed jubilantly within its rooms.

It was at Yasnaya that Papa had written his great fiction, where our mother had raised her young family, where at night, the rooms reverberated with the sound of their lovemaking. It was there that they talked incessantly, so close it was if they had known each other before conception, where he had taken her unformed mind in an attempt to sculpt it.

I too grew quiet, saddened by the melancholy that I knew clung to me just as uncomfortably as did the newly formed crystals on the tips of my fur cloak. As I stepped from the troika, I flexed my frozen toes, trying to shake off the nostalgic feeling, trying to revive reluctant flesh. How careless my parents had been I thought, casting aside their relationship as if it were of no more importance than a rough draft, spattered with ink stains, re-worked several times but ultimately one to be discarded. It was clear to me now that the last shreds of hope, the ashes of a marriage in its death throws stuck to my parents like a shadow undiminished by the position of the sun. If I returned again and again to this house, it was in a futile attempt to gather in my arms, the last remnants of childhood. As futile as carrying unbound sheaths of wheat and watching helpless as it fell to the ground.

12

Olga Feodova met us with a lantern hovering under
the porch like a diminutive cockroach albeit one in a bright
Pavlovsky shawl. She clucked and fussed and pulled at my
clothes as I knew she would, and I gave myself up to her
strong bony hands as I had done ever since I was a child.
With every step, I shrank in size until I was once more a little
girl in need of comfort. I forgot for a moment that I was a
woman in love, a painter, that I was here with my lover that I
was grown up. I let her spin me this way and that to unwind
my clothes as though they were swaddling blankets, to lift the
cloak from my shoulders that had now become too heavy to
drag, to smooth the strands of wet hair through her fingers. I
let her unwind my scarf which was now prickly and stuck to
the back of my neck with wet, melting ice crystals and I felt
the familiar sounds of the house wash over me, as every
muscle and nerve in my body gave itself up to the delicious
sensation of coming home. Every single creak and scrape
were joyous to me in that initial greeting and I welcomed it
all.

Seeing Repin hovering behind me, Olga's head shot
up from its usual owl-like position, folded somewhere into
her scrawny neck. Her black, deep-set eyes swivelled
suspiciously from under whiskery eyebrows to send him
hostile looks, weighty with disapproval. She sucked in her
cheeks with undisguised dislike. If Repin believed Papa was
the member of the family whose approval he needed, he was
quite mistaken. Olga placed a protective, excluding hand on
the small of my back directing me crab-like fashion, to a chair
by the fire that blazed in the entrance hall. She directed the
servants to light candles, to bring bowls of hot chocolate and
honey buns, to carry our bags upstairs and then she sank on
arthritic knees to remove my boots. I stretched out in the tall
wooden chair, my arms hanging limply by my side and lifted
my foot.

Glancing up, I caught Repin's look of complete astonishment. "What?"

Olga looked from my face to his as though she'd been caught stealing flour.

"It rests so easily doesn't it?" he said, and he looked away, his gaze sweeping over the large, warm hallway with its dominating family portraits, rugs and books shelves. Mama had displayed Papa's china with its imposing coat of arms in floor-to-ceiling glass cases. There were sabres, stuffed animals–relics of Papa's hunting days and artefacts collected from trips abroad. There was no escaping the fact that everything about the house heralded privilege no matter how Papa tried to disguise it. But puzzled, I still followed his gaze. I had never seen Yasnaya Polyana as anything but a home. Father's ideological struggles took place in Moscow, on the road to the Steppes, within the arms of a peasant woman, but not here. Not until now that is.

"I don't understand."

Repin raised sardonic eyebrows and an expression I'd never seen him use with me before, one of barely concealed contempt. My heart plummeted to my stomach as the feeling of unease that I generally associated with my parents' quarrelling came over. Reluctantly, I pulled my foot from Olga's lap.

Repin made no effort to remove his coat, nor his hands from his pockets. He thrust his chin forward, unable to even point to the objects of his derision.

"All of this." He jabbed at Olga with his fist through his coat.

"Olga?" I said and it was my turn to be astonished. "Why, she's our nanny. She's a member of the family. She's been with us forever. Papa inherited her–" my voice dwindled as I realised how that sounded.

Repin shook his head. "Exactly! Your father–" he began choking on the word. A pulse began to beat at my temple. It was all right for me to criticise Papa, but I didn't want anyone else to. Repin had been respectful in the past.

"What about him?" I sat up in my chair, my voice steely, the muscles in my stomach contracting uncomfortably.

Olga Feodova sat back on her heels; her hands placed
proprietarily on my boots. When I indicated that she should
leave, by trying to shake them off, she held onto my feet
defiantly.

"He plays at being the peasant. He dresses as a
peasant in clothes made specially for him and yet comes back
to this!" Again, Repin made a jabbing gesture. "To be waited
on hand and foot! Quite literally. It's the worst kind of
hypocrisy. He can dip in and out of any of the lives he
chooses to live. Which is more than the common man can. It's
an unspeakable indulgence!"

"You knew what he was like," I said quietly. "You've
even painted him! Besides we're talking about my father. Not
me. Why are you so angry?"

Repin turned bewildered eyes to mine as if seeing me
for the first time and a cold hand of dread replaced my
apprehension.

"It's because I thought you were different, and I see
you here and I realise–"

I snatched my foot away.

"What Repin? What do you see here? This is my
home. I can't help where I come from! Surely, it's better to try
and do something about the injustices around us rather than
ignore them? Papa did try to reduce the number of serfs he
owned but when he offered them their freedom, many
mistrusted his intent. Most of them refused to go." I switched
to French, flicking a glance at Olga's bowed head. She being
one of them. Repin looked blank whether deliberately
misunderstanding or not. I knew he wouldn't admit to
understanding the language even if he could. I switched back
to Russian. "He has set up peasant schools on his estates,
even a publishing venture to print only the Russian classics.
Yes, he's inconsistent but he means good, he does good. Or
maybe you think my mother is more authentic."

Repin made a humourless guffaw which made Olga
growl defensively and move even closer so that she was
practically hugging my knees. I frowned in irritation wishing
I could shake her off completely. I'd forgotten this dog-like
devotion in her.

"Your mother?" he echoed rudely his Ukrainian accent grating.

"My mother doesn't pretend to be anything that she isn't," I continued firmly. "She's not trying to be a peasant nor live like one and yet she does everything possible to help them. During the great famine she organised food lorries to be delivered to the Steppes. She wrote to newspapers appealing for donations. She contacted textile manufacturers to provide underclothing for those suffering from typhoid, she–" I took a deep breath.

"How commendable," said Repin and I could tell he wasn't at all impressed. "Tanya, Tanya," he said at last taking his hands out of his pockets and moving towards the fire to warm them. It was only the fact that he was so engrossed in our conversation that he allowed himself this moment of self-indulgence. I knew he could be stubbornly proud preferring to suffer discomfort rather than enjoy the comfort of my father's home. "Can't you see? Your parents, like so many elitist Russians are just play acting. It's not enough to do these random acts of charity."

"Why not? Don't you believe in the nobility of the peasant soul?" I meant it sardonically but Repin flung me an impatient, disgusted look.

"There's nothing noble about the peasantry," he said angrily. "Why your father insists on glorifying it and turning it into something it can never be, baffles me. I come from peasant stock and I have no illusions whatsoever as to the people they really are. And there is nothing either noble or spiritual about them. Years of famine and abandonment of the land has destroyed any nobility of spirit, I can assure you. The peasant village is a dreary, morally bankrupt place. It is cruel and mean but what is worse, there's rarely any escape from it and that breeds a particular kind of Russian hopelessness."

Repin unwound his muffler dropping it soundlessly on the rug. Olga covered the small distance on her knees to pick it up and then move back to me. We both looked at her with varying degrees of exasperation. Repin's was one of exasperation that she should perform such a menial task, mine that she was performing it all for Repin. My eyes narrowed.

"You did," I said quietly.

"I've escaped nothing. I carry the village on my shoulders, in everything I say and do. Open your eyes Tanya, the world is changing! Russia is changing. Yasnaya may be the country but it is not Russia. People like your parents have got to want social change, want to live it, really live it! Here!" Repin struck his chest moving to warm his back and lifting his coat so that snow dripped it onto the flames causing them to crackle and smart and I could smell the fabric from his clothes as they grew hot. "They have to feel it where it counts. This isn't a game, Tanya," he continued earnestly. "The aristocracy has to be prepared not only to give up its privileges but more importantly, its property."

I swallowed, suddenly afraid of something I could neither identify nor understand.

"Could they do that do you think?" he said. "Could your parents give up Yasnaya Polyana?"

I glared at Repin and his ridiculous suggestion. By even voicing such a question he showed that he saw only what he wanted to see. Worse, that he didn't see *me* at all. My father could no more give up his estate than he could cut off his right arm, nor could any one of us. I thought I'd explained the love we held for this place, that it was simply our life's blood. What hadn't he understood? I was fast regretting bringing him here. I was prepared to share what was to me, a magical, insular place, something that was more important than painting itself. If he failed to appreciate that, then there was nothing worth preserving between us.

"You're actually sounding just like my father," I said pushing Olga away and standing up.

"So are you."

For a moment we glared at one another and I stubbed the toe of my boot bad temperedly.

"Drink, now?" said Olga Feodova.

*

'But then begins a journey in my head…' Though my limbs were indeed so travel weary that I didn't think I could ever walk again, my thoughts began their own fervent pilgrimage, to keep 'my drooping eyelids open wide…' A slate grey line edged windows which were frozen solid, blotting out the landscape. The silence enveloped everything in timeless suspension so different from the linear dissection of hours in Moscow, which were always announced by the intrusive cuckoo clock. I pushed back the bed covers. I lit a candle, shoved my feet in fur-lined slippers, and flung a shawl over my shoulders. Fear of rejection, fear that he might not love me, made me hesitate as I stepped into the corridor. As if from a long distance, I could see the mirror image of my flame, but at a higher angle, bobbing from side to side. It was a few seconds before I realised it was coming towards me.

"I was coming to find you," he said.

"I was coming to find *you*."

"You were too far–"

"It was so lonely–"

We both spoke at once, relief causing my voice to tremble. At first, there was only the faintest spark in the surrounding blackness and then it gradually grew brighter and larger until it became an exact replica of mine. Repin laid a hand on my shoulder turning me away from the direction of my room. Gently, he took the candle from my hand.

13

Bread baked in traditional bird shapes lay gently cooling on the kitchen table, the sweet smells evocative of my childhood. Olga Feodova stood in front of the stove melting huge slabs of chocolate for my morning beverage. There was also a tray crammed with poppy seed biscuits and bowls of berry jam. It was hearty food designed to keep your energy levels up in the cold. It might be Lent but here at Yasnaya, buried deep in its snow drifts, spring was still a long way off.

"Repin?" I hardly dared enquire. Olga glared at me as though I had said I wasn't hungry or didn't want her chocolate. She jerked her head in the direction of the library.

"In there. What he is doing I can hardly imagine. He didn't want breakfast. Is that a Ukrainian thing?"

Of course, in Olga's book, this was the very worst of his (numerous) character flaws. Never mind the way he spoke, which given that Olga was no Muscovite herself could hardly be held against him, or that he spent most of his time in the childish pursuit of painting but not to manifest a manly appetite (at least not for food) was to sink to the lowest denominator. I quickly made appreciative sounds, not that it was difficult, when Olga scooped the thick chocolate into a bowl and handed it to me all steaming and delicious. Momentarily, my fingers brushed her gnarled, rough, beloved hands and I held her gaze.

What did Olga Feodova really feel about our family? It had never occurred to me to think of her as a person, person. It went without saying that we didn't consider her a serf, but she was most definitely part of the furniture. Did she have a family of her own? I found it hard to imagine. Had she ever been in love, had she had a child? I glanced at her narrow, flat hips. Probably not. Did she have friends, a gossip group, did she go to church? I couldn't answer any of those questions and I rather doubted Mama could have either. I expected Olga to be at Yasnaya as I did the house to endure (notwithstanding a renewed interest by Papa in gambling). She was as an integral part of its structure as were the apple orchards, the skating pond or Papa's library. It was the way it was when our father was a boy, and it was the way I anticipated it to be in the future. Until now, that is. Until Repin had hinted at change of which I was ignorant.

"Olga Feodova," I said taking my bowl to the kitchen table and clearing tins and baking trays and other cooking paraphernalia to make room. I was in no hurry to find Repin nor move from the warmth of the kitchen. It was a warmth generated by the oven in which food was cooked on coal, stoked by a fire that never went out. Above it was a space large enough for a person to sleep. I knew that Olga slept there most nights even though she had a bedroom of her own. I was awash with happy, nostalgic memories of the many, many times I had stood beside her making cakes or dropping eggs and generally getting in her way. I plunged a spoon into the dense hot chocolate, pulling at it with my teeth. It made my whole mouth thick and furry. I ran my tongue over my lips savouring its buttery sweetness.

"Have you a husband, Olga Feodova?"

Olga Feodova spun round so quickly that the jug of cream she was carrying spilled down her front. Her skin turned livid, then white, then resumed its natural jaundiced colour and her head sank like a turtle's onto her chest. She began visibly shrivelling so that only her bright shawl stirred with any kind of life.

"Olga Feodova!" I said in alarm leaping up to take the jug from her. "I didn't mean–"

"Who's been talking? Who's said what?" Olga hissed in a low, suspicious voice. "If it's Katya in the dairy–then I'll–" Olga's eyes completely disappeared into her head. "Then I'll boil her eyeballs in vinegar and stew her Achilles tendon. I will–"

"*Blin*," I said in awe. I was only grateful that I'd never done anything to invite such criticism. "I've heard nothing at all. I was merely wondering if–"

Olga wiped her hands on her apron and pushed me back in my chair.

"Oh, I see how it is," she said suddenly deflated. "It's almost Easter, so your thoughts have turned to romance." Her face unfolded as her eyes turned in their sockets, reappearing slowly. "You're thinking of marriage yourself. You might even be considering that man from Kharkov."

I considered this diminutive creature. At least she had remembered his birthplace. I took it to be a good sign.

"That man from Kharkov as you put it, is actually a very famous painter."

"He could be Count Sollogub himself and it wouldn't change my opinion of him. It wouldn't make him good enough for you, Tatyana Lvovna Tolstaya."

I scraped back my chair. "Things are changing, Olga Feodova," I said haughtily. "The old ways are going, the old snobbery. If two people really care–"

"'If two people really care'…" she echoed. "Don't make me laugh! Love never had anything to do with marriage!" she snorted. "At least not for your kind. And if it does…Look where it has got your father, may the bones of the saints rest in peace. Love! And on top of it all, his play acting!" She shook her head so vigorously that for a moment she was a speck of whirling colour. "You weren't born when the countess, your mother first came to Yasnaya," she continued twisting her hands, the knuckles already misshapen appearing even more pronounced. "Your papa got it into his head that he would farm himself. He dismissed all the labourers and the result was a disaster! He'd never tended a pig in his life, so the pigs all died. He didn't know how to cure hams, when to plough, even less when to reap! So, he got bored and escaped to Moscow. That has been his pattern. He wears a smock, those famous bast shoes when he 'communes' with us peasants but when he dines in the city, he wears the finest clothes made from cloth especially chosen in Paris!"

"Not anymore," I said quietly. The warm, cosy feeling I'd felt earlier, had solidified more quickly than my hot chocolate.

"Your dear Papa tells a good yarn but they're fairy stories. There is a-b-s-olutely nothing fun about being a peasant woman." Olga pronounced the word just as my mother did and I realised that Mama must have got it from her. "She works her fingers to the bone, tolerates being beaten–you've heard the proverb: 'Hit your wife with the butt of the axe, get down and see if she's breathing. If she is, she's shamming and wants some more!'" Olga gripped the side of the kitchen table as if to stop herself from grabbing a knife and stabbing something. "And what is the worst, the very worst, is that if her husband goes away, she is obliged to have relations with her father-in-law! Yes, you may well wince. Believe me if you were a peasant wife, you'd be doing more than that! Wake up Kotchka, this isn't poetry."

I took a deep breath. "For what it's worth, Repin thinks just the same as you do. I mean not that he believes in wife beating. Or... the rest."

Olga threw up her hands as if to shake me. "Of course, he does, Tanya! It's because we're both peasants! But you–you are different. You can fool yourself all you like. Love! Happiness! Pah!" She spat on the flagstone floor. "Not with the likes of a man from Sloboda Ukraine! Never! And don't come crying to me when he breaks your heart. Because he will. You just don't see it. After a rain on Thursday." She finished with one of her favourite expressions. Which meant never ever. She was certainly hammering the point home.

"Oh, I don't know," I said lightly, maliciously and not altogether truthfully. Finally, ready to go and find Repin, I rose from my chair. "I think I'm beginning to see things exactly as they are. Besides, even Mama accepts that Sergei is to marry a village girl."

"Is to marry a *what*?" Olga spun round on childlike feet, slamming into me so that I toppled back in the chair. Her small, strong hands gripped my shoulder anchoring me to the spot. I tried to nod but found that I couldn't even turn my head.

"It's Kitty Shishkova the girl from–"

"I know who you mean!" snapped Olga. "She wears dresses without collars or cuffs. The whore!"

"I don't think she's quite that," I said taken aback. I had to agree though with her observance of dress. At the time, it was customary for well born women to wear something white around the neck. "I don't think you should even blame her. You know what Sergei's like. When he wants something there's no stopping him."

Olga's grip tightened so that I cried out. This seemed to have an immediate effect because she released me suddenly, groping her way to a chair opposite. I rubbed my neck, but Olga seemed oblivious of me. Absent-mindedly, she broke off a bit of a carefully constructed bread waiting to be glazed. I watched amazed as she took another mouthful, washing it down with a slurp of the eggy milk mixture that would give the pastries their shiny finish.

"Just like your mother," she said thoughtfully. Mama? Surely Olga must mean my father? "Two peas in a pod. But what a to do. It's one thing for the father to play at peasant life but another for the son to live it! What has happened to this family?" Olga turned her whole head towards me owl-like. "She should never have moved to the city," she said darkly. "I knew no good would come of it."

Olga made to break off more bread, but I laid my hand on her forearm.

"Talking of the city," I said. "You've reminded me. Mama wants you to come back with us."

Olga raised an eyebrow. "Us?"

I blushed. "You know what I mean."

"The only time your Mama needs old Olga Feodova is when-" She stopped abruptly, an expression of horror coming over her face.

"Is when...?"

"Am I interrupting?"

We both turned as Repin appeared at the kitchen door. He had a lazy smile on his face and his one slouchy eye on the side I loved, was turned to me so that my stomach did a summersault in spite of it being full of chocolate. I also quite forgot my curiosity as to what Olga had been about to say.

"Something smells delicious," he said disarmingly. "This khleb is better than that of my own village! It's all in the hands, eh, Olga Feodova?" He crossed to the table and sliding into a chair, patted her bony fingers. "The bread must be kneaded in such a way, isn't that so? And then permitted to rise and then–"

Olga Feodova snatched away her hand. "Yes, yes Ilya Yefimovich Repin. It is exactly as you say." She leapt to her feet and wedging her shoe against the table leg used all her body weight to try and lever Repin to his.

"And the bird shape? Why is that Olga Feodova."

Olga looked blank. While she had been baking bread like this during Lent all her life. I knew she had no idea why. For once she turned expectant eyes in my direction.

"It's tradition," she said uncertainly.

"Yes," said Repin pleasantly. "But why in the shape of a bird?"

Olga pretended not to hear.

"It's to symbolise the return of migratory flocks," I said.

"Ah, we don't do that," he replied, "in Ukraine."

"I will bring you chocolate and the rest of this bird, *bread* I mean–to the library," said Olga breathlessly. "No need to wait till Easter we might as well eat this batch now, what do you say Kotchka?"

I opened my mouth to say something but Repin, enticed by the convivial warmth was just settling in and seemed in no hurry to leave the kitchen. Olga appeared to think otherwise. Literally digging in her heels, so that her toes were sticking straight up, she tried a different position tugging at his right arm with all her might. Repin could have lifted Olga with that one arm alone and I was afraid that if she were to suddenly let go, she would fall flat on her back.

"I have heard so much about you. Tanya didn't stop talking during the whole of the troika ride." I threw Repin an irritated look, but he continued unperturbed. "You are part of the family, aren't you? Then you should be painted too. Did you know that Tanya is painting Lev and that while she paints him, I paint her?" Luckily, he didn't say that I had actually begun my lessons painting Arkady.

Startled, Olga stopped pulling at Repin momentarily losing her balance. He stooped to steady her as she scuttled away from him in panic. Repin misinterpreting her reaction as one of affected vanity, pressed her all the more.

"Come, come," he insisted now taking her arm. "Surely you must have been told that you have a..." Repin took in the billion or so wrinkles that criss-crossed Olga's face- more numerous than the marks left on the ice rink after an afternoon's session. I wondered what words he would use to describe it, let alone paint it. "I have to tell you Olga Feodova, that I only draw from life. I am no good at the imagination. I have been told that my faces tell a story. Just as yours does, even if you don't realise it. Surely you would want your face to be immortalised. For people to say, 'Ah, so that was Olga Feodova?'"

"No, no, no!" Olga shook off Repin's hand as though it were diseased. She wiped her hands repeatedly on her apron and then her face as though trying to erase all contact of him, all memory.

But now Repin, equally impassioned could not stop.

"You see, Olga Feodova, I want the world to know the peasant's face for what it is." Again, Repin made to touch her but the old woman sprang away. "No scenic landscapes, no winsome little thatched cottages in the background, just the peasant's face." Repin paused triumphant, imagining he was getting through to this fiery, bad-tempered little babushka.

I looked at her anxiously. She had spread herself against the chimney breast just like the glazing mixture, before it cooks, diluted and invisible. Repin towered above her.

"My kind of painting will no doubt shock," he said happily. "After all, only a short time ago this same person was treated as a slave. But that's the point, the peasant is a human being, every bit as important as the landowner or aristocrat. She suffers just as many emotions, just as much loneliness and confusion. Everything is the same. Art can do this you see. It has a purpose, a duty even, to show this. I'm tired of big biblical scenes. Russian artists should concentrate on the ordinary Russian people going about their ordinary daily jobs, no matter how seemingly dull or worthless. Just like yourself Olga Feodova. That's why you are so important."

Repin, I knew had lost Olga at 'biblical' but he took a a step closer. Olga ducked under his arm.

"No, no, I am not, Ilya Yefimovich. I'm not important at all." Olga's tone was sharp, acerbic. She slammed what was left of the bird-shaped loaves into the oven, forgetting the all-important glaze. Of which she'd drunk half anyway. And then I remembered and understood. I got swiftly to my feet.

"Come *deroghoe*," I said using the word with which in the past, my mother had so often addressed my father. "I'm starving. You have made me so…" I added in a low voice and in French so that Olga wouldn't realise she was being dismissed.

Repin looked confused, partly because I had unexpectedly called him 'darling' and partly because I had spoken in a language he barely understood. Either way, my tone, implied something intimate. I blushed for good measure, lowering my eyes. I grabbed a couple of rolls and bowls of chocolate and to emphasize the point, kicked open the kitchen door.

He rushed to hold the door and for a moment as he stood close beside me and I breathed in his smell, I felt dizzy with desire.

"You've forgotten something," I hissed. "Something fundamental to the peasant's belief."

"What?" He shook his head utterly puzzled, following me into the small sitting room, a room heavy with Papa's presence. Papa would drag his desk here to escape the cries and demands of young children. In Moscow, he had sewed off the legs of his chair so that he was closer to the table. Here, all he had to do was borrow one of the chairs from a nursery that had never been dismantled. He was also the only man I knew emaciated enough to fit into one. Above the mantlepiece was a picture of Dickens, one of Papa's heroes. I set the chocolate and rolls on an ottoman in front of a blazing fire. Outside it was snowing and the delicate birch trees surrounding the house were strung together in a cobweb of frost. I imagined the branches suddenly moving like a ballerina and shedding icicle sleeves.

"What did I miss?" repeated Repin.

I settled comfortably in my usual chair, taking time to drape my shawl gracefully around me before nursing yet another bowl of chocolate.

"Surely, you of all people must know," I said pushing a chunk of bread into thick chocolate. "A peasant never wants to be drawn? Not on paper on canvas, after a rain on Thursday. Never, ever."

Repin frowned. "Why is that? I don't recall…"

"Simply put," I said my mouth full. "She believes that the Devil steals a person's soul when her image is portrayed on paper. I'd wager this house that she believes that you Ilya Repin, are the Devil himself!"

I had meant it lightly but Repin seemed far from amused. "Oh excellent," he said morosely. "And I was hoping to win her over." He leant over to break off a bit of bread choosing the beak. I had taken a wing and now all that remained was the plump body. Olga had used icing sugar to denote feathers. "It's a shock to discover people like Olga still believe in all that superstitious claptrap." He sighed heavily and stared bleakly into the fire.

"What does it matter? It was a simple misunderstanding. She'll soon forget about it." My tone sounded persuasive though knowing Olga Feodova as I did, it was highly unlikely she would ever forget. She had a unique talent for nurturing a grudge.

"It's not that." Repin stretched out his legs towards the fire, his hands thrust deep in his pockets.

I swallowed. "You could alarm me, *deroghoe*," I said with a smile, but my heart was suddenly heavy. When he turned his head, instead of the rush of warmth I expected at my use of the endearment (the second time in less than an hour), his look was cold, appraising even, as though he were eyeing me up for a portrait. A portrait on commission that is.

120

"There's so much work to do. I'm overwhelmed. I thought it would be easier."

I set down my bowl and covered the small distance between us dragging my shawl behind me. I was on my knees at his feet. In much the way Olga had been at mine when we arrived. I clasped my hands on his knees.

"I know," I said hurriedly. "But today is the first day and we got up late and the light is strange and the candles are still burning so–"

"That's not at all what I mean," he said impatiently, shifting his knees and my hands with them, so that I sank back on my heels, rebuffed.

"Then what?"

"Oh, don't be like that!" he said impatiently.

"Don't be like what?" There were sudden tears at the back of my throat and my stomach clenched as it did when I was with Papa. How was it that in a moment everything could change? It was my turn to stare despondently into the fire. "What is it Repin?" I said forcing my tone to be gentle. "I'm sorry but I don't understand."

Repin got to his feet and began pacing the room. From time to time when he caught sight of some family memorabilia, he would shake his head, smiling to himself without humour. He leant his head against the cold windowpane as if welcoming its cooling effect and then turned, still leaning against it, to look down at me. The collar of his jacket was turned up rubbing his chin.

"The dream is one thing," he said enigmatically. "The reality quite different."

"That tends to be the nature of dreams," I said lightly.

"There is still such a divide," he said gloomily as if I hadn't spoken. "Social, intellectual, cultural–it's an enormous gulf. I'm not sure it can be crossed."

I swallowed. "A gulf? Between us?"

Repin ran his fingers threw his hair. "No. Yes, of course, between us!" he said angrily. "No, what I mean is between someone like Olga and someone like me and you and your father. It's more than just language. It's more than my sweet people of Ukraine–"

121

I moved back to my chair. "Oh, I see," I said relieved. He was often maudlin when he thought about his birthplace but could be easily distracted. I was determined to return us to the closeness of the night before. "It's because I spoke to you in French."

"Don't be ridiculous!" Repin said exasperated. "You're being deliberately difficult and not following."

"Well, what if I am?" I examined the toe of my new kid leather shoes, exquisitely simple and all the more valued for not being made by my father. "We're here at Yasnaya to *escape* domestic rows, not create more of them! I thought we were here to paint, to be together, to be close." I whispered the last word which I knew was having the desired effect. Repin was still frowning but his eyes at least flicked over me. I held out my hand to him. "Come here," I said softly.

For a moment he continued to watch me until gradually the creases on his forehead smoothed and a smile flickered on his lips. With his back to the window, bending a knee, his hunched shoulders propelled him forwards.

"You do look lovely by the fire," he conceded. "The light is good now and the colour of your dress exactly matches the cushion behind your head. And you've got just the right amount of white," he made a flickering gesture with his fingers. "The froth around your throat."

"Could you paint this then?" I said touching my neckline. "I've always found lace such a difficult thing to paint."

"It's all about technique and yes, I could paint it. I could paint you." His eyes travelled from my eyes, to my neck to my breast. He found my fingers and moved them to my side. "Finding you attractive is not the problem," he said gruffly his lips so close to mine I could feel his eyelashes on my cheek.

"Then what is?" No sooner had I spoken than I regretted opening my mouth to do anything other than kiss him. Repin sprung away from me.

"It's this!" he pointed to the room, to the frozen landscape. "It's Olga! It's the maddening, infuriating, exasperating backwardness of Russia!" Then spying my

122

empty bowl, he pounced on it clutching it to his chest. "It's these bowls!"

"Bowls?"

Repin traced a finger despondently over the embossed coat of arms. "Don't you see? There is so much change happening in our country and you are completely blind to it! Olga is too. You both live in separate worlds of your own. I thought that the social revolt would come from the peasants themselves but now I see that they can't think for themselves, not while they're still governed by outmoded superstition! Did you know that when villagers from my own hamlet were told that the Czar should be deposed, they could not comprehend life without him? They think of him as a god and would not budge even though they were offered land and labourers. Look at Olga, she won't have her picture painted!"

"You can't use Olga as an example..."

"Why not? She's the *perfect* example! Do you know anything about her? She's lived with your family for two generations, do you know where she even *comes* from?"

I squirmed in my seat. "No but–" I frowned. "She comes from Yasnaya!" I added triumphantly.

Repin crossed his leg inelegantly, leaning away from me to stoke the fire. I wanted to tell him that he could ring for someone to do just that but felt he might happily push me into the grate if I did.

"I'll tell you about Olga Feodova," he said stonily. "She's famous, infamous even in some parts. I bet you didn't know that she was married when she was just thirteen years old to a man she met for the first time on her wedding day. This man, this *ogre*, beat her every day and locked her in her room for days on end without food, while he slept with his niece. After a few years he got a job in Siberia and one night, he locked Olga naked in a barn while he cavorted with prostitutes. God only knows what the temperature must have been. She was pregnant at the time and lost the child. Pregnant again when he died of syphilis some years later, she borrowed the train fare to Tula and from there made her way back to Yasnaya whereas you rightly said, she'd been born. She miscarried and was never able to have more children."

I shook my head, tears blurring my vision. "I'd no idea."

"My point Tanya, is that this sort of thing happens in rural communities all over Russia. There is nothing at all unique about Olga's story. A peasant woman is treated as a beast of burden in the village, but on an estate, she is then at the mercy of the landowner himself. Peasant life is not to be glamorised and has little value to the average aristocrat. I want my next painting to be vast and bold and provocative. I want to depict suffering but dignity too. I want to show men who are more than just human haulers. I want to rediscover somehow, the true Russian spirit. More than anything I want change to take place quickly!"

"So does my father," I said firmly.

Repin rounded on me. "Your father!" he exclaimed angrily. "With all this!"

I snatched my shawl from under Repin's leg where he had sat on it.

"Yes, with all this," I said coldly. "And 'all this' as you put it, didn't seem to matter in Moscow. Why does it here?"

Repin sighed. "Here it's so *obvious*. You seem so much a part of it, to belong to it so completely. You'd never give it up." He seemed so concerned, so fearful, that my annoyance dissipated.

"It's only a house," I said more gently.

"You know that's not true," said Repin sombrely, "it's much more than that."

And he was right, of course. For a moment we sat in uneasy silence while my emotions shifted away from love and towards active dislike. And back again. Despite a merrily burning fire, draughts of cold air still managed to drift through the room. My feet were frozen but when I thought of what Olga had endured and knew that Repin would in any case remind me, I stopped myself complaining. We were also in need of fresh candles. Wax had slid down the candlesticks pooling on wooden surfaces. I folded my velvet skirt around my legs for warmth. If it weren't for Repin, I'd have asked a footman to fetch my fur wrap, a maid to refill the chocolate, a valet to bring me books from the library, someone else candles, in short serfs to hover.

"All right," I ventured taking a deep breath. "As you're so anxious that the different Russias be united, that we all be equal, then why not think of you and me as a social experiment? Surely if a random couple such as ourselves can't live together convivially, how can you expect all of Russia to? But I warn you," I added lightly, "I require much work, much persuasion. I have endless arguments in my head to counter yours. I have years of ingrained privilege coursing through my veins. And it's not just my intellect you must seduce, you understand, it's a question of …"

And then boldly because I was tired of our conversation, just as a child does, I took his face in both my hands and turned it to mine.

14

In the days that followed, rumblings of unease about Yasnaya and my relationship with it, began to take hold and flourish. Yasnaya was so much more than a house and I didn't need Repin to underscore what I already knew. In his eyes it was an insulated, beautiful and privileged world but it was also mine. A place where I felt safe. It echoed with happier memories, happier ghosts of a time when I believed my parents still loved each other, when they were young, when the future was nothing but bright and hopeful, surrounded as they were by their growing brood. I drew strength from every step I took on untrampled snow, from the walks through the birch woods to the newly frozen ponds. Every breath of icy air was invigorating to me. I wanted to stretch out my arms and embrace the house and keep them forever locked within the periphery of this tiny boundary. In so doing, I might just keep the very world at bay, that my teacher was so desperate to bring in.

I visited room after room, from the undisturbed nursery with its board games, children's books, rocking horse and dolls to the main dining room, and the living spaces scattered with over-stuffed sofas and chairs. It was as though, if I stood still long enough and blew hard enough, I might breathe life once more into the inanimate objects that to Repin represented yet more acquisitive signs of privilege and to me triggered off memory after memory of joyful family gatherings.

There were portraits of Papa in his officer's uniform and not only of his father before him, but generation after generation of counts and princes. There were regimental swords and sabres, there were pictures of favourite horses, of wonderful balls in exquisite palaces. There were artefacts acquired on long journeys to far flung corners of the earth–far beyond the Steppes and Siberia. But these were the props and underpinnings as he saw them, of a society dedicated to pleasure, to further impeding progress. Again, I insisted, it was my history, my society, my world. It was a world waiting once more for its inhabitants to use and enjoy; a world that would not be permitted to flourish, if a new one was to be created in its place.

Repin and I set up a studio in the small dining room. This was the least cluttered place in the house, virtually stark by comparison. At first, Olga followed me from room to room, like a shadow in reverse, attempting to anticipate my every move and with the sole objective of keeping Repin as far away from me as possible. When a letter from Mama arrived however, she changed from being morbidly gloomy to manically industrious. She seemed to spend hours in the attic rooms looking for things, packing trunks and even rearranging the nursery. Repin put it down to the ravings of a mind halfway to senility but he was tolerant of her given her origins, given that she (like him he reminded me daily) was a peasant and urged me to be patient. Every day she asked me when we planned to return to Moscow.

My painting of Papa was going better than I could have hoped. While I been unproductive in Moscow, my inspiration dried up and contrived, here at Yasnaya, nestling within the haven it offered, I saw my father as he truly was. At first the influx of emotion that other pictures of him evoked in me, was confusing. On the one hand, I was confronted with the eccentric, intolerant and prematurely ageing parent that nonetheless dominated the Moscow house. Even if that parent as Mama liked to say, was captivated by his own entrancing inner life. On the other, I felt the haunting presence of the fun loving, boyishly charming man I had known when I was little.

Either way, his was a deeply critical, snobbish and difficult influence whose love of humanity really only embraced the peasantry while he reserved his true and most genuine contempt for his family. And all the time the real tragedy of his life was the conflict that raged within him– the endeavour to marry morality to his art. In this, I came to accept that Repin and my father were not so very different. As I would discover, Repin would spend the rest of his life, trying to balance a profound social conscience with an equal desire to paint.

And so, while my canvas was small and my palette extensive, Repin's was of epic proportions with drawings in sepia. Drawings he had collated over the years were pasted over the walls to inspire and prepare him for his next project. He had lived, for several months near the town of Stavropol some six hundred and fifty versts from Moscow, with a team of barge haulers. Not only did Repin grow fond of these men, he learned their stories. One had been a priest, another like himself had started life as an icon painter. These men took on saintly characteristics and for the duration of our stay at Yasnaya, Repin became increasingly preoccupied with them. While my picture of Papa seemed trite and unimportant by comparison, Repin's huge sketches took on a socio-political significance that I knew would have a long-lasting effect.

Even hastily drawn in pencil, the fresh sketches for the eventual oils, rendered me speechless. The haulers were ennobled in feature and stature, suffering etched in the deep lines of their faces while the grace of their bent bodies was physically tangible. These were no ordinary human beasts of burden but men more dignified and more worthy of respect than any aristocratic writer could be. The irony and contrast of our respective portraits could not have been greater. Repin was no longer bothered whether I painted in the dark, candlelight or early morning and he had soon abandoned the idea of painting me at all.

My portrait of my father was a labour of love–at any rate an attempt to retrieve and therefore honour, whatever love I still felt for him. Repin's was an urgent need to record, what he saw, as the Russian people's suppressed creativity. We worked differently too. While I sat practically immobile in my small corner of the room–a neatly defined section with its carefully stored brushes and rags and in silence, Repin moved across the floor as though he were a gymnast. He leapt from sofa to sofa regardless of his boots. He stood on chairs, windowsills, even the piano. He whistled endlessly under his breath or grunted answers to questions raised only in his mind. He measured with his hands, cloths, patterns, bits of string. He huffed and puffed and sighed, ran his hands through his hair, scratched at his week-old beard drawing blood. He flexed his hands until the joints cracked. He hardly ate a thing. After ten days he was gaunt, but his eyes blazed with excitement, driven by an inner impetus stronger than him.

He was on a mission to reach out to all, to teach his fellow Russians through his art, how to really live and feel. But this could only be achieved, he felt strongly, once social inequality had been righted. My portrait showed a literary man in repose–Repin's, men harnessed into leather straps, wearing little more than cheese cloth smocks and rag-made shoes, yet full of vitality. From time to time, as if remembering I was still there, Repin would slide across the strip of uncarpeted wooden floor to my side and glancing down at me, frown, gather my face in his two long-fingered hands and kiss me. His eyes boring into mine would close and he would outline my breast with his thumb sending shivers to my very toes.

And so, the house and land that I had dreamt of sharing with Repin, was re-visited only by myself. In the afternoons, when I could no longer see and Repin was at his zenith, I would slip out of the tall French windows, wrapped in furs, to walk in the now frozen garden. Not even the hedges and parterres were visible beneath the snow drifts and only the exquisitely slender branches of birch gave shape to an otherwise monotone landscape. In total silence, through endless variations of white, I would make my way through the orchard and rose garden and down the long avenue of poplars. Behind and above me, the house was an elegant, protective shadow waiting, watching, ever vigilant.

When I grew tired of lugging my feet through heavy snow, I would retrace my steps to where the paths diverged, one leading to the pond, the other to Papa's magic wood and the place where he and Mama had planted their respective trees. Smoke spewing from the chimneys was always a heartening sign too, marring the otherwise oblique palette of white and pebble grey sky with smudges of black. And everywhere, silence enveloped Yasnaya in a tranquil vacuum far away from the commotion and upheaval that Repin assured me, raged through the rest of Russia. No clocks here to propel us towards our destiny. Only the occasional raw squawk from a bird or unidentified animal was a reminder of the existence of wildlife.

One afternoon, as I was creeping onto the verandah as quietly as possible, wanting to slip unnoticed into our studio, Olga Feodova pounced on me as if from nowhere. Silently, she unwrapped layer upon layer of my sodden clothing and scraped snow from my boots. It was only as she was shaking out my fur cloak that I realised she herself was dressed to go out. She had on her brightly embroidered turban which covered her forehead entirely and shawls were wound on top of this for additional warmth. She always seemed a completely different person when dressed like this, younger somehow but more anonymous. On this occasion, she also seemed agitated, distracted, and in a great hurry to get me to do something. Only I wasn't sure what. It was then that I noticed several trunks in the hall. It gradually dawned on me that Olga might be in the process of leaving. Catching my eye, she took me firmly by the arm.

"There are poppy cakes and tea," she said hurriedly. "I have taken them into... him." She jerked her head in the direction of the small dining room. Olga Feodova only ever addressed Repin as the 'Ukrainian' and she rarely brought him so much as a cup of kvass. I shot her a surprised look as I deliberately and slowly peeled off my wet gloves. "Come, come, Kotchka," she said impatiently virtually snatching my gloves from me and tossing them onto the hall table. "The tea and cakes will get cold."

"You have been cooking?" I asked much too irritated by her bossy manner to humour her. Of course, she'd been cooking!

"Yes, yes," she said almost pushing me through the door. "The little one in the kitchen can't make blin to save her life. And as it's the last day–"

"Last day?" I echoed over my shoulder as with one final push, I found myself vaulted into the small dining room. Repin looked up or rather down, sharply. He wasn't exactly hanging from the chandelier but almost. He was poised precariously on a series of stacked chairs with an intriguing arrangement of long-handled brushes, elevated above the canvas. He held onto the delicate crystal which swung hazardously from its velvet rope.

"Don't move!" he warned as he squirted thick black ink through these pipes and then smoothed them over with an outstretched foot.

Olga's tray of tea things was just as precariously resting on a fender seat by the fire. She emitted a cry and rushed to move it. I was more concerned with the number of tapers positioned around the room and wondered at the wisdom of any lit candle with so many loose bits of paper floating about but refrained from comment.

Repin could barely conceal his irritation as Olga weaved her way among the various easels. She was unusually clumsy pouring tea, not quite closing the samovar spout so that liquid created a puddle on the rug perilously close to one of his paintings. She then began slapping cakes on plates with such ferocity that crumbs flew everywhere. She'd have been better off tossing pancakes in the kitchen with 'the little one' as she dubbed the under cook. In a rush to re-fill my tea, she tripped over a pile of books. I had barely finished my cake, my fork half-way to my mouth, when Olga whisked away my plate.

"Olga Feodova!" I protested. "I was enjoying that!" I caught Repin's expression. He was annoyed with us both. He declined her offer of a drink and I knew he wanted us gone as soon as possible. Ink was fast drying on his picture and he had to mix the sepia with water, climb up his improvised ladder, apply it, smooth it with his foot and all this while hanging on to a swinging light.

"Yes, so you're finished. Very good. We go now," she said stacking the tea things and chipping a few cups in the process.

"Go?" I echoed. "Go where?" I was amused by her frenzied energy.

"We go tonight to Moscow," she said breathlessly. "On the overnight train from Tula. It takes longer but we're there by morning. Your bags are packed. Even yours," Olga flicked a look in Repin's direction. "Seven Asses has been… roused…" she added which I took to mean that he was relatively sober. "I didn't know what you wanted done with all this. He should go for a walk." Olga reverted back to her habit of speaking about Repin as if he weren't present. "Then Seven Asses can put this stuff in the troika." And Repin will have you killed, I thought to myself. Repin was looking at the old woman oddly. Yes, I thought. He might just kill her.

"I'm not going anywhere," he said flatly. "Not until this is finished."

Olga Feodova stumbled with the tray. His response, in whatever scheme she was cooking up, was clearly not one she had anticipated.

"You don't understand," she said panic making her speech rapid and sharp. "We must go tonight. We have no choice."

"But why?" I asked calmly warming my cold feet by the fire, feeling sated despite the manically consumed tea and cake. I looked forward to an evening with Repin, drinking cherry brandy from Chekov's estate and talking about his day's work. Mine never warranted more than a few lines. "What on earth is so important that we have to leave when it's already dark?"

Olga looked frightened unused to reasoning her position. Opposition coming from me too, was something she had not foreseen.

"You must believe me when I say it *is* important. I could tell him." Once again, she jerked her foot in Repin's direction and then crossed herself unexpectedly as if she'd inadvertently come into contact with the devil.

"No," I said firmly, annoyed. "You can tell me."

Olga gripped the tray so fiercely her bony knuckles turned white and the veins sprung upwards under the diaphanous skin.

"There have been developments," she said darkly. "In Moscow. Your lady mother, has sent for me and as I cannot leave you here with–with him." Her eyes again swivelled to the base of the 'ladder'. "Then you must both come with me."

"Now this *is* nonsense!" Repin dropped the extended paint brush carefully to the ground and then eased himself to the floor, chair by chair. He wiped his hands on a cloth and shook his hair from his eyes. "Olga Feodova," he said sternly. "You are a woman of the world are you not?"

Olga Feodova mumbled something unintelligible and stared at her feet, almost bent double as though at any moment she would show us how she could touch her toes.

"Then what can you possibly imagine goes on between your mistress and me?"

"Oh!" Olga's head shot up as if it had been yanked by a string. "Oh!" she moaned.

"Quite," said Repin taking a used cup from the tray and returning to the samovar to fill it. "Now, what is all this rubbish? If you want us to suddenly cut short, what is proving to be a profitable and most delectable holiday, then you're going to have to come up with something convincing. And no, we are not leaving on any train tonight. It's cold and it's late. Sonya Andreevna will just have to wait. Or you can return alone."

I threw Repin a relieved, grateful look. Olga reeled as if slapped. She had never known my countess mother to wait on anyone.

"That's the end of it!" he said firmly. Olga's eyes narrowed, swivelling to meet mine with what was as close to an appeal as she could muster but I shook my head.

Repin took a long slurp of tea.

"I'll stay until I can safely move my canvas. I do see that you must have your reasons for getting back, so Tatyana and you can travel on ahead." He must have felt my glare because he added hastily, "but it's up to the countess to decide when."

Olga made a face and muttered something under her breath to the tune of it being a little early to be assuming any airs and graces and over the bones of the saints would she allow me to marry a peasant. She then lapsed into her dialect, a language I couldn't understand but the fierceness of her expression suggested that if there had been animosity between them, hers was now an all-out declaration of war.

"And I'm not deciding till tomorrow," I said emboldened by Repin's authority. "And don't wake me early!" I added to Olga's cross, retreating back. "I won't have decided by then."

The door slammed shaking Repin's precious canvas. I closed my eyes bracing myself for a violent response, but the canvas did not fall and when I dared look again, Repin was smiling.

"What can have caused the creature to react in such a way?" he asked with fleeting curiosity but then, setting down his teacup on the piano, he crossed the room to crouch on his knees at my feet. "I meant what I said," he said charmingly, taking both my hands in his and raising them to his lips. "It *has* been a delectable holiday."

I freed a hand to trace his mouth with my finger.

"Then kiss me," I said.

15

Travelling with Olga Feodova was a very different experience from travelling with Repin. She sat bolt up-right for one thing, like a skeletal, intractable buddha. I had declined her offer to sit beside her, horrified that I might inadvertently fall asleep on her shoulder. As a small child I should have liked nothing better, but I was peeved with her and could hardly engage her in conversation as it was. She spent most of the time mimicking my every move. Pretending to sleep myself and out of sheer boredom, I played a little game with her, trying to will her to sleep. I would close my eyes hoping that she would follow suit but every time I opened my eyes, no matter how randomly, hers too would spring open. I tried to catch her out on several occasions but either she was used to not sleeping or she could sleep with her eyes open.

Every nerve in my body vibrated with irritation and in response to the swaying train. The drowsy warmth of the compartment and the velvet blinds keeping the frozen exterior at bay should have aided my sleep, but they did not. I was annoyed, irrationally I knew, with my mother for summoning Olga back to Moscow. I was annoyed that Repin and I were forced to be apart–the first time in our short courtship and I was especially annoyed with the cantankerous old cockroach in front of me. Her brooding coal black eyes had me pinioned so that I squirmed as though I had the pox. When not holding me captive with her malevolent presence, she spent the rest of her time sewing what appeared to be a tiny set of doll's clothes.

This time too, the journey seemed interminable. I was tired before we even set off. Snatches of unsatisfactory conversations with Repin repeated themselves in my head and the small, over-heated compartment in Olga's company,

was claustrophobic. I thought of my incomplete portrait of
my father and was dissatisfied with that too.

　　I had begun the portrait, in part to document Papa's
hair growth (which now seemed a poor excuse for a picture)
and in part to prove my hand at portraiture. Painting that had
given me such pleasure in the past, now seemed problematic
and to demand something extra from me that I wasn't certain
I was able to give. Increasingly, I felt Repin's criticism not
only of my family but of our whole way of life. Insulated as
we were at Yasnaya, it was easy to discredit his warnings of
the new Russia that he assured me hovered as close as Tula.
He said if I only opened my eyes, I'd be aware of the dissent
that was seeping through the hitherto subservience of our
peasants. He said I was a fool not to wake up and make
changes before they were made to me–changes to *me*, I noted,
not to *us*. I wondered how it was that in Moscow we had only
been fascinated by each other and not at all about politics. I
wondered unhappily whether our love would survive.

　　And all the while during that long night, I searched
Olga's face for some indication that she too was changing–
that her intractable loyalty was being eroded by new ideas.
She fell asleep long before I did, removing her tightly bound
turban almost absent-mindedly as she did so. Her elongated
eyes slid shut and her head fell forwards on her chest. With
the dawn, cracks of light slipped through the edges of curtain,
igniting sections of her iron grey hair with strips of colour. I
was especially startled by the thought that she might even
have been pretty once. I thought of her violent, short-lived
marriage.

　　With a shuddering jolt and screech of brakes, the train
came to a spectacular halt. Olga Feodova was thrown
forwards. Instinctively my arms shot forward to stop her
from landing on my lap. Ha! I thought, when she realized
that I'd been awake before her, I've won! She emitted a low
cry, scrabbling on the seat for the shawls and ribbons with
which to embalm herself. Once her hair had been plastered to
her skull with pins and material, she thrust her sewing into
the long, grubby carpet bag she used for traveling. She
lurched for the window tassel, yanking it so that the blind

shot up with a ping and daylight blinded us both. She covered her eyes stumbling back as if allergic to the sun.

"We go now," she announced bluntly. Poking her head out of our compartment, she called for Seven Asses who had accompanied us on the journey as our personal porter. Blearily he emerged from his end of the train, still drunk but a few sharp taps on his head from Olga Feodova quickly sobered him up. Or enough to send him, somewhat unsteadily, in the direction of the luggage wagon.

I stamped my feet together to shake off the pins and needle sensation that had begun to crawl up my legs. I stifled a yawn oblivious to the bustle around me as travellers poured from carriages eager to stretch their legs. And then, just as we had left the platform and I was being guided by Olga at breakneck speed towards the station exit, with a less agile Seven Asses trailing behind us, I was distracted by the sight of crowds of students waving huge home spun banners. I pulled back, twisting to see more as she propelled me onwards. My heart began to hammer uncomfortably in my throat.

"Papa's name is on the banners," I said trying to keep the panic from my voice. "What does it mean?"

Olga pushed me ahead of her. "Nothing," said Olga tightly. "It means nothing. Keep walking and pull up your hood. Hide your face."

"But what has happened?" I insisted. "Is this the reason I've had to return?"

"Of course not." Olga Feodova grabbed my hand as though I were a small child and like a child, I dragged my heels, my fingers on her tiny wrists.

"Papa's name is on everything!" I said in disbelief and looking around, I saw that it was not an exaggeration. Billboards and life-size cut-outs spun in the wind. There were pictures of him on the front pages of the day's newspapers and on banners strung from iron beams. I couldn't help thinking that the portrait of my father might be useful after all. Olga Feodova pressed on determinedly.

Seven Asses who could neither read nor write caught up with me, tugging on my cloak so that I was forced to stop.

Breathless, he set down the luggage luge. Standing on one foot he scratched his ankle with the other. He looked from my face to Olga's retreating back, trying to gage our reaction while his was a mixture of fear and confusion.

"It's all right," I said reassuringly eager to get home now as quickly as possible and discover what was really going on. But Seven Asses seemed to have other ideas. He pushed his cap back on his head and scratched his head. Along with everything else, I wondered if he had fleas. He belched loudly, clutching his belly. For a horrible moment I thought he might be sick. He swayed, was supported by the luge and righted himself like a sailing ship coming about. He let out his belt by a couple of notches. I began to walk on, not wanting to lose Olga in the swirling crowds.

"There have been rumours Mistress," he called after me. I turned abruptly, the familiar anxiety returning. Seven Asses was still rooted to the spot, scratching his belly.

"What do you mean? Is it to do with this?" I walked back to him, motioning to the posters behind me, the extreme cold, hunger and a sleepless night all now well and truly forgotten.

Seven Asses shrugged. "Maybe."

I considered touching him, but he looked so completely unappealing I couldn't bring myself to even get close. I could smell body sweat and alcohol even from a short distance. Instead, I resorted to drawing myself to my full height and speaking in the tone my mother often adopted with the Yasnaya servants.

"Tell me!" I said sharply. "What have you heard?"

Seven Asses visibly shrank. "They say your father, the count has been ex-communicated," he said meekly. "That the Emperor himself is angry and that the countess has a–"

"Has a…?"

"What a lot of nonsense!" said Olga Feodova pivoting back to us, skirts flying like a whirling dervish. "Bones of the saints! Seven Asses is the biggest fool on the estate. Why would you listen to a thing he says! He's a good for nothing drunk! He's wasting our time because he's too lazy to pull this thing!" Olga kicked the luge with her foot and set his hat straight on his head. "He's keeping us all waiting. Why your good mother insists on retaining this waste of space is beyond me. You're a free man, Seven Asses. You should make your home elsewhere."

"And you're a free woman, Olga Feodova!" He lunged towards her. "Make your home with me!"

"I use the brain God gave me," she said in disgust. "Why would I want to mess up my life a second time?" She set his hands on the luge poles and gave him a push as though he were a mule. "Walk on!" Olga re-arranged my hood. "You too, little mistress."

"Why won't you tell me?"

Olga Feodova's mouth clamped shut in that unassailable manner I knew only too well. Not even the threat of a night in Siberia would compel her to talk. She spun on her heel and set off at a virtual gallop so that I had to run to keep up with her, with Seven Asses listing somewhere in front.

An enormous crowd had gathered at the station entrance. People positioned near the front held a huge canopy above them. My father's name was on that too. I shuddered suddenly with cold and apprehension and an overwhelming urge to be enveloped once again at Yasnaya and in Repin's arms. At the thought of Repin I wondered fleetingly if he'd known anything about all this. For someone who claimed to have his finger on the collective Russian pulse, I marvelled that such news could have escaped him.

Our Moscow coachman was waiting and gratefully I took his extended hand to be helped up and into the cocoon of dark and warmth. Olga spread fur rugs across my knees, gave Seven Asses another clout around the head for his trouble and positioned herself on the leather seat in front of me, disappearing under layers of blankets. The horses trotted off, lifting their feet reluctantly in the thick snow. I gripped my hands together in the delicious heat of my fur muff and closed my eyes.

It seemed that within seconds we were driving down the avenue of birch trees to Khamovniki and our city house. As the coachman emitted a loud shout, spurring the horses into a gallop, I noticed we had passed a small group of men crouching in the snow. Peering back out of the window these men had leapt to their feet and were running after us waving notebooks and cameras.

"Journalists!" spat Olga making a swatting gesture as if they were rodents to be chased away.

"And why exactly would journalists be camping out in these temperatures, at this time of the morning and on our land?" I asked pinning Olga with my most decisive stare. The old woman had the grace to squirm. She busied herself with her carpet bag shifting her bottom as if it were too bony to make sitting comfortable.

"It's not as if I'm not going to find out," I added rapidly losing patience with the whole cloak and dagger act which at this stage in the day and on an empty stomach was growing increasingly tedious. Olga Feodova tucked her hair under her turban and made a clucking sound. "Look we are here," she said.

The carriage swept into the half-moon drive in front of the house rather than clatter into the courtyard. Servants, I was relieved to note, poured from every direction–grooms to attend to the horses, Mama's maid to indicate which bags were to go up to her and which to my room and house butlers to pull a now flagging Olga from the carriage and unload the hampers of food she had thought necessary to bring from Yasnaya. I heard the men grown under the weight of jars of preserved fruit, kasha, sweets and poppy seed bread. The bag of paints and the canvas of my father, I carried myself.

Tired as much by Olga, as by the journey itself, I let everyone pass in front of me, intending to venture into the house when it was at last quiet outside. Only the stamping, snorting of the horses as they were led to the stable block made any audible sound. The air was cold and crisp; above me swirling snowflakes waited to descend. Ice sat in a thin film along my eyelashes, on the ends of my fur hood and muff. My tummy rumbled pleasantly, and I thought of the hot breakfast that must surely await. I thought of the questions I would ask my father. It seemed much had been happening since I'd been away. I wondered when Repin would come. It was so quiet that for a moment I was disorientated thinking myself back at Yasnaya and that I would find Repin waiting for me in the small dining room. I closed my eyes trying to invoke everything about him: the smell of his neck, the feel of his hair as it rubbed my throat, his lips when they smiled in that lopsided way they did when he was aroused, his hands moving to take possession of mine.

"Do this for me now and you can have one later." Arkady's familiar drawl resonated clearly from behind the courtyard wall.

My eyes flew open. Had the power of suggestion actually worked? Worse still, had I conjured up the wrong man?

"It doesn't work like that."

But that was Mama talking now. Mama in a tight, sharp, narrow voice. My heart thudded dully. It was not a tone he should trifle with because I, who after all knew her better, knew exactly what it meant. He should stop. Not press his point, whatever it might be, any further.

"Yes, it does. You can have as many as you want–we can." Arkady corrected himself hastily. "Just not now. Despite everything, you must see that."

"Oh, I see all right," Mama's voice was so low I had to strain, standing very still, to hear her.

"Well then," his relief was evident. His voice rolled in rich, creamy waves.

"It's not like ordering a cab. It might never happen again. Not at my age. It just doesn't."

"But what about your family? What about your children?"

"Don't you think I'm not tortured by the thought of them? Every minute of the day I wonder how they will react. They're the *only* ones I think about. I'm surprised you mention them though. They weren't a consideration before." Mama's voice was tart. Oh, no, Arkady I wanted to warn him. Turn away now. This is a side of Sonya you really don't want to see!

"Yes, you're quite right. They weren't before but that's because you said this couldn't happen."

"We've been through this," said Mama wearily.

"Yes, and we'll go through it again. Until I understand what has happened exactly."

"There's nothing to understand. You know what we did and the result…"

"No, not what we did." Arkady's tone was harsh. "What *you* did. I don't feel I've had any say in this. I feel used, deceived, that you lied."

"You think I wanted this!" said my mother, her anguish clear.

I wanted to round on the man, stand in front of my mother and protect her. I moved, my boot crunching the snow.

"What was that?" I imagined Mama taking an instinctive step closer to Arkady, looking up to him with her large, agate eyes.

"It's nothing–one of the grooms probably. Don't be so jumpy."

Losing my nerve, I kept quiet. I heard the rustle of clothing and held my breath. There was a pause. I can't imagine they kissed. They seemed too angry for that. After a while, Mama's voice returned muffled, less clear.

"You're not being fair. You wrote once that you wouldn't be against this. Do you remember? That time when you were in the Crimea? You knew how I felt, and you said you wouldn't be against it. Not at all. Those were your words."

"And I'm not!" Arkady said in exasperation. "Just not like this!"

"It's because you want to be free!" Mama sounded as petulant as Masha and I wanted to shake her. I could hear the tears hanging behind every word. "Well, have your freedom. I don't want anything from you. Go! Go back to your estates and your women and your fine living! I'll resolve this myself."

Again, there was a pause. Perhaps Mama turned to leave and Arkady pulled her to him. After a few minutes, I heard her blow her nose.

"Perhaps we should think about my original idea. We talked about it at the beginning. After all it's not as if it hasn't been done before. Half of Petersburg–"

Mama blew her nose again loudly, so that I couldn't hear Arkady's proposal, but I heard my mother's incredulous response.

"But he'll know!" she said. "It's been so long. And now…"

"There's still time," said Arkady. "And you're a very beautiful and beguiling woman." I could imagine Arkady kissing the top of Mama's fur cap believing he was winning. "I've not doubt at all that you can do this thing, if you put your mind to it."

"You don't know what you're asking." There were more sniffs. "Is that what you want?" My mother sounded deplete of emotion.

"I agree it's not ideal, but I can't think of a better solution."

"And afterwards, you'd be happy for things to continue? You would never be able to say. You could never claim…"

There was a much longer pause. Perhaps Arkady was as much at a loss as I was to understand what she meant, to what she was referring. But then that was what happened with eavesdropping. I wasn't supposed to understand their conversation,

"I hadn't thought that far."

"No, I didn't think you had." My mother's voice was totally devoid of the affection with which she generally addressed him–an affection I used to find annoying it was so sickly sweet but its absence alarmed me even more. "Men never do."

"Don't walk away like that."

Arkady's footsteps moved towards hers and stopped. "I have to go, you know that. I'm late as it is."

"It's a long journey. You shouldn't be going."

"Why not? Oh, I see you're concerned! How very sweet!" Mama's voice was laced with a sarcasm I was certain Arkady hadn't noticed. I heard his drop theatrically.

"Of course, I'm concerned! So, you won't go? I have my usual box at the opera Saturday and there's a new little vodka bar in Arbat. I mean you'll think of your health of-"

"How silly you are!" Mama said smartly. "I'm not ill. And of course, I'm still going, in fact almost immediately. Seven Asses will accompany me as far as Novgorod. Will you come to the station? Or maybe not, the press has gathered, so Lev tells me. The story is out. The question it appears is not so much whether or not the church has acted correctly but rather who in Moscow has not read *The Kreutzer Sonata*. I mean have you?"

The mention of father's name was clearly inflammatory.

"So, you're doing it for *him*!" Arkady said enunciating every word in lacerating tones. "Why then, this charade? Why couldn't you just say?"

"For *him*? Don't be ridiculous! I'm doing it for my children!"

More nose blowing. They were silent so long I thought they'd finally gone in until I heard Mama's voice, stronger this time, more forceful.

"Do you realize that he has given away all copyright to the people? Much of his estates? That unless I do this now, we will have nothing to live on!"

"It's an excuse."

"It's the *truth*!"

"That may be, but the Czar himself has seconded your husband's excommunication, forbidden *Sonata*'s publication. How do you think you can possibly change his mind? Don't you realize the gravity of what he's done? This isn't a case of upsetting a few leftist art critics! Wake up Sonya! *Novoe Vremia* is saying that there are two Czars in Russia and one of them is Lev. They say that the Czar can do nothing to rattle Lev Tolstoy's throne, but Tolstoy certainly is shaking the Czar's!"

"It certainly is astonishing."

"It's more than that!"

"I mean that his writing can have such an impact."

"Well, it does. And not least I suspect on his own family. They say that all of Russia is feeding on the book - that everyone debates it. They're saying that his is a Christian anarchism and therefore a direct attack on the establishment. But I suspect that excommunicating him will only make him even more popular. They say that even President Roosevelt has been drawn in, that he considers Lev depraved."

There was another uneasy silence. Who wouldn't agree with that?

"But Chekov likes it."

"Chekov would, given how closely it resembles his own shambolic arrangement!" Arkady changed tack, perhaps realizing that he wasn't one to make moralistic pronouncements. "Given all that, how by the bones of the saints, do you expect to persuade the Czar? I'm amazed he's even granted you an audience."

"I don't know," Mama said coldly. "But I can certainly try. I shall go on bended knee. I shall beg him."

"But to do what? You can't uncensor something. The story has been banned. And that's the end of it."

"It has," agreed my mother. "But that has only increased its popularity and his! I need the Czar to lift the censor, so that the story can be published even if in some larger anthology. We need the royalties. It's my only hope." Then, as if remembering something, she said less stiffly. "And to think, that when I was a girl, Lev promised I would dance with the Czar! He said I was like Pushkin's wife and that everyone would fall in love with me." Her voice went all dreamy.

"Yes, well I'm not sure I want to end up dying in a duel like Pushkin did." Arkady's reply hinted at some humour. "At least not yet."

"I just never thought my first meeting with him would be like this."

"No, and it doesn't have to be. Don't go! I can't put it more strongly. To hell with Lev's copyright, let him sell his property, give his money to the poor, join a monastery for all I care. We'll manage."

"And you'd support my children too?"

There was an uncomfortable silence, and I could imagine Mama standing as tall as her fur lined boots would allow and fixing him with a censorious gaze we knew only too well. "No, I thought not," she said.

"Sophia, don't."

I started. Arkady had called Mama by her formal name. She was always Sonya to our father and to their friends. I wondered if she'd noticed. I rather hoped she had. When Arkady repeated her name, I knew it was to an empty space.

16

I waited until I was certain that Arkady had followed my mother, before venturing into the courtyard. By now, my hands despite a fur muff, tingled with cold and I stamped the ground to get the circulation going in my feet. My cheeks smarted as if stung by hundreds of bees, my lips felt tender and cracked. My thoughts had taken a gloomy turn. Even I could tell that at times Arkady and my mother appeared to be talking at cross purposes but I was clearly in no position to question them. Gloomier still was the notion that the only knowledge I seemed to have of my mother these days was through snippets of conversation and-overheard ones at that.

"Tanya!"

I spun around. "Papa?"

"I've got rid of them!"

At first, I couldn't make my father out at all against the snow drifts and then he emerged, a lumbering Quasimodo in his ridiculous handmade shoes. I clapped my hands together for warmth, dispersing snow crystals like so many glowing insects. I was eager to be inside now but he, on the other hand, seemed completely oblivious of the cold, shuffling amiably towards me as if we were both out on a pleasant country walk. What was less aimable was his wild expression. His eyes were the colour of sea buckthorn, his complexion sallow. Wisps of hair sprouted at intervals over his face, even growing from his ears. But as ever, it was his beard that drew my attention. It was now so long that it lay limply like a scarf over one shoulder. I looked again. Had we agreed an exact length before we returned to Yasnaya? I was surprised that the thought wasn't entirely pleasing. We had all become used to time spent apart, relying on his frequent absences for peace of mind. Perhaps, he'd forgotten. Perhaps, I would.

"Got rid of what?" I spoke precisely hoping that my tone indicated I wasn't in the mood to linger. That I was cold, not surprising the inclement weather and that it was even dangerous to be outside for much longer.

"The horses of course. Oh, I know I said I would some time ago but it's not until this arrived that I appreciated how quickly I was going to have to carry out my plan."

I had no idea what the 'this' was but then Papa always said he could see things that we mere mortals could not. I was about to murmur something along those lines, when he suddenly turned to heave something out of the snow.

"It's a present," he said a little shyly dusting off the seat of a bicycle. "From the Moscow Society of Velocipedes. Isn't it marvellous?"

I looked from his excited, expectant face to the inanimate contraption and back again.

"Yes, it is," I agreed hesitantly. "But … er… is it entirely practical at this time of year? I mean will it even move in the snow?"

"Bones of the saints, Tatyana, it's *English* for heaven's sake! Of course, I'm going to use it in the snow!"

"I see."

Which wasn't the right response.

"You're always hovering, Tanya," he said gruffly. "It's never a direct trajectory with you."

"I'm sorry." I pointed with my foot. "And…" I thought desperately of something positive to say. "And this … can be ridden on the road? I mean with the sledges and horses and carriages?"

He stroked the handlebars reverently. "Ah… well funny that you should ask." Papa cleared his throat. "I have to practice a bit more. I'm not quite ready."

"Ready for what?"

Papa shifted uncomfortably. "A test. I have to pass a test. And the bicycle has to be registered and I have to pay tax on it."

"Oh." I wondered how that would sit with our mother and all their wrangling over finances.

"Of course, I will learn properly at the Manège– incidentally it's where I learned to fence as a young man." He turned to go.

"What's it like?" I said feeling guilty at not appearing more enthusiastic. "Not the Manège. I mean the sensation of riding this?"

Papa smiled boyishly. "It's nothing but innocent, holy foolishness."

I couldn't help but be disarmed by his unashamed pleasure. "Are you any good at…this 'foolishness'?"

Papa smiled. "I have to confess…I am not." He giggled. "I know, I know. It's hard to believe but true. The thing is Tatyana, I don't know what happens when I'm sitting with my feet on the pedals. I imagine something in front of me, even if it's not there. But most of the time it is! I feel a pull towards it–an *irresistible* pull. There is nothing I can do to avoid it. Not, that is, until a collision happens."

"Oh Papa," I said amused. "And does this happen often?"

"Every time. There's a woman who is also learning to ride a bicycle. A very fat woman in a hat with feathers. Naturally, it's the fault of the feathers. I see them trembling in the wind. I try not to, but I feel the bicycle pulling towards them. And then we're done for. We collide!" His voice dwindled at last running out of steam. "Is he still here?" he added darkly.

"Who?"

"Your mother's boyfriend." His voice dropped to a conspiratorial whisper. "Prince Demidov."

I thrust my hands deeper in my muff, clenching my fists for warmth. And courage. I also had a question. There was something I needed to know. "I've only just arrived back from Tula. I've not yet been to the house. But…"

"Yes?" He looked at me closely his myopia getting the better of him. I returned his look, keeping mine steady.

"There were journalists at the gate, Papa," I said. "And at the station when I arrived."

"Pah!" said my father dismissively. He waved a hand as though, if I tried, I couldn't have conveyed a more trivial piece of news.

"It doesn't trouble you?"

My father looked genuinely amazed. "Why should it?"

"I know you've received death threats. At least I don't *know* for certain, but I saw the headlines at the station. They say you've also had horrible letters, that even Metropolitan Levin has written a prayer for your death! I saw it Papa. Doesn't *that* alarm you?"

My father leant his shiny new bicycle carefully against a snowbank and took me by the arm. He was so uncharacteristically calm, that the old anxious feeling replaced any lingering hunger that might be scaling my stomach wall.

"I'll show you what alarms me Tanya!" he said pulling me towards one of the outbuildings. Not letting go of my arm, he reached above him for the lantern and unhooking it, lowered it in front of us. I could feel muscle pulsating under his shirt and part of me wondered at the vigour of this seemingly frail old man. It was only the beard that was deceptive. His eyes burned, driven by the fervour of his beliefs. My father stood straight and tall now, his shoulders broad, still manly. He kicked open a storeroom door, pushing me ahead of him.

"You see Tanya!" he said angrily. "Do you see?"

It took me a few minutes to be accustomed to the darkness.

'Looking on darkness which the blind do see...' I half muttered to myself. The line had become a sort of mantra for Repin and me. And thinking of Repin, I was suddenly overcome with desire to be with him and an equal aversion to being cooped up with my father in this small, dank space. The stable door had clattered shut and my heart began to pound unsteadily in my chest.

"What?" Papa's voice rose unsteadily.

"I don't understand," I said confused. There were hundreds of canvas bags. Maybe more. All piled one on top of the other. "Is?" I hesitated, knowing how important it was to answer correctly. "Is Mama storing grain again? Is there…" I wracked my brain to remember what Repin had said about the Steppes, the peasants, anything. "I mean… is there going to be another famine?"

Papa dropped my wrist. "'Is there going to be another famine!'" He tucked his hands behind his belt, rocking on his heels in characteristic pose. "No, of course there isn't! No, this is much more important!" He raised his arms as if summoning the heavens. "Those bags aren't full of grain!"

I looked again. My heart was beating painfully. If not grain, what then? Clothing?

"No?"

"No, you ninny!" said my father so that I would dearly liked to have punched him.

"Oh, ye gods and little fishes!" howled my father kicking a sack so that it fell on its side. He bent down to untie one. "Look! They're full of letters! Hundreds and hundreds from villages all over Russia! Letters of support, I'll have you know. Do you realize that people who have never read a book in their lives are reading mine? There's even a sect calling themselves after me. There are now thousands of these pacifists. Don't you understand, Tanya? The church itself is in danger of imploding and all because of *my* writing! Everywhere I go people turn out in hoards to cheer me– more people come to see me than they do the Czar!"

I looked at him in disbelief. I wasn't sure that I wanted to imagine thousands of fanatics wandering around proclaiming anything in my father's name. Dropping my muff so that it hung off my wrist and removing a mitten, I hunkered down beside him. I blew on my fingers to warm them before picking up a dirty, ink-stained envelope.

"And that's a good thing?"

My father looked at me puzzled. "If it changes the way we think about social injustice then yes, of course it is."

I stood up. There appeared to be bags behind, in front and above me.

"Repin thinks so too," I said with a sigh thinking of Repin teetering on top of a ladder to sketch his barge haulers.

"Of course, he does!" said my father delightedly. He took the letter out of my hand, replacing it carefully in a bag. "I've said it before but I am more convinced than ever. All art *must* have a moral sense. I'm glad you're here Tanya, as you can bear witness to what I have to say. Take note. From now on, I will never write another line of fiction. Ever."

He had said this before, many many times but as we stared at each other, the unbidden presence of my mother, rose between us. I didn't want to remind him that mother would have a great deal to say on this (as on any) matter. That provided he didn't give away more copyright to his fictitious work, then she probably wouldn't mind what he wrote.

"But I don't understand. If you say that your fiction has drawn all these followers, attracted all this attention, then why stop writing it? And doesn't it concern you that the authorities have banned your *Kreutzer Sonata* just when it is bringing you such acclaim?"

I held my breath wondering if I'd gone too far but my father turned his whole head towards me, sucking his teeth.

"Not remotely. That little story reminds me too much of your mother as it is."

I wanted to ask him which bit exactly and hoped that it wasn't because Pozdnyshev, the insanely jealous protagonist, strangles his wife. I also knew that despite Mama's supposed bravado, she had been deeply hurt by the book. Not least, because as Papa was happy to tell anyone who cared to listen that he advocated abstinence in all things and had taken a vow of celibacy. I had come to understand why Mama might seek comfort elsewhere.

"But you've become infamous because of it."

My father smiled contentedly. "I know and if it means that people are drawn to my other work and my way of life, then so much the better. I have seen what an obligation I have as a writer–the enormity of my responsibility. Take Dostoevsky or Gogol, to me they–"

His smugness irritated me. What was good for him was not necessarily a prescriptive for the rest of the family. Especially not our mother. I inched my way to the door.

"Music doesn't," I said my hand on the door handle.
"I'm sorry?"

I cleared my throat. "Music doesn't *just* have the moral sense you suggest. It provides a sensual pleasure too surely and yet it can reduce us to tears, render young girls temporarily insane, send armies marching, not unwillingly, to their death. Why is that?"

My father held the lantern above my face so that I blinked. "Music can inflame the passions, certainly and it follows therefore, that it poses a moral *threat*."

I looked at him in astonishment. "You don't really think that?"

My father snorted unattractively. "Everyone knows that music has long ceased to reflect cosmic and social order. If anything, I'd go further and say it seems to produce a quasi-*electrical* effect. And it's well known that stimulation–rather I should say over stimulation (just look at your mother) is the principal cause of sickness, immorality and even death! Music is to blame for this which is why I distrust it so completely."

"But you love music!" I protested remembering the many evenings our parents had played the piano together often well into the night. In particular, I remembered the great Wanda Landowska bringing her harpsichord to play for us at Yasnaya. Mama had even photographed her, a sombre Papa standing behind her in his usual Cossack garb, hands thrust in the belt of his smock.

He frowned something suddenly occurring to him. "Does HE play?"

A retort to the effect that of course he did, bounced off my tongue. Arkady, as befitting any gentleman of his class was brought up playing a musical instrument to a proficient standard. But Papa barely digested what I had to say, his attention deflected once again by the sack-loads of correspondence. He picked up a letter bringing it close to his eyes.

"Can't..." I renewed my efforts. "Can't art just give pleasure? And if it does arouse strong emotions then surely it has succeeded? Just as powerfully as..." but then I stopped.

The conversation was drifting to one with which I was all too familiar. Repin and I often debated the merits of music as opposed to art. I voted for music while Repin believed that there was an area of the nervous system to which the latter communicated more violently than anything else. He was equally fascinated by the human body and the unmoderated behaviour of animals. His portrait of Ivan the Terrible was a case in point. Perhaps he and my father had more in common than I cared to think.

"Tanya, Tanya." My father shook his head tucking the letter into his pocket, despondent again. "You simply don't understand! Russian writers have an urgent, *desperate* fight on their hands, a sort of Christian mission. There's no time for anything else. Without it, they, we–*she*–are all animals!"

I stared at my father. It could so easily have been Repin talking. How had life for these men become so complicated? As for my father, there seemed very little evidence of the so-called 'radiant inner life' my mother claimed drove his genius. On the contrary, he seemed tortured by every aspect of his existence. Well animal or not, at this moment, my requirements were very simple. I needed breakfast and urgently.

"I think I can hear Mama calling," I lied. "I heard her say something earlier about a train journey."

"What! Do you mean she's leaving? Alone? Or maybe she's going with *him*!" My father pushed past me almost knocking me over. He wrestled open the door and I gasped as cold air once more stung my raw cheeks. "I will not allow it!" Taking the lantern with him, he rushed out into the morning.

Inwardly, I shook my head, Papa was clearly still jealous of my mother and yet he wished to live a separate, monastic life. It didn't make any sense and it was selfish on his part. But it was all too problematic. I yearned for the quite routine of life at Yasnaya. The way it used to be. Before Papa became obsessed with the idea that owning private property was immoral and that Mama's vivacity and love of fine things, her yearning to live in society not on its fringes, was something to be mistrusted.

Slowly, I followed my father's footprints in the snow and although it seemed as though we had been hours talking, the weak wintery sun indicated that dawn was still only just breaking. It was weeks since I'd last been to the city and I wondered how many guests might be staying. I anticipated a full house as Mama gathered friends wherever she went. I also wondered what they might have been roped into doing. At Yasnaya there was always mushroom gathering or berry picking depending of course, on the time of year. In winter there was also skating or sledging, in the summer tennis or swimming. There was a fluidity to time spent, guests coming and going, always welcome, a huge samovar refilled as required, food laid out on tables, women arriving with needlework, men with books and conversations that could last hours. And in the evening, with the sound of the bell, tea once again: sweets and cherries or raspberries.

My tummy rumbled in delicious anticipation as to what I would find for breakfast. I called out 'hello the house' or something to that effect and heart thumping, slipped into the vestibule, shedding my cloak and outdoor shoes. I padded into the drawing room but excitement rapidly gave way to unease when my call went unanswered. And it wasn't just my soundless footsteps that felt out of kilter. The house was hushed, closed even, as if its very life had ebbed away. Everything was as it always was. The furniture hadn't been covered in dust sheets, there were still flowers in the hall. I wasn't sure that I could even have put my finger on it, but there was a heaviness in the air and even the cuckoo clock seemed to have lost time.

I went into the dining room just as the woodcock made a long plaintive cry, then got stuck and I had to reach up to pop him back in his coup. The long hand made a sudden bid for freedom, stabbing my finger and I sprang back in pain. I turned to the sideboard. Peering into a jug of hot chocolate I grimaced. There was a layer of congealed skin along the top that made my stomach turn. Even the poppy seed cakes looked fusty and the kasha several days old. Where *was* Olga and her hampers? More importantly, what had happened to Masha and Sergei?

155

Carefully removing the skin from the milk, I dipped the least stale bun I could find into chocolate and was about to take a bite, when I again heard my mother's voice in the corridor.

"So, you will not listen to me on this." Arkady's voice was rigid, unforgiving.

"It's not that I *won't*, I just can't think about it now, Arkasha," replied Mama gently enough.

"Why? Is that because you've already made up your mind? Without taking into account what *I* want."

"Yes. No, of course not." I could envision my mother shaking her head flustered. "I have to go."

"And you insist on this other thing too, then."

"Yes."

There was a rustle of material, the scraping of furniture and footsteps.

"Then you are not the person I thought you were," Arkady moved out of earshot.

"Arkady, how many times do I have to explain? I'm doing this for the children. Lev lives in another world half the time–*all* the time, actually. He has absolutely no concept of what it is to run a household. Nor is he involved with the children. Oh, he's good at organizing games–at least he used to be–but only because he enjoys them himself. Otherwise, he's not interested. I proofread *all* his work. And now that he's giving up all copyright, it means there won't be any money either! It's my only chance to negotiate a small income."

"I still don't see how speaking to the Czar is going to help that."

My mother sighed. "We've been through this!"

"Yes, and we'll go through it again until I've understood why."

And again. Overhearing their conversations, I wondered if all adults were this repetitive.

"Look, Arkasha," continued my mother. "Contrary to what you might read in the papers, it's actually the *Czarina* who doesn't like *Sonata*. She was shocked by the book (weren't we all) and wants it banned. It would also appear to be the one publication to which Lev hasn't relinquished copyright. The royalties from the book go to the children. And it's a surprising success. I'm not sure whether or not that's due to its notoriety or literary merit, but it's already on its' fifth run."

"Yes, but at what cost, Sonya? It's appalling how you are portrayed. Doesn't that upset you?"

"Of course, it does!" My mother said passionately. "I used to be a very private person. I never confided in anyone - not even Olga Feodova!" I could hear the smile in her voice. "Lev has chosen to humiliate me in the most shameful and public way. It stings me to the core."

"Then why do it?"

"You know why." My mother was becoming irritated.

"It's not worth it." Arkady was harsh again.

"Yes, it is. Besides, by protesting, by showing outrage, I only give credence to the story. By supporting the book, by encouraging it, it stays just as it is, a story. Nothing more."

There was more rustling of material, the creak of a floorboard. I crossed the room on tiptoe and pressed my ear flush to the door. My heart was beating so fast that it filled my head. I had to confess that there was a certain thrill to eavesdropping. Every muscle in my body strained to hear their conversation. There was also a downside.

"I can't be with you."

I sprang away from the door doubting that I'd heard correctly. Mama's unattractively shrill response assured me that I had.

"Arkasha what are you saying?" she cried. "I don't understand! You know how important–"

There was a pregnant pause.

"I know that you've chosen *him* over me and if you can't admit this, then you've been lying to me all this time. More importantly, to yourself."

I heard my mother gasp, her next words enunciated clearly. "How *dare* you speak to me like that! You've never used that tone with me before."

"You've never given me cause to."

There was a frosty silence.

"If that's how you really feel, then I *will* be with Lev," my mother said coldly after a while. "You leave me no choice."

"Don't fool yourself, Sophia, you've always had a choice. We're in this situation precisely *because* of your choice. Be with Lev, I don't care. Actually, I never really believed you'd leave him anyway. But you'd better get cracking with the other matter," he said mockingly. "Before your particular goose is well and truly cooked!"

"Oh, I don't know," said my mother calmly. "I think there's plenty of time for everything. To begin with, I think I shall have an interesting chat with the Czar after all. I shall tell him that this... event is the real postscript to Lev's *Sonata*. I shall also tell him that Lev can write all the fiction in the world but that in reality, he observes celibacy with as much sincerity as he does everything else."

It was obviously Arkady's turn to be surprised, a surprise that rapidly turned to anger.

"Are you implying? Do you and Lev? Are you saying that you... *lied*?"

"I'm saying that Lev is still my husband," said my mother, her voice rising to match his. "I never lied but I didn't stop you from believing what you wanted to either!"

"But you've always said how the revelations on your wedding night destroyed you and how there were at least a dozen–" Arkady's incredulous tone dipped suddenly so that I couldn't hear the rest of the sentence.

"Then one more won't make any difference, will it!" my mother snapped.

For a moment, given the lengthy silence that followed, I thought all was well between them. I hoped they were embracing, that my mother had buried her face against his neck and that at this very moment, he was tilting her chin to look into her beautiful eyes. Instead, when he spoke, Arkady's voice was indifferent.

"I don't think I ever really knew you," he said and my heart sank.

Stop! I wanted to cry. Call a truce! Please? And do it quickly before you both say unforgiveable, unforgettable things. But there was still time. I could still stop them. I took hold of the door handle twisting it violently–too violently for the door gave way with a thud, and I catapulted into the hall. Arkady looked up astonished, his gaze softening when he saw that it was me. I blushed at the familiar, intimate look he gave all females.

"Kotchka," he said in Russian and I realized then, dispassionately, that all the while my mother and he had been talking in French. But his use of my mother's Russian term of endearment was all at once familiar and reassuring. "You have indeed landed on your paws like a little kitty cat!"

I shot my mother an apprehensive look, then did a double take. I frowned. Even in the short time since I'd last seen her, there'd been a dramatic change in her appearance. There wasn't one, specific alteration but so many that I stared trying to make sense of the transformation. Her eyes were bright with unshed tears and her cheeks were flushed which was entirely normal for my mother when she was emotional. She perspired freely and her normally smooth hair clung to her neck in tendrils and not in an attractive way. But it wasn't any of those things, it was more that everything about her seemed to have spread. Her face had widened so that the nostrils flared and her once angular cheekbones were now rounded and plump. Her bosom heaved, promising to burst from its tight corset if she so much as breathed and her waist had entirely disappeared. Her once exquisite footwear had been replaced by ungainly boots and she was dressed in travelling clothes, her fur cloak draped over her shoulders. Arkady by contrast, was as sleek and feline as ever; the true cat amongst us.

"I heard voices," I said which was true, feeling myself redden.

"Good heavens!" said my mother brushing tears from her cheek. "God isn't speaking to you too?"

Arkady raised a sardonic eyebrow. "'Too?'"

"Oh, you understand nothing, Arkasha," said my mother impatiently. Arkady turned away from her, his eyes hooded and unreadable.

"That, my dear, is becoming increasingly obvious."

I held out a hand, powerless to stem the hostility between them.

"I'm like a fly," my mother hissed ignoring me and suddenly desperate all over again. "Can't you understand? I'm buzzing in a spider's web and the spider is sucking my blood."

"Are you, Mama?" I replied nervously. "I mean I know you're not a fly–obviously." I watched in alarm as colour spread under the translucent skin of her face and then just as quickly drained away. "You aren't going somewhere?" I said rapidly changing tack. Please don't. Please hug me. Please say that you've missed me. "I've–I've just come back from Tula," I added helplessly. "There were banners everywhere at the station–all about Papa."

Arkady shook his head, collecting his hat and gloves from the hall table. "No, I'm the one leaving," he said opening the front door. There was a blast of icy air and then warmth again. Turning back abruptly, he swooped past my mother and taking my hand raised it to his lips. For a moment our eyes met, and in that instance, there was no artifice, only pain and his eyes filled with tears. "Good-bye little Kotchka," he said. "Learn to be happy." And placing his astrakhan hat jauntily on the crown of his head, my mother's lover vanished into the snow.

17

"Is it true?" said Masha one afternoon, when coming downstairs, I found her sitting on the bottom step. I had taken a nap after lunch and then begun working again on the portrait of my father. My objective now was to depict him in a harsher light. His beard had obviously grown but there was a dourness to his features I believed absent from my earlier sketches. Perhaps what I was feeling though, was also an obstacle. Everything was tinged with gloom. I wanted Repin. I even missed Sergei. I hated being the most responsible adult in the house. Mama's departure had left a palpable void. It wouldn't be long before we'd be back to spartan meals of cold blini and gruel. Olga Feodova (and her food hampers) had accompanied our mother on her journey to Petersburg so there wasn't even the sound of her scolding to fill the dreary silence. The house felt abandoned and sullen. One of Mama's favourite Meissen plates lay in pieces on the drawing room floor, its companion intact on the windowsill. As the hours passed (and no servant came to clear up the mess), the exquisite bits of china some with a complete tiny flower, others with only a hint of gold to suggest the wonder of its former pattern, began to symbolize the fissure that had developed–that there was something irrevocably damaged at the heart of our family. It wasn't as if we'd been blissfully happy before, but the cracks were effectively painted over, and the overall image was one of accord. Now, the silence seemed to reverberate only with the imprint of arguments.

"Is what true?"

Wiping my paint-stained fingers on my smock, I hunkered down beside her tucking my skirts around me. When she raised it, her face was pale and tear stained. She cradled her favourite doll.

"Is it true that Mama has a baby in her tummy?"

I swallowed and continued rubbing material on my hands at a loss as to how to answer. The words hung violently in the air. And yet Masha had merely stated what we must all have secretly understood by our mother's broadening shape and newfound plumpness.

"Sergei's Kitty is going to have a baby," I said playing for time.

Masha frowned thumping her doll against the balustrade. "I'm not stupid!" she said crossly. "*I* told you about Kitty. I'm talking about Mama. She's having a baby, isn't she?"

"I suppose so," I agreed reluctantly, my head suddenly spinning with all the consequences such a declaration implied.

"It's disgusting," said Masha.

"Oh, I don't know," I replied lamely. "I think it'll be fun to have another brother or sister in the house."

"Why?"

"*Why?*" I met Masha's glare with surprise. "Don't you *like* babies?"

"Not his babies." Masha jerked her head in the direction of the front door, and I knew that by 'his' she meant Arkady's.

"We don't know anything about that," I said firmly. "And you're not to say anything. Not to anyone."

Masha made a face. "I already have," she said proudly. "To Sergei. He's coming home as soon as he can. He was only at his club," she added quickly thinking that I was annoyed he'd been disturbed. I gave my hands a final, irritated rub. I felt a mixture of panic and relief, but I also thought of our father. "Oh, Sergei doesn't mind," said Masha again trying to reassure me. "He said he'd already lost too much money gambling and it was still early. He said he had to borrow–"

"You shouldn't have done that," I interrupted but I wasn't sure which bit of her news alarmed me more. Any meeting with Sergei implied a scene of sorts and his histrionics coupled with our father's fury, made for an exhausting encounter. There'd be no Repin to comfort me later either. "The last thing we need is Sergei here. We need to be calm and wait for Mama to come back."

"Do you think she is? Coming back, I mean."

"Oh darling, of course she is!" I gathered Masha in my arms. At first, she resisted but then she clung to me. Her small body shook with quiet sobs. "There's nothing to worry about. Nothing has changed."

"Of course, it has!" Masha said fiercely pushing me away and wiping her eyes with the back of her hand. "There's going to be a baby! Everything will change."

"But not the people around you," I said gently. "They all love you just the same as before."

"That's a lie!" Masha began to pound her doll. "Everyone lies all the time!"

I sighed. "Adults are… complicated. They do their best but it's not always very clear–"

Masha's eyes narrowed. "Why are you so odd?" she said. "You always say such odd things."

I picked up Masha's doll offended but thought better of fuelling an argument. The doll's blue eyes were wide and staring. "What's happened to her eyelashes?"

"I cut them off," said Masha in a matter-of-fact tone.

"Because you were angry?"

Masha shrugged. "Maybe."

"Have you eaten today?" Her cheeks looked suspiciously flat. I had helped myself to some very stale tuzhiki left over from Lent, but I now wondered if anything else had come out of the kitchen that day. Father certainly had a half-starved look about him but then he always did. It was sometimes ironic to think that our patronymic derived from the word for 'fat'.

"Come on!" I said pulling my sister to her feet. "Let's find you something to eat." But Masha yanked back her hand holding on to the banister for good measure, wedging her feet in between the spirals.

"I'm not eating till Mama comes back," she said.

"But darling that could be ages!"

Masha glared at me. "So, you know then! She's not coming, back is she? She's gone with IT. You lied!"

I closed my eyes. "I'm not lying. I said 'ages.' A figure of speech. What I meant is, that I don't know when she'll be back. She's gone on the overnight train to Petersburg alone, not with Arkady. It takes a long time to get there and then she's waiting to see the Emperor so–"

Masha suddenly let go of the banister and sat back down on the stairs with a thump. "Oh…" she breathed. "And will he be wearing his clothes?"

"His clothes?" I echoed. It took a few seconds before the penny dropped. "Let's hope so. Have you got to the end of the story?"

Masha shook her head. "Mama read half and then got tired. She said we would finish it another time."

I touched Masha's head remembering that despite her maturity, she was still only a child. Once again, I gathered her to me and hugged her. For a moment she allowed her small, warm, body to relax against mine and then pulled away abruptly.

"Look, we'll get ourselves something to eat, we'll try and fix dolly's eyelashes and then I'll read you the rest of *The Emperor's New Clothes*. Would you like that?"

Masha nodded vigorously.

"By the way, Masha how did you know where to find Sergei?"

Masha grinned, pleased with herself and tapped the side of her nose in a gesture reminiscent of Olga Feodova.

"Tell me!" I said smiling. I grabbed her by the waist so that she started giggling and dropped her doll. I knew that if I tickled her long enough, she'd probably wet her knickers.

She was still laughing moments later when Sergei burst through the door. He stood tall and broad in his winter coat filling up the entire door frame. Snow glistened on his moustache and sable collar. He removed his hat, shaking his luxuriant black hair like a dog. His eyes were bright with emotion and even I, a mere sister, could see how attractive he must be to women. He pulled off his gloves, rubbing his hands together and then sat down on the hall bench to remove his boots.

"Well, well! Like uncut dogs!" he exclaimed.

I disengaged myself from Masha and patted her knee, concerned to see the panic returning to her face.

"Not really," I said deliberately calm, although for once I agreed with him. The oh-so Russian expression might have been created for our family alone. "I think Masha may have over-reacted. I mean, it's always wonderful to see you but if you're worried about us then you needn't be. Papa doesn't seem to mind the furore at all. On the contrary, he's pleased he criticized the Czar and is delighted to have had death threats and he's not at all troubled by the press camping at the gates. Actually, he seems to enjoy the fact that they're out there freezing while—"

"Bones of the saints Tanya!" he interrupted wildly looking and sounding uncomfortably just like our father. "You know that's not what I meant. Our mother—"

"… has gone to Petersburg," I finished quickly.

If Sergei had suddenly become our father, then my nervous chat was all our mother's. "In fact, you've just missed her," I prattled on. "She was here earlier but she had to leave as she has an audience with the Czar himself. And in the Winter Palace! Oh, what I wouldn't give to see the Peacock Clock! You'd love it Masha. Do you know you can hear three birds: a rooster, an owl and of course, a peacock?"

"Only three?" Masha thinking of our own Tyrolean masterpiece wasn't impressed.

"Yes, but the whole thing is set in a magical garden! When the chiming starts the owl turns its head, then the peacock spreads its tail and finally the rooster crows to signal the end of night and the beginning of day. The dial of the clock is hidden in a mushroom but there are other animals too. Mother—"

"…is a slut." It was Sergei's turn to finish my sentence for me.

"Oh…" I said as if he'd slapped me and I sat down abruptly on the step beside Masha. I'd been so distracted by remembering the description I'd read about the famous clock that had once belonged to Prince Potemkin, that I'd momentarily forgotten about Sergei.

"What's a…?" whispered Masha.

"What's she doing here?" Sergei jerked his head in Masha's direction without looking at her. The 'she' made Masha immediately burst into tears.

"Well, 'she' lives here, in case you'd forgotten!" I said crossly. "It's you who's the stranger!"

"Christ!" said Sergei. He took off his coat lobbing it carelessly on a chair and then began fumbling in his trouser pocket for tobacco.

"You know Mama doesn't like it," said Masha through her tears.

"Then all the more reason to do it!" replied Sergei tersely. "Shouldn't you be in bed?"

"No," said Masha sticking out her tongue in a way I was itching to do myself. "It's far too early. I think you should go back to your club."

"I'm not going anywhere until I've sorted things out."

"What do you mean?" I said uneasily. There was a purpose to our brother not normally noticeable in someone so indolent. "There's nothing for you to do. For any of us. It's not our busines."

"It's absolutely our business, our family's. I will have, I *must* have satisfaction."

Which could only mean one thing. "Don't be ridiculous!" I snapped. My mind raced. I wasn't sure if it would help matters if I said that Arkady had gone because I wasn't certain that he *wasn't* coming back. His kissing of my hand had seemed final to me but then you could never really tell with proper grown-ups. "There's nothing to sort out," I said firmly. "As you can see, everything is entirely normal."

Sergei inhaled deeply and blew a smoke ring which curled and floated up towards Mama's velvet curtains. I could imagine her delicate nostrils flaring as she detected a hint of tobacco.

"Normal?" he said quietly in a tone just like our father's. And just like our father, I knew that his quietly simmering anger would find an outlet no matter how hard he tried to suppress it. "Normal?" he said again, his eyes narrowing into slits. "She's destroyed everything!"

"No, she hasn't," I retorted fiercely. I wanted to say that he was a fine one to talk given his own circumstances but thought he might end up challenging me, not Arkady and mean it! "We don't know anything for certain. No one has said, have they? We're all just guessing. It's not up to us to do anything other than wait for her to come home. Besides, Sergei, if you're so sure, why don't you ask Papa? Or aren't you brave enough?"

Sergei took several furious puffs one after the other before stubbing out his cigarette in one of Mama's delicate Meissen dishes. He rang the bell.

"I need a drink. Where's Seven Asses? Where are any of the servants anyway?"

"Papa's given them a holiday," said Masha helpfully. "You know he always does that when Mama goes away."

"Bloody useless!" exploded our brother. "How on *earth* am I expected to have a drink then?" Masha and I followed his look to the sideboard crowded with decanters and bottles of vodka. All Sergei had to do was extend an arm. His eyes widened belligerently but neither Masha nor I moved. "I don't believe this! To think that anarchy has spread this quickly! And in a mere twenty-four hours! It makes my head spin to think how quickly Russia will be spoiled. Papa's a fool to believe in all that nonsense!"

There was a sudden clattering outside on the porch. There was also a strange squeaking noise that I knew couldn't be coming from the dining room as I had disabled the cuckoo clock. Masha moved closer to me, cradling her doll, her eyes once again swimming with tears. Sergei lunged towards the door. Anarchists so soon? I felt a moment's dread. But then a bicycle wheel covered in snow, levered open the door. Muttering in Russian, and half blue with cold, our father stumbled after it.

"Papa!" Masha cried running towards him.

"Bones of the saints, man!" said Sergei taken aback. "What the–" and he moved quickly to pour him a drink. He thrust a tumbler of vodka to our father's lips as I took Sergei's coat and wrapped it around Papa's thin shoulders. He looked small and bewildered; his face framed in a halo of sable fur.

167

Papa's beard had completely disappeared inside his clothing, but his hair hung in strands of frozen icicles. His sunken cheeks were streaked with dirt, the nails on his hands broken and dirty. I recoiled at the stench once he'd kicked off his pig skin boots. He seemed delighted by the attention.

"My children," he said over and over again. "Oh, my children!"

Sergei and I exchanged looks–his still defiant, mine warning.

"Have you ever seen anything like it, Seryozha?" my father said pulling Sergei's jacket so that our brother was forced to bend down to him. Papa had inadvertently used Mama's nickname for him and I could see that my brother was touched. He wasn't the only one. "It's beautiful. I am not one for technology, but I must say that the line of beauty of this stupendous machine quite… quite moves me." To my alarm there were tears in his eyes. "I shall write about the bicycle. I think it has affected me more than the story about Stryder."

"I thought you said no more fiction," I reminded him smoothing his hair reluctantly.

Our father's eyes widened. "Oh, but it won't be fiction!" he said downing the vodka in one and holding out his glass for more. "I shall write about art–the truth about art to be more precise."

For a change.

Sergei shook his head, reaching for the vodka himself. "I don't understand. What's the connection between art and a bicycle?"

Masha shimmied herself onto Papa's knee, but his arms didn't go around her in the automatic way our mother's did. He let her balance unsteadily, using his leg as a seesaw. The motion made me feel dizzy. After a while, she removed the glass from his hand forcing his arms around her.

"You really don't see it?" Any affection our father may have held for Sergei in that brief, euphoric moment after coming in from the cold, quickly evaporated when he realized he was dealing with an intellectual light weight.

I averted my gaze not wishing to be drawn into any more of Papa's tiresome rants and alert to the fact that Masha on an empty stomach, could also turn very quickly.

"No, he doesn't," Masha said emphatically at which our father pushed her off his knee.

"There is *so* much in life to be ashamed of!" he said his eyes bright. I had a sneaking suspicion that he knew about our mother after all. "Look, I sleep, eat, ride, play the piano, quilt–"

"Quilt?" echoed Masha. "And that *hurt*, Papa!" she said indignantly rubbing her bottom but staying put on the floor, legs akimbo.

Papa ignored her. "And I write of course, but I'm still bored. It's all meaningless. All of this!" His arms shot out to encompass the room and in particular Mama's knick-knacks. "You must see that we all live in a state of sin and that sin is loss of love!"

"Our mother isn't short on love," muttered Sergei under his breath.

And neither are you, I might have retorted.

"None of it means anything! Not family, not artistic creation–it is all worthless unless life is reduced to the starkest and barest simplicity." Papa's voice rose triumphantly. He hoisted up his sopping peasant's trousers and smock. The belt had slid halfway to his knees. He began to pace the room, running his hands through his thin flowing hair as droplets of ice melted down his bony chest. Sergei went to warm himself by the empty fireplace and gave the bell an authoritative pull. I wasn't brave enough to remind him that no one would come, that the fire would not be lit.

"I made a mistake." Papa stopped suddenly in front of Masha prodding her with his foot for which trouble he received a furious glare. "I wrote about Stryder," he said.

"Yes, a horse." Sergei's eyes were beginning to glaze over. Whether from vodka or boredom, I wasn't sure which.

"But that was short-sighted of me," continued Papa. "Because in *reality*, all I was doing was writing about *society*. Whereas the *bicycle*, is the perfect fusing of simplicity and functionality. Like the Russian people!"

Sergei snorted. "You are joking, Papa," he said again pulling the bell to no avail.

"Oh, Seryozha," said Papa sadly. "The Russian peasant knows God in a way we cannot. His wisdom is a million times more sophisticated than all Western philosophy put together. It's our only salvation."

"Amen to that," said Sergei, thinking no doubt of Kitty.

"Suffering is our only salvation."

"Yes, yes, yes." Sergei taking hold of a fresh vodka bottle, smashed his glass against the stone fireplace. Masha began to whimper but our father, grinning like a fool and perhaps imagining himself back in his regiment, followed suit. In no time they had decimated Mama's entire crystal collection. The only positive outcome being that Sergei seemed to have forgotten his desire to challenge Arkady to a duel.

"We're going to slip away," I whispered to Masha.

"I'm going on a pilgrimage," announced Papa.

"*Again*?" mumbled Sergei listing towards the mantelpiece.

"Yes," said our father who by now was even drunker than our brother. "I shall follow the Icon of the Three Hands."

"Masha, my girl, it really is time for that hot drink." I pulled her to her feet and quietly and unnoticed, we crept away from the hall, making our way through the darkening house to the kitchen. Her small hand in mind was damp and her doll bumped along the wooden floor. She clung to my skirt as I felt along the corridor, groping for familiar landmarks, the brass candle holders embedded in silk wall hangings, the odd picture.

Rummaging in the dark for matches was the greatest test of memory. I opened drawers without seeing them and thought of Repin and my first ever art lesson and our discussion about the imaginary sight. Where was that tool now when I needed it? But without the luxury of time, the serenity to contemplate elongated spaces from a distance, I was indeed blind … 'Looking on blindness which the blind do see…' Where *was* Repin? When was he coming back? When was our mother?

All at once, nothing was clear at all and it wasn't through lack of light. I tried to imagine negative shapes, to orientate myself not by what I knew, but by what I didn't. Everywhere I turned was yet another shadow. Furniture loomed larger than life and more eerie by night. The kitchen, which in former times was a bustling hive of activity, producing delicious food, was now sterile and cold and I could no more bring it to life than I could make my mother love my father.

Everything had altered once again, and the sudden appearance of our father was just as alarming as was our mother's absence. I realized then that a house could do very well without a male presence. But I was at a loss as to how to begin. I had no idea how to light the wood burner, or how to transform the chicken that lay belly up on the marble slab, into a succulent roast or what the many little pots covered with muslin represented. Our father could do without food, in fact he seemed to thrive on fasting but the rumblings in my stomach were increasingly painful and I was beginning to feel light-headed. I felt tears of fatigue and frustration prick my eyes.

Why, oh, why did our father have to write stupid stories that enraged so many people and why did our mother have to rush off on a fool's errand?

"I want Mama," said Masha beginning to cry.

So do I, thought I. Oh, so do I.

18

The days that followed merged into weeks with still no sign of our mother, nor Repin for that matter. I received a cursory note to say that he'd received an unexpected commission, one that would take him to St. Petersburg. He assured me that all was well between us. But it didn't seem as if all was well between us, nothing seemed well at all between any of us and as the days passed and fewer servants came to the house, everything seemed to slide into a grey, hazy cloud of neglect.

Mealtimes were no longer assigned to the dining room. With the abrupt demise of the cuckoo clock, the harmonious rhythmic and regulated routine of our household also ended. Papa appeared from time to time, foraging for strange, mouldy bits of food or to brew his undrinkable coffee which he never finished anyway, leaving it to decompose in the sink. He seemed not to notice the absence of servants nor our mother. As the house grew dirtier, and dust gathered in tracks over the furniture, Masha too grew more and more withdrawn. Her large, almond-shaped eyes filled with an aguish I could do nothing to assuage. Not even my feeble effort to glue back her doll's eyelashes cheered her. Her quiet acceptance of the inevitable chilled me and I began to doubt that she would ever recover her mischievous disposition. Despite our sometime sisterly spats, it tore at my heart strings to see her so miserable.

Sometimes, I would venture into our mother's boudoir, holding my breath half hoping, half fearing that she would have come back or better still, had never left in the first place. I loved to imagine Mama sitting at her dressing table, powdering her bosom getting ready for a party or ball. The room was heavy with the scent of her perfume. Her robe still lay discarded, lifeless across an armchair, her shoes, on their sides peeped from under the bed. Books lay where she had casually left them, their spines arched, straining to support the pages beneath. The curtains were closed, fossilizing the contents of the room in stale air and everywhere candle wax solidifying in their holders, stained the curved edges of tarnished brass. It was as if sleeping beauty had arisen and vanished never to return.

Sergei, left the house after a week, still bemoaning, the 'state of affairs.' Or 'Mama's affair' as he put it and hadn't been to see us again. I was relieved. It had taken Masha and me most of the following day to clear up after his drinking. It had amused my father and brother to stay up all night, locked in the hall discussing not only the perfect line of beauty but Kitty's magnificent breasts. When they still hadn't gone to bed by the time I came down to breakfast, and I overheard Papa confessing to a lifetime's obsession with a peasant woman married to a serf at Yasnaya–an obsession that from what I gathered seemed to centre entirely on the quality of her bare, tanned legs–I let myself out of the house and went for a walk.

It interested me not at all that he should immortalize this woman in a short story called *The Devil*, nor that he should publish two different endings. If there was a devil at the moment it was my father and I was beginning to accept that he was nothing but a cauldron of conflicting infantile emotions–none of them of any use to us. I wanted him to show some emotion that was not entirely self-motivated, and anger would have been as good as any a place to start.

But as the days passed and the chaos, together with unwashed clothes increased, it was I who became increasingly angry, angry especially with my father whose hermit-like existence absolved him of any sort of familial responsibility. I wanted him to fight for our mother, for once to act as if he were the head of the house, to restore order and above all, to bring us Olga Feodova. There was now barely enough water to bathe in and we were fast running out of candles. I had stopped trying to plait Masha's hair–there didn't seem to be much point, it was so matted together.

As the nights and days merged into one, as the light became an unchanging palette of oblique grey and as the snow melted into the gritty slush of spring, we wandered the house like lost souls, slowly disintegrating with neglect. Only the weekly delivery of vegetables and dairy produce, thankfully not cancelled by our father, guaranteed any sort of edible food. But it was all cold and unappetizing. I longed for the sweet smell of poppy seed cakes, the mouth-watering aroma of shashlik, of pastries, of blini, of soups and pies, of sour cabbage that stank out the house for hours afterwards, for fish in aspic and kulebyaka and for desserts: the fruits and tarts and ice creams and all the meals that we had ever turned up our noses at and taken so extravagantly for granted.

I longed for the smell of beeswax emanating from the aged knots of our inheritance and the fragrant, intoxicating scent of exotic house plants. I longed for the visitors who queued outside to visit Papa–some illustrious, others ordinary but all welcome. I longed for the ritual of tea as the great, silver samovar was carried into the day room and the swish of silk as my mother swooped into the hall, her train lingering over a carpet that I now felt would grow if I watered it. But what I needed most was for the sinking darkness that I forgot when I slept, but to which I clambered every day on waking, to disappear for good.

"I want Mama," became a new plea in the morning and at bedtime. "When will she come?"

"I don't know," I replied wearily, losing sense of time, wondering who smelt more, Masha or me.

"I want her now." Masha's eyes kindled momentarily with a tenacity I had always admired.

"Then tell her," I said impatiently, without really thinking, just eager to blot out my sister's voice and enjoy once more, the silence in my head.

Masha glared at me but rose from the window seat where she had sat most days watching for any sign of a carriage, to rummage in Mama's desk for paper and ink. She sat in our mother's chair; one leg tucked under her.

"Make sure you write in straight lines," I said. "So that Mama can understand you."

174

Masha gave me a withering look and bent her head in concentration, peering in the dim light to dip her pen in fresh ink.

"But we don't know where to send it?" Her head bobbed up in panic.

I met her desperate gaze steadily, wracking my brains to think of a place that sounded credible.

"We'll send it to…" I did a mental check list of possibilities. "The English Club in Petersburg," I said triumphantly. "Everyone passes through the club at some stage. It's where she'll go to meet her friends. For all we know, she may even be staying there. She *will* get your letter, Masha. I promise you."

Masha pursed her lips and turned back to her task, pleased with this explanation. For the next half hour, Masha busied herself writing and re-writing her letter. I heard the scratch of pen on paper, the occasional grunt as she smudged ink and had to begin again. I observed the careful way in which she used blotting paper, pressing it lovingly against thick parchment. She took out an envelope from Mother's velvet writing box and wrote out the address in large capital letters.

"Shall I read it?" I offered. "To check for spellings?"

Masha started and to my surprise colour flooded her neck and cheeks. I held up my hand. "I'm sorry darling, I'm sure it's all perfect and Mama will be thrilled to hear from you. We'll walk down to the gatehouse after lunch and leave it with the coachman."

"What if he's not there?"

"Then we'll give it to the man who delivers our vegetables."

"But he only comes once a week." The warble had returned to her voice.

"Then you'll just have to wait," I said impatient now myself. My head had begun to throb quietly. I couldn't solve these many problems and I didn't want to.

Masha bit her lip. "She will get it, won't she?"

I nodded vigorously. A lie of omission… I was pleased that this simple errand had produced such a positive effect.

I left her happily composing more letters and went up to my studio. And was tempted to go downstairs again. It was in such a state of disorder, I hardly knew where to begin. Coffee cups (had I really used so many?) played hopscotch along the floor, snaking their way among rusting tins of paint. I couldn't see any brushes at all until I discovered a jar of them, caked in paint and stuck to bits of newspaper. And yet, and yet…there was still the slightest, most delicious whiff of turpentine. My heart skipped a beat. I angled my easel closer to the window wiping grime from the sill, my breath setting on the pane as quickly as tempera.

Going through these well-versed steps in preparation, my excitement grew. Here at last was something that might fully occupy me. But when I pulled out the picture of my father that I had brought from Yasnaya Polyana, I viewed it with disdain. I had begun with such optimism, trusting in my talent as a painter to convey a more urgent message. Now, it no longer seemed to matter. I would have to begin again or paint something else before I did.

Meeting resistance as I tried to slide my father's portrait back into its traveling case, I reached into the cylinder to remove what seemed like paper wedged at the bottom. Almost ripping it in my effort, what emerged from under my hands, what appeared to grow even as I unfurled the paper, was a drawing of Arkady. It was no more than a rough pencil sketch, but the shape of his head was accurate as were the hooded eyelids and striking, arched brows. The long nose gave way to sensuous, full lips and a cleft chin. I smoothed out the paper, pinning it to a board and unfurled a fresh, canvas nailing it to the easel.

I closed my eyes. During that first lesson with Repin he had told me to use every sensory devise other than my sight. He had told me to breathe the canvas, feel the smell, to touch my thoughts. I struggled to conjure up a clear picture of my mother's lover and then, slowly, fragmented images in distressed light crowded my vision. Of all the people to whom sensory devices should apply, it was Arkady and I remembered him not as the stranger who had skated with my mother but the man who had raised my hand to his lips. I had breathed in the strong, lime scent of linen mingled with the aroma of Turkish cigars and horse. There was something inherently virile about him. At the same time, and while I didn't completely trust him, there was also an unexpected sensitivity that redeemed any harshness of character.

I could understand why my mother had found him irresistible. It wasn't just his lack of hair. Everything about him was as different from Papa as it was possible to be. All this I wanted to portray, and I had only one portrait in which to do it. And then it came to me. I would not treat my study of Arkady in the way I had Papa's. Everything about Arkady denoted flight, restlessness, repressed energy. Rather than a head and shoulders portrait which I felt wouldn't do him justice anyway, I would depict Arkady skating. One leg would be slightly stretched behind him, his face at a three-quarter angle. Head into the wind, a half-smile would play on his lips as though he had caught sight of or remembered something amusing.

For the first time since leaving Yasnaya, I was excited by my work and during the weeks that followed, after a cold lunch, I would disappear up to my study while Masha scribbled more of her mysterious letters at Mama's desk. Gradually too, I began to take an interest in the house and managed without any help, to tidy and clean as best I could. I aired Mama's boudoir, drawing back the voluminous silk curtains so that they billowed in the ever warming, spring breeze. I dusted the hall, blew away giant cobwebs and beat the rugs as I had seen Olga Feodova do.

Things had also improved in the kitchen. When the man came to deliver his weekly supply of vegetables, I persuaded him to show me how to light the stove. We could now have hot drinks and soups, although I had not yet learned how to pluck a chicken successfully. And when the first shoots appeared in the garden, Masha and I ventured into the orchard for morning walks. We sat silently under apple trees willing the fruit to ripen and watched as magnolias sprang along delicate branches and all the while the unspoken words hung between us.

When will Mama come home?

Neither us of brave enough to voice the fear…

Or is she never coming back?

One afternoon, when I was enjoying the lengthening light and carefully painting the cerulean blue of Arkady's scarf, a tap at the door jolted me from my secret world. I was pleased with my progress. I felt I had captured the graceful, fluidity of a skater. The man's face was now in profile, but his body faced the viewer and there was no mistaking the strength of his shoulders and taut upper body. His left leg was bent at the knee, the thigh lean, the skates at perfect angles to the ice. In the background, the snow-capped trees blurred with the iron railings of the botanical garden. The peculiar light of late afternoon, of which I had become obsessed recently, unified the winter scene. Only the presence of the man indicated an almost unbearable vitality. The patches missing, however, were significant. I found it impossible to paint the fur sable of Arkady's collar or the velvet lining of his coat. I thought of omitting these two elements altogether, but the painting and its subject would be somehow diminished if I did.

"Not now Masha!" I called, my paintbrush in my mouth as I rubbed oil and pigment onto a cloth.

But whoever it was turned the handle.

"I said–"

"It's not Masha," said Repin stepping into my study in much the way he had first appeared all those months ago.

I bit my paintbrush in shock as paint dropped onto the canvas.

"Bones of the saints!" I said spitting the brush out of my mouth and jumping up.

Repin too leapt forward reaching for white spirit and a clean cloth. Calmly he dabbed at my canvas, using fresh pigment and a fine brush. With no effort at all, he had cleaned the damaged patch and filled in the blot with perfect shading. With a few choice strokes he had done what would have taken me days to accomplish.

"Oh…" I said in awe.

I felt the butterfly touch of his hand before he moved to the window, his back to me. I felt a surge of disappointment. I had fantasized about his return but it was never like this. He was controlled, distant. Fine needles of apprehension raced under my skin. Blood rushed to my cheeks and a gentle pulse mounted in my head. I swivelled my easel towards me.

"Where have you been?" My tone was accusatory, angry even. The momentary urge to throw myself into his arms, vanishing the minute he turned his back on me.

"Petersburg," he said with some surprise. "I thought I told you."

I gawped in astonishment. "You did, but that was weeks–*months* ago." I couldn't keep the plaintive note from my voice. "When I left Yasnaya I assumed you would follow. As in soon after. I never thought it would take this long! Did you, did you–" my thoughts darted from one suspicion to the other. "Did you at least finish your barge picture?" Which wasn't at all what I had wanted to ask.

Repin frowned, turned to the easel swivelling it to face him. Were we going to play a silly game now of back and forth? Thrusting his hands in his pockets, he began to rock back and forth on shoes that creaked. I took a closer look. New and expensive shoes and very unlike Repin. Everything about him or so he had led me to believe, was a direct reflection of the social protest he espoused–namely that art must engage with the people. These shoes did not express such a sentiment. His eyes following mine, shifted away.

"You too have wasted little time," he said ignoring my question.

"Doing what, exactly?"

"You really think his eyes are this colour?"

"Blue, yes." I tilted the easel towards me, having to check in spite of myself and annoyed that Repin was still able to cause me to doubt myself. "Periwinkle blue to be exact."

He raised an eyebrow.

"Oh, don't be ridiculous," I said crossly. "You didn't answer my question."

He began to jingle keys and whistle under his breath–both habits new and irritating.

"I couldn't finish 'The Haulers.'"

"'Couldn't?'" My voice was soft, deceptively soft.

"Well… could have, I just didn't have enough time."

"You began something else?"

Repin shrugged. "A commission–an important one."

"Oh, yes," I said. "I thought you didn't–"

"No, well I don't. This was different." At last, he took his hands out of his pockets. "Look, I didn't come here to argue." His gaze wandered back to my picture.

I scanned his face nervously to see if I could guess his reaction but once more, he turned away from me this time folding his arms across his chest. He examined the view as though it were new to him. Which in a way, I suppose it was. Snow was melting fast in huge, sinking piles like quicksand. The days grew longer suffused with a new light and every gust of air brought with it the delicious scent of white narcissi. All over Khamovniki, almond trees were in bud. Renewal and regeneration were everywhere except where it was needed most.

"No?" Suddenly weary, I sank onto the window seat saddened at how things were turning out between us. We had left each other in harmony, wanting more of each other. I had spent sleepless nights aching for his arms, for his smell, for his neck against my lips and the feel of his thigh between mine. "Why have you come?" I said sharply.

For a moment I thought he hadn't heard me, and I drew breath to repeat myself when he moved abruptly to sit beside me, his leg touching mine. He took my hand in his and when I tried to pull away, he held it firmly in both of his.

"To bring you back," he said his voice suddenly gentle.

"I don't understand," I said my voice unable to stop sudden tears. "I thought you were angry."

"I thought you were."

I shook my head. "I'm not–I was. I didn't hear from you."

Repin turned my face to his. "Look at me," he said brushing tears from my cheekbone with his thumb. The rhythmic movement was soporific. It was a long while before I spoke.

"You said you came to bring me back?"

Repin continued to caress my face and soothed by it I kept my eyes firmly shut but they flew open when he said, "To Yasnaya. I promised your mother I would bring you to her as soon as possible."

I covered his hand with mine drawing it away from my face. My heart had begun thumping uncomfortably.

"So, she's come home?" I said groping for words, for meaning.

Repin nodded.

"Has she been at Yasnaya long?"

"No, not long." Repin's voice was tight.

"Is she staying then? Why didn't she come here first?"

Repin shifted uneasily. "Your mother's not well," he said at last. "I've been at Yasnaya for some weeks with Chekov, as it happens. We-she needed a doctor." Repin could not meet my gaze.

"I see..." I said anxiety turning to all out fear as I tried to make sense, not of what Repin was saying but of what he was not.

"I-I bumped into her in Petersburg," he said. "Actually, I was on my way here to Moscow."

"And she persuaded you to accompany her to Tula?"

"No. Yes. Not exactly."

I could imagine how it had been. I knew just how persuasive my beautiful, vulnerable, alluring mother could be. I remembered too, the night when Repin and Arkady had stayed to dinner and how she had captivated us all. I remembered how seductive Repin said older women were. Splinters of jealousy chased away concern.

"And you've been with her all this time?"

"Yes. I-I was working too of course."

"But not on 'The Barge Haulers'."

"No."

I rose slowly from the window seat. "Do you have any idea what it's been like for us here?" I said my incredulity at his feeble explanation giving way to unbridled anger. "Papa's half demented, there are no servants and apart from the weekly delivery from Tula, we've had no contact with anyone. Not even Sergei has been to see us except for a one off, drunken session with Papa. And talking of our father; Papa is totally oblivious of anything not related to his writing or apostatizing as it's become now. He sometimes, but not always, remembers to bring up water from the well and it's been an even colder winter than usual. And we're running out of candles and basic food stuffs! Masha spends most days glued to the window in the vain hope that our mother will come home. And here you're saying that you've been too busy working to send word!

"That's not what I said." Repin was frowning and a thick vein that I had never noticed before pulsated at his temple. Looking at him more closely, I noticed a couple of days' worth of hair growth, that his clothes were hanging off him and that there were deep shadows under his eyes. Normally, concern would have softened my resolve but I was too annoyed to think of anything but expressing my feelings - months of pent-up anxiety and loneliness getting the better of me.

"And as for my mother…!" I rounded on him. "What is she thinking of? We haven't even had Olga to look after us. I can't quite believe that she would just return to Yasnaya without a single letter of communication! Masha has written to her every day! Has she said anything about that or is she so wrapped up in her new life she's forgotten about her old one? She couldn't wait to get away from the country and now she's back living there!" My voice had risen unattractively, I knew, but I couldn't help myself.

"Your mother did get the letters," said Repin quietly, the pulse at his head increasing.

"Then why didn't she come home? Why didn't you encourage her to? What on earth were you thinking? Bones of the saints, Ilya!" I used his given name for the first time and for a moment we were both startled. "You were *staying* with her! You had a responsibility to us, to me! I just hope your silence isn't evidence of guilt."

"What do you mean?" It was Repin's turn to sound annoyed.

"I know how you like older women."

182

Repin let out an exasperated grunt. "How on earth do you reach that conclusion, if I'm with you?"

"But that's the point. You're not with me, are you?" I said bitterly. "You've been with my mother!"

"You're ridiculous," he said turning once more to face the window. "Hysterical and it's most unbecoming!"

I grabbed his arm. "I'm neither of those things!" I shouted. "I want an explanation! You can't just reappear as if nothing has happened. It doesn't make sense! How can you show such little feeling! Tell me! Tell me!" And then in spite of myself I began to sob and laugh all at once as if my body and mind were in the grip of a wild creature. As something stronger than myself took over, there was also a kind of relief. I could give into it; I didn't have to be strong any longer. I began to shake and gasp for breath. I tried to speak, to make myself understood though my head felt woolly, my tongue thick. I lashed out at Repin too, until a hard, quick slap jolted me back to reality and I was left exhausted and weeping.

Repin pulled me to him then, imprisoning my head against the coarse tweed of his country clothes. For a moment I allowed myself to forget that we were quarrelling, that I had just spent months on my own, and that no matter how much I had yearned for him, I wanted my mother more. I cried then for the past and for the future, for the shattered remains of what had been our family. We had been unhappy, but as Papa had understood once, unhappy in our own way. I cried because on the threshold of an adult world, it still held as many mysteries as it uncovered.

Repin's hands were in my hair, stroking, smoothing, as he held me. I felt the even beating of his heart under my cheek.

"I'm sorry," he said over and over again. "I am so sorry. I didn't know what else to do. It was an impossible situation. She made me promise. I knew we should have told you. It was wrong."

Gradually, I stopped crying as I registered the logic of his words. I took a final shuddering breath and sat back, leaning against the large open shutter, my knee hooked in front of me as though I were riding side-saddle. Along with concern, I read elements of secrecy in his expression. He reached into the deep pockets of his baggy trousers groping for tobacco.

"Do you mind if I smoke?" he asked glancing round the room at the various canvases propped up against the walls, wondering what damage a quick puff might do to my paint.

"No," I said impatiently. "Who made you promise?"

Repin stuffed tobacco into a clay pipe with shaking hands but try as he might, he could not make it light.

"Oh, let me," I said grabbing it from him and tightly packing the loose strands of tobacco. I held the match, cupping the pipe basin with my other hand and putting it to my lips. I ignored Repin's uncharacteristically prim protest as I blew smoke in his direction. The rapid rush of nicotine gave me a sudden violent calm. He reached over and removed the pipe from my mouth. "Who made you promise?" I repeated.

Repin placed the pipe between his teeth, swore as it was extinguished and once again tapped it against the side of the windowsill.

"I didn't want to have to tell you this way," he said. "It's not easy."

"Who?" My heart was being stretched as it was, but I was now morbidly composed. So, he was in love with my mother. I knew it! I was suspicious before but now…Shock gave way to clarity. Eventually, as my whirling thoughts settled, I knew what I would do. I would sell the pictures I'd amassed and with the proceeds I would go to Rome. I would escape from my claustrophobic, manic family and its all-consuming dramas. I would learn to draw all over again and try and obliterate everything Repin had taught me. Once I had somehow made my father understand that he had responsibilities, not only to the Russian people, but to Masha too, then I would leave for Italy.

Perhaps it was the steeliness in my tone that made Repin withdraw his arms from me. He considered me thoughtfully. In the growing twilight he looked older and greyer. Better suited to my mother.

"Olga," he said. "It was Olga Feodova who made me promise."

His words hung in the vortex between us and I did a mental gulp. "Not ... not my mother?"

Repin frowned. "No. She wouldn't have been capable."

And then, as I studied the face of a man I thought I knew so well, I began to interpret his little expressions in a different light. Where I had seen treachery, I now saw only suffering. There was the uncomfortable suspicion that I might have been terribly wrong. Repin reached for my hand, kindly, firmly. Not as a lover.

"There is something you must know," he said gently. "Something you should have known before but somehow we–they–oh I don't know–I wanted to protect you. I thought you wouldn't have to know."

It was my turn to take his hand in mine. I moved closer to him touching his face and not as a friend, I kissed his cheek.

"I'm sorry," I said.

Repin pulled away, catching my hands in his and kissing them. "No, I am sorry little one," he said his voice breaking. "When I am with you, I realize you are a woman but when I'm away from you, I think of you as a child and much more vulnerable. We're not good apart. Everything becomes distorted. Believe me when I say I only wanted to spare you..."

"Spare me from what?" I whispered. And nothing, nothing in the world could have prepared me for his next words.

"There is no easy way to say this, Kotchka," he said his fingers preventing my lips from coming closer. "No easy way at all." His voice broke. "The fact is, that your mother tried to kill herself." His face began to swim before my eyes. "She tried but did not succeed. Not in killing herself, that is."

19

As far as Masha was concerned, our mother had come home and we were on our way to Yasnaya Polyana to see her. So, for her sake, I swallowed my shock, and did my utmost to pretend there was nothing wrong. Food was always a distraction with Masha and the newly opened Saratovsky station built to connect Moscow to the south-east, teamed with food stalls. There was even a booth selling pirozhki–little parcels of puff pastry stuffed with meat and cabbage which Repin had loved as a boy. Masha and I preferred kulebyaka, a pirog made with salmon, hard-boiled eggs and buckwheat. I'd not tasted anything quite so delicious in a long time. The scalding hot pastry melted in my mouth and if the salmon was several days old and the rice a little dry, I didn't care. I was just relieved that the fish head hadn't been baked in the pie as was usually the case. At any rate, it made an exotic change from our recent staple of improvised borscht. I could have eaten ten of the things and was immediately cheered by the thought of Olga Feodova's cooking. There was her zakusi to look forward to and Chekov's famous dried cherries with syrniki–those delectable crisp little rounds filled with creamy quark.

But while I travelled a mental smorgasbord of culinary recollections, the only thing that Repin chewed on was a thumbnail. His arrival in Moscow had meant that I was able to share the responsibility of my sister's welfare but he had wanted her to remain there. He said that just now, Yasnaya was no place for a child. I pointed out that neither was Moscow with a delinquent (mostly absent) parent in charge of a sinking ship. Besides, how could Yasnaya *not* be home with Olga Feodova at the helm and our mother, no matter how fragile, in residence? I understood that Mama had lost her baby but I wasn't at all curious as to whether or not

Arkady knew this or cared or had even been in contact with her. I was just giddy with relief that she hadn't succeeded in what she may or may not have attempted, that Repin had come back for us and that we did not have to spend one more night in the gloomy Khamovniki house.

As we hurtled through the dark, however, the reason for our journey once again seeped through my sated senses. My thoughts became increasingly maudlin. With every emission of steam, every train whistle, I was assaulted afresh with the notion that our lives were somehow running in parallel to our father's fiction; that if one were not already imitating it, then the other would have had to invent it. Once, I had feared that our mother would end up as the tragic victim in *The Kreutzer Sonata* murdered by her husband. I had never ever imagined that she might share the fate of Anna Karenina.

In fact, the more I thought about it, the more I convinced myself that my parents' story seemed to be concluding in much the same way as Vronksy's and Karenin's. Or was it that Papa just kept writing the *same* story? Over and over again. On that basis, perhaps he was right to abandon writing fiction precisely because he was incapable of writing anything original. I had to concede that we did provide ample material but still...

During that endless journey, my head swam with disquieting thoughts. I began to wonder at Papa's careless disclosure of family events and secrets, maybe even creating situations just so that he could write about them. But no, I chided myself, that was going too far. Even now, he couldn't possible have known how this latest drama would unfold. On the other hand, he of all people *would* have known the doubt that plagues Anna even at the last moment. 'She wanted to fall half-way between the wheels of the front truck...' were his words. I shuddered as the train chugged along the final segment of track. Shuddered and remembered how Anna feels horror in those final moments asking herself why. Did our mother also ask herself why? Did she not think of us? Had Anna not thought of the children she was leaving behind? Was it fair to surmise that our mother did not, or possibly could not, love us enough?

I roused myself just as the gold onion domes of the Kremlin complex gleaming through a final outpouring of steam heralded our arrival into Tula. Early morning also brought with it the delicious aroma of cinnamon from pryanik or the gingerbread for which the region was famous. Gathered along the platform, brightly clad babushkas and cooks in Tatar caps sold various varieties wrapped in linen cloths. Repin had been amused to learn that the city had once presented Catherine the Great with a cookie weighing sixty-five pounds. Masha liked that gingerbread in all its shapes and sizes was used to teach children the alphabet. Or more precisely, they could only have some, once they'd learned their letters.

This time, Seven Asses met us with an open top carriage, apathetically hurling our bags into the space beneath his feet. Masha nestled contentedly against me. Already her eyes sparkled and her cheeks continued to bulge with a pryanik Repin had bought her as we left the station. Following the peasants habit (originally as a result of sugar being an expensive commodity), she also sucked on a sugar lump. Like them, she made it last, keeping it lodged at the back of her teeth to reuse the next time a cup of tea was in the offing. Her face was lopsided as a result, making her appear simple. I was just glad she was eating again.

Repin shot me disapproving, disgruntled looks, his gaze shifting from Masha to me, to the passing meadows and forests. I willed him to stay focussed on the scenery. The closer we drew to Yasnaya, the more his agitation grew. Studiously, I ignored his huffing and puffing, his crossing and re-crossing of his legs, his exasperated grunts. Masha certainly didn't notice anything out of the ordinary, amusing herself by making faces behind Seven Asses's back and holding out her hand so that her fingers caught the breeze.

Her excitement was contagious and smothering my apprehension, I anticipated only the joy of seeing our mother, of eating Olga's food, of being once again with Repin, grumpy as he was and lastly, to getting back to my portrait of

Arkady. I hoped to surprise Mama with it for her name day which was at the end of the month. I had given up on my picture of Papa. For one thing, I was too cross with him and for another, I now didn't really care if he left Moscow or not. Increasingly, he was becoming an invisible father and more available to the public than he was to us. We certainly learned more about him from the tabloid press than we did from his infrequent appearances at mealtimes or from his fantastical, extraordinary conversation.

Yasnaya Polyana in the spring was a glorious place and my heart sang as the horses slowed to a canter. Soon we had passed the avenue of Dutch limes and the four chestnuts that had originally come from Riga. Peasants had begun clearing moss and cutting away the winter's dead wood. The air was potent with their own particular brew of clay, lime and cow dung which they used to smear the trunks of the apple trees. It was a smell that I had grown up with, and it, and the sight of the new green grass, the blue sky, and the bright skirts of the girls working alongside their menfolk, made me want to leap from the carriage and dance a barynya. But turning into the white stone gate posts I gasped, blinking in disbelief.

"What are *those*?" I asked in horror. Since I'd been away, hut after thatched hut had sprung up marching through the fields as moles tended to across our lawns. Repin didn't bother looking in my direction.

"Oh those," he said despondently.

"Yes, those," I replied testily. "They'll have to go of course."

"Not, of course," said Repin wearily rubbing his temples. "Your father has been somewhat extreme in his generosity to the peasants. The huts belong to them now. Given half a chance he'd have them living in the house. It seems he's doing everything possible to give away his wealth."

"Yes, but not in our direction," I muttered thinking of the ridiculous measures to which Masha and I had gone in order just to eat. "Besides, doesn't that please you? Isn't this what you wanted?"

"Strangely, no," said Repin and for once I believed him. "Forgive me Tanya but playing at being a peasant doesn't impress me. Your father gets bored quickly enough and sprints back to Moscow so that he can write leaving your mother–well leaving you all."

A sudden jolt and the carriage lurched sideways so that I was thrown against Repin. For the briefest, sweetest moment his hands were on my body. But if I thought he would hold me tenderly, even encourage me to sit beside him, I was mistaken. He pressed me firmly back in my seat. I stiffened my resolve to stay calm and concentrate instead on the scenery. There was also the delight I always felt at the first sighting of the house. Excitedly, I hung over the carriage, twisting this way and that, to get a better look. The pussy-willow was already green and wisteria was coming into bloom intertwined with tuberoses and honeysuckle. In the joy I felt at being home, I pushed Repin's rejection to the back of my mind. Perhaps I was over-reacting, perhaps he was just tired. Perhaps it was I who was over-sensitive.

"Look!" cried Masha excitedly. "It's all exactly the same!"

"Did you really think it would have changed?" I asked smiling but she only voiced my own fears.

"Wait! Just wait!" said Repin as Seven Asses pulled on the reins, and the horses stopped in front of the summer entrance. I had a moment's déjà vu seeing the balustrade of cookie cutter figures dancing around the verandah. "There's something–"

But Masha scrambling over me jumped from the carriage. Ignoring Seven Asses's attempt to pull down the step, I followed suit, eager to see our mother, to be in the house, to walk in the garden, to embrace everything. I yearned to sleep in my old bed, in clean sheets and to hear real owls at night and not anticipate the tortured sounds of the now defunct cuckoo clock. With every step I took, I became the little girl I once was, returning home after a day's outing, eager to see my mother. As memory after memory crowded in on me, I thought only of that need, forgetting about Repin, about Moscow, about everything that had gone before. I wanted Olga Feodova to emerge wiping her hands on her long apron and to hear my mother's tinkling laughter as she greeted us from the drawing room.

Repin tried to grab my arm as we all but collided in the hall but I slipped easily from his grasp not even stopping to remove my shawl. I ran from room to room calling for my mother, stopping only long enough to allow my fingers to caress the odd piece of furniture as the enveloping twilight shrouded the house in shadow.

Although it was still cool enough to warrant a fire, the grates were empty. It wasn't as if there was a shortage of firewood either–just no one had bothered to bring in any logs. There was also a strange musty smell as if, despite the wonderful spring weather, the rooms had not been aired. Winter drapes were still in place. All spring cleaning seemed to be taking place outside. I felt an odd disquiet begin to flutter in my stomach as with growing alarm, I called for my mother and Olga. Why was it so quiet? Even if my mother had been living on her own, there was a distinct lack of servants. At this time of day, they would normally be busy putting the house to bed. The small dining room would be laid for an early supper, fires lit in the bedrooms, shutters closed. The sound of footsteps as between-maids busied themselves turning down beds and re-hung discarded clothes, was notably absent.

Breathless, I ran up two flights of stairs to my bedroom. To my dismay, it was exactly as I had left it months before. No servant had been there since. The bedclothes were turned back just as they had been on the day I left for Moscow with Olga. The flowers had turned to mulch in green rimmed vases and dead flies lay in clumps along the rug. Cobwebs hung in graceful loops from the tops of picture frames. There was the unmistakable scratching of mice behind the walls.

"Mama!" I called my voice cracking, growing ever more fearful as I flew back down the stairs. All reason left me; all need for pretence in front of Masha. "Mama!" I hollered putting all my energy into my lungs just as I must have done as a toddler. I felt a toddler–in the desperate need I had to

191

find my mother. But somewhere, from the depths of the house, it was Repin who answered, his voice that of a disembodied stranger–a stranger from another lifetime, and totally disassociated from mine.

I banged open my mother's bedroom door holding my breath, my fingers digging into my wrists to prepare myself for… for what? My heart was beating so loudly it seemed to fill the room, my ear drums–the entire house. I let my shawl slip to the floor as sweat coursed down my back and the space between my breasts. My blouse clung to my arms. I wiped my eyes with the back of my sleeve. It took me a few moments to become accustomed to the eerie light and then the muffled sound of sobs stopped me short. From moving to the mound on the bed.

"Masha?" I whispered. My sister lay on the floor, by the bedhead, curled tightly as a clam. And then I wondered if my heart really had stopped. Prickly sweat bored through my skin as the world begin to spin. Just in time, to stop myself fainting, I managed to grab hold of the four-poster. "Is she…?" I stammered. There was no visible sign of life coming from the inert figure on the bed. A tangled mass of colourless hair was just visible on the dingy pillow. The body was so tightly bound with bedclothes that they might just as easily have been a shroud.

At first, I thought Masha hadn't heard me but then she shook her head almost imperceptibly and her whole body began to shake. She made no effort to rise, hugging her knees, her face still hidden. I bit my lip so fiercely I could feel drops of blood on my chin, but the pain propelled me forwards. I leant gingerly towards the bed. Just as I was about to touch the body, it moved, taking a deep, shuddering breath so that I sprang back both horrified and elated at the same time.

"She's alive!" I hissed. Masha shook her head refusing to look up. "She is! I promise you. Masha look!" I moved to the window and opened the shutters a fraction to allow in some cool air as much for my mother as for myself. Gradually, the nausea passed and the sweat dried on my skin. "Look!" I repeated. "She's breathing… you can see."

I hunkered down beside my sister wrapping my arms around her. She was shaking violently as though she'd caught a chill and for a moment our hearts mirrored the other's beat. I felt the pulse at her neck, her small hands clinging to mine and blew strands of her hair from my mouth.

"You smell!" she said at last breaking away. "Don't hold me."

"Mama's alive," I said quietly. "Come on, we've got to find Olga."

"I want to stay here," she said through pursed lips.

"Well, you can't," I said firmly. "Mama needs her rest."

"How come? She looks like she's been sleeping for days!" Masha's voice was muffled. "What if she never wakes up? What if she wakes up all alone?"

"We'll find Olga and get you something to eat and then you can come and sit with her," I said pulling Masha reluctantly to her feet. She was a dead weight against me, unable or unwilling to lift her head. I dragged her to the door. "Come on Masha," I said impatiently. "I'm not going to carry you."

"Do you promise she's not dead?"

"She's not dead," I said quietly.

Together we lumbered down the corridor. Unable to see much, my other senses were heightened: a musty odour throughout, sticky surfaces and the sound of unwelcome rodents scuttling along floorboards. In the dark, I groped for familiar contours, the French sideboard, the narrow chairs on either side. I located matches in a cabinet drawer. Fearful of accidentally setting Masha's hair on fire, it took me several attempts to light a candle. Her head lolled against my shoulder but with no warning at all, she would suddenly jerk forward her plait swiping me in the face. Behind me, footsteps stopped in front of closed doors, then retreated. Rounding a corridor, Repin shone a light in our faces. Masha's was ashen.

"I've been looking for you!" he said tersely.

"Where's Olga Feodova?" I responded equally terse. Under the pretext of nuzzling her close, I covered Masha's ears with my hands. I didn't want to alarm her any further with my questions. "What like cut dogs has been happening here? Why are there no servants? The place is in scarcely a better state than our Moscow house! What are you not telling me and why is our mother so ill? You never said-"

Repin tried to take my arm but Masha was glued to me.

"We have to talk," he said thinly.

"I'm all ears," I said sarcastically.

Repin again tried to take my arm but again Masha was in the way.

"What's the matter with her?" he said, his head jerking in my sister's direction.

"What do you think's the matter?" I hissed. "She's in shock! Much more important, what's the matter with our mother?"

In the lamplight, it wasn't only Masha who looked ill. Repin's eyes were bloodshot and there were deep creases from his nose to his mouth.

"I can only assume that Olga Feodova has gone to fetch Chekov," he said. "In her absence, the servants have left. They're a fickle lot at the best of times but then you know that better than me. I don't think they'll have gone far. To the huts I should imagine–the ones you saw as we drove into the village. They'll be back soon enough now that Seven Asses will have told them you're home."

"I do know," I said with feeling. "But they're also loyal. We've not had trouble like this before. They've never simply vanished! It doesn't make sense."

Repin's silence spoke volumes.

"There's something else, isn't there."

Repin sniffed in the way he did when he didn't really want to answer something. I would have smiled were I not so suspicious.

"Yes."

"Yes?" The light above us flickered, Masha was growing heavier by the minute as was my hunger.

"Vadim, the foreman and others cut down thirty birch trees," managed Repin at last. "Olga reported them to the police."

Reaching up, I drew the lamp closer to his face so that I could read his expression. "Why would she do that? You couldn't resolve the matter?" I know I sounded cold, autocratic even. But this was not what I'd expected. Nothing was turning out as I expected.

Repin frowned. "Well, yes, I might have been able to had I the authority but Olga ignores me. I would have done things differently. I would have given them a good fright but forgiven them."

As would I... My head jerked. "And they aren't? Forgiven I mean?"

"No."

Repin's mouth brushed my ear, whispering so that Masha wouldn't hear. "Apparently, what they did was a criminal offence. It was too late. The local policeman was sympathetic but there was nothing to be done."

I moved my head away. His whiskers tickled my skin.

"The trees will grow."

"Eventually. Of course.

"So?"

"So," said Repin and this time it was he who was cold. "All the peasants involved were sentenced to six weeks in jail and a twenty-seven rouble fine."

"Twenty-seven roubles!" I exclaimed in horror forgetting about Masha. "No wonder there aren't any servants here! *Now,* I understand what's been going on!" I thought rapidly. "Then we must help the families. They must be suffering terribly."

"Yes," agreed Repin. "We must, but not today. As to your mother..." He motioned to Masha. "Let her lie down and you and I will talk."

"Then help me," I said suddenly weary and shifting my sister's weight so that she fell mostly on Repin.

"I'll carry her, if you'll take this." He handed me the lamp and scooped her up easily in his arms.

Together we made our way to Masha's bedroom. The contrast with mine couldn't have been greater. I pulled back a quilt I remembered Mama embroidering–a cornflower blue picked out with tiny white daisies and sheets that were starched and fresh. Repin laid Masha carefully in the bed. I removed her shoes, tucked the covers over her and kissed her cheek.

"She'll be fine," said Repin a little too impatiently. "Come, what she needs now is sleep."

"I suppose so," I said unconvinced but sensing my hesitation, he orientated my shoulders in the direction of the door.

Holding the lamp in front of him, he led the way downstairs. He seemed very familiar with the design of the house, confidently moving to the first floor, along the hallway to the small dining room–the room, that because of our painting, we had made our own. Repin slung the lamp onto the mantelpiece and in its triangle of light, I made out the familiar easels–his and mine and ladders from Repin's heroic attempts at painting 'The Barge Haulers'. A covered canvas I didn't recognise was propped against the wall.

"Your latest work?" I said half in wonder, half in envy. And something else. Just a tiny bit of resentment. Because while I'd struggled to look after Masha in Moscow, here he had been, in my home, happily painting. Repin muttered something unintelligible.

"But not 'The Barge Haulers'." It was a statement because I knew the answer. "The shape is different. More… portrait size." Vast too by the looks of things.

"No. Yes. I mean you're right, it's a different shape. A commission. Makes a change to be paid real money."

I wanted to ask him what he considered to be 'real' money but thought better of it. I would see the picture first. Ducking behind him, I had crossed the room, and my fingers were actually touching the protective cloth when I felt Repin's hand cover mine.

"It's not finished," he said pulling me away. "And it needs to be. It's being collected by the end of the week."

"Oh," I said taken aback. "Can't I see it?"

"Tanya…" I caught the exasperation in his voice and not being able to see his face clearly, clung to every nuance. The tightening in my belly had returned and the recovered ease between us entirely vanished.

"We've always shown each other our work," I said petulantly.

Repin made a spluttering sound. "It's not that I won't," he said. "But the light–the non-existent light–look, I'll show you if it means so much." But his tone only emphasized how unreasonable he thought I was being.

I curled up on the sofa by the window. He was right, of course. Such poor lighting was not the way to appraise a new piece of art. I could make out the darker shadows of the room only because it was so familiar. Suddenly weary, I leant back against worn and loved cushions.

"You can tell me now," I said quietly. "What happened to my mother?"

Repin lowered himself on the sofa opposite mine. He had repositioned the oil lamp but there still wasn't enough light to encompass my teacher. My teacher, not my lover… who was sitting not beside me, but at a distance. I heard the scrape of his shoe against the wooden floor, the chafing of fabric as he crossed his legs.

"You might as well tell me everything," I said patiently.

There was the slightest hesitation. Repin cleared his throat and I knew he was running his hands through his hair in the way he did when he was nervous.

"I bumped into your mother in St. Petersburg," he said.

"I thought you were here finishing off 'The Barge Haulers'," I interrupted sharply.

"I *intended* to," replied Repin patiently. "The thing is, that I went to Petersburg to see…to see someone about this commission. Look Tanya, I was just as surprised, but it was an opportunity I couldn't overlook. Anyway, the point is that I saw your mother in the lobby of the Astoria. Our stay overlapped and she suggested we travel to Yasnaya together which I was very happy to do, obviously."

"Obviously."

"I could hardly refuse your mother when I was staying in her house!" said Repin tetchily.

"No, you're right, I'm sorry." Except I wasn't. Blood had begun pounding at my temples, my throat was dry. I clenched my hands in a futile, physical attempt to combat an irrational surge of jealousy that had begun fizzing inside me.

"For a time, it worked well. I had so much to do. Your mother, the little I saw of her, seemed happy. Your sister wrote her frequently which I know cheered her. She very kindly consented to my staying on to finish the commission which I had won after some competition I might add, and she made plans to return to Moscow."

"When was that?"

There then followed such a long silence that I thought Repin hadn't heard me. I was amazed he didn't hear the fizzing in my belly that was reaching boiling point. I repeated my question.

"Easter."

"I'm sorry?"

"Easter," he repeated gruffly. Boiling and beyond. I felt my heart clamber to my throat and the blood regurgitate in my head.

"So…" So…Just shortly after Masha and I arrived in Moscow…

"I'm not sure exactly what happened," Repin said smoothly. "Olga was busy opening the house properly after the long winter."

"I don't see the house exactly 'opened' as you put it. Far from it, actually."

Repin ignored me. "And then, one day everything changed."

"What do you mean?"

Repin crossed and uncrossed his legs. He untied his cravat.

"I may be wrong, but I think it had something to do with a letter."

I stiffened. "One of Masha's?"

Repin shook his head. "I don't know. I don't think so. Your mother received an inordinate amount of post. There was a lot of correspondence to do with your father but that was dealt with separately. Fan mail was deposited in one of the peasant cottages and she had one of the girls sort it out. Not all of them can read but she taught them to decipher your father's name. The letters that came directly to the house though were of a personal nature. All I know is that one in particular distressed her a great deal. She was deeply shocked. She made light of it and Olga didn't seem unduly worried until…" Repin's voice petered out.

"Until…?"

"Until she was found unconscious."

My head shot up. I'd been thinking of my last encounter with Papa in Moscow and the sacks of correspondence that couldn't be contained in a single stable yard.

"Where?"

Repin hesitated. He scratched his neck. He hated wearing a stiff collar and would invariably pull it away from his face as though willing his neck to shrink.

"Where?" I insisted.

"Tanya–"

"I'm not moving until you tell me." And then of course I wished he hadn't.

"By the lake."

The words ricocheted around my head. The *lake*? I didn't understand. Like Repin's portrait wrapped in canvas, I felt but could not see, a hidden landscape whose true significance eluded me.

"B–but it's too early for swimming…"

"Yes."

"Was … was she out walking?"

Repin said nothing. Were we playing some sort of game where I asked the questions and he answered 'hot' or 'cold'? I was determined.

"If not walking, then what?"

"She'd gone skating," he said at last, the sofa creaking again but still Repin stayed where he was.

"Skating?" I echoed. "On the middle pond?" Ripples of relief drowned the beginnings of a terrible suspicion. It was the place of choice for swimming rather than the rivers or other ponds because it was shallow, shaded by the willows that grew along its banks and there was even a rustic bath house for changing. Mama had taught us all to swim there. It was small, contained, safe.

"Not the middle pond, no," said Repin. "The Upper one."

It took a while for his words to register. "But it isn't safe there. Everyone knows that!" I shook my head. "I don't understand."

My thoughts continued to summersault. Spring always came abruptly to Russia. I had been in St. Petersburg when it had snowed in May but the very next day had been balmy with the ice melting in large floating islands along the river. I frowned.

"The ice was already beginning to crack even when we were here last. It would have been unstable." I thought of the last time I'd seen our mother skating like a girl, being pursued by Arkady, her bright scarf flying out behind her, fur cap glistening in a halo of snowflakes. "She–she could have fallen through–"

And then, even as my words fell in a void, I knew that's exactly what had happened. What she had intended. I couldn't speak. And somehow, deep down, I think I had always known how it would be for her. From the moment we met Arkady, from the moment my father threw pails of water at her feet laughing as she jumped clear. But ever since we had entered the house, I think I had convinced myself that if I could keep Repin talking, the reality of what had taken place would be lodged somewhere other, in a place and time I would neither have to confront nor acknowledge. Above all, a place where I was still a child. I clung to that moment a little longer because when it was truly known, when Repin confirmed it, then I would be grown-up. There'd be no going back.

"Olga sent for Chekov but there was nothing he could do. She had lost the baby. Olga said it was for the best–that she was too old, that the scandal–" Repin thumped his knee. "Look, I didn't want to be the one to tell you all this."

"Why not?" I cleared my throat. "I'm glad it's you." I wanted to sit beside him. I wanted to put my head on his shoulder, to squeeze my fingers between the buttons of his shirt and feel the pulse under his skin. I wanted to turn back the clock to when we were completely happy. But of course, I couldn't, and nor could he.

"And ever since, she has been bedridden," said Repin ignoring my comment. "Some days she appears in good spirits but then she regresses. Olga has tried to make your mother better." He didn't have to say, 'to make her want to live.' "I can only assume she's given up and gone for Chekov."

"I see," I sighed deeply. "And Arkady? Does he know do you think? Would he come if he did?"

Repin shrugged. "I have no way of getting in touch with him. I've left messages at the English Club, but they've not been collected. No one has seen or heard of him since the winter. I heard a rumour that he had gone abroad but it was only that. I'm sure that if he knew…"

Knew? What? The truth? What then?

"Yes," I agreed after a while. "I'm sure he would."

"And Papa?"

Repin shrugged. "He must know something."

I shook my head suddenly overwhelmed by the direction my thoughts had taken.

"What is it?" Repin could hear my bewilderment. And pain.

"It's just," I took a breath. "It's that the parallels between what is happening to us in real life and what Papa wrote about in fiction, are uncannily similar. I thought the lines were blurred as it was in *The Kreutzer Sonata,* that he unashamedly wrote about what was happening in reality to us, but now it seems it's the other way around. We're actually fulfilling what was written. Like a prophecy. I mean Papa is Karenin, isn't he? Our mother is Anna, Arkady is Vronsky." The words tumbled out keeping up with my thought process. Had my mother like Anna, also had second thoughts at the moment of throwing herself on the ice? Like Anna had she questioned her actions even when it was too late?

"Yes," interrupted Repin calmly. "But there's a fundamental difference. Your mother is alive."

"Anna has a baby" I continued not hearing him. "She's with Vronsky and Karenin forgives her. And she *still* kills herself."

Repin sucked his teeth. "You know very well," he said. "In the book at least, it was much more complicated than that."

"More complicated than *this*?" I knew by his silence, that Repin agreed. After all, what could possibly be more complicated than what was actually happening? The house felt cold, the darkness complete, and there was absolutely no warmth coming from my one-time lover. "What," I said horrified that I could even think it. "What if she tries again?"

"That won't happen!" said Repin roughly.

"You don't know that! How can you know that? And don't say it's up to us, her children, because that's too much! Too much of a responsibility! It's not fair–it's–" my voice rose hysterically.

And at last, Repin moved. There was an expletive as he banged his knee before landing almost on top of me. I was half crying, half laughing, confused by him, but mostly by myself by a growing, suffocating sense of panic. As if a Vodyanoy, King of the Deep covered in revolting algae was slapping me down with his scaly tail.

"Or a Schuka," I whispered against Repin's chest. If there was ever a creature, I'd feared even more than Vodyanov or Baba Yaga when I was little, it was Schuka.

"What?" Repin pulled away from me.

"The horrible pike fish capable of swallowing a man whole."

"I know who you mean."

"That's what it feels like. Now. At this moment. As if it–they are all coming to get me."

Repin pushed my head back on his chest, his arms strong around me.

"Nothing is coming to get you," he said gently. "You're home now. I'm here. "

I made an effort to blot out any more images of sticky slimy pools inhabited by terrifying water spirits. Gradually, in his arms, relief washed over me and I was calmed by the slow, steady tempo of his heartbeat under my ear.

"I wish you'd told me," I said eventually.

"So, do I now," said Repin gruffly. "At first, Olga Feodova thought it was just a matter of days before your mother recovered. But soon the days became weeks. We lost track of time. It was a mistake to keep it quiet. I see that."

"I'm not a child," I said. "You mustn't keep trying to protect me. I'll only find out anyway and then it's much worse. It only makes me think that you have something to hide."

"I'm sorry," he said.

"And you haven't seen the letter? I mean do you think it influenced her decision. Could it have been fro-"

Repin's lips brushed my hand. Not my lips, not even my cheek but it was a start. "Not now, it's late. We can talk more in the morning. Go to bed," he said. "And no, I have no idea who the letter was from."

20

While I found comfort in my childhood home, reassured by the sounds of a house I had grown up with, I sought double reassurance in Repin. Obsessively, I went over every inflection of his voice, chipping away at every mannerism and turn of phrase. I re-examined, re-evaluated it all and found him lacking. There was a time when he had looked upon me with desire, when everything I said seemed to hold some peculiar fascination for him, when my every gesture was an invitation to love making. Earlier, had it not been for talk about my mother, I knew I'd have barely held his attention. It would seem that not even our passion for art was enough to unite us.

He had also become secretive about the projects he was working on where once he'd been open and enthusiastic. Most depressingly, he seemed bored with the whole idea of teaching me anything new at all. I was stunned by how quickly our friendship had disintegrated. It was the ebb and flow of intimacy I found difficult to negotiate. The words Repin used were logical, compassionate even, but my gut told me otherwise. His ambivalence towards me, only increased my own. For fear of the answer, I did not dare ask if his love had turned to loathing.

'But then begins a journey in my head…' As I tossed and turned alone in bed that night, I came to the conclusion that our love had indeed petrified. What remained was a shadowy imprint of something so remote that I wasn't sure it had even existed. I yearned for the time that seemed a lifetime away now, when everything was breathless and new, when even the scent of his skin would ruffle the pit of my stomach with fairy fly strokes of desire. For the first time, in this house, he had said good night and turned away from my room. Nothing had prepared me for the loneliness of those retreating footsteps.

But pondering on Repin, sifting through the dusty sediments of our love affair was a distraction, a device to ward off the landslide of pain that hovered ready to cave in on me. My mother. The reason I had returned to Yasnaya in the first place. There. I had said her name. I could avoid her no longer. She was there in my head. Except that of course, she had never gone away. And in accepting the idea of what had happened, my mind screamed with disquieting thoughts. I punched the pillow, releasing the familiar scent of verbena and lavender but not even those soothing smells could appease my fevered head, nor stem the onslaught of troublesome questions.

I lay in the dark, arms outstretched as if to ward off the burgeoning shadows crowding my bed. What was it that Repin had said? That the character of Anna Karenina and my mother *were* different. But were they? I wracked my brain to remember the sequence of events in my father's novel. I knew it was based on a real-life character who had killed herself. A story, that beginning with the familiar love triangle, becomes enriched by all the other marriages around it.

Mama had been deeply affected by the book. At some level, had it influenced her subsequent actions? But then again, she had no real reason to feel so despondent. I knew her situation may have *seemed* hopeless but, in the novel, as with the real-life event that had inspired Papa to write about it, Vronsky had wanted Anna to divorce Karenin. Far from rejecting her, he had desired nothing more than to give his child (and their future children) his name. And the husband (at least the fictitious one) had proved to be a noble person, kind and forgiving loving enough to want happiness for the erring wife. In the end, it is not gossip, nor society's shunning of her but Anna's own character - her increasing jealousy, insecurity, fear of ageing - predetermined from the opening pages– that is her downfall.

Was it also my mother's? I was suddenly wide awake, fumbling in the dark for matches and a candle, dressing gown and slippers. I'd had an alarming thought. Perhaps, the real reason Mama and Arkady had quarrelled was not because she had sought an audience with the Czar about *The Kreutzer Sonata*, but because she needed His permission to divorce Papa. Perhaps Arkady (unlike Vronsky and unlike Karenin) hadn't wanted her to. Divorce that is.

Was *that* the reason Mama had been so miserable? Ultimately, had Arkady rejected her? Had Papa? But that didn't really make sense either. For all his ranting, I knew that in his strange way Papa loved her, more than that, he needed her. Certainly, when he'd written his fiction, they had worked closely together discussing ideas, characters, endings. Mama had always said she was a true writer's wife. That it was her vocation, giving her a sense of purpose. Perhaps without it she had felt redundant. But then, she had begun writing her own stories. And she had us. Sergei, Masha and me. Even without Arkady, surely that was enough? We were enough? Then what of the letter? What was it that had caused her such despair?

A funnel of cold air spiralled up the staircase when I opened my bedroom door. But for the odd cooing wood pigeon, the tweet of an owl, the house was quiet. Sporadic streaks of morning light breaking through gaps in the curtains, guided me downstairs. If Olga Feodova really was back in charge, then the kitchen was where I was headed. I hoped there would be freshly baked savouries on the range. I would make a hot drink and put order to my disruptive thoughts.

While the rest of the house was still cold, warmth emanated from the kitchen. And delicious smells with it. Here at least, nothing had changed and as I had dreamt on the train, trays of syrniki were cooling on the counter. A squeal of pleasure escaped me. What was it to be? Cheese pancakes with sweet sour cream or donuts? I bitterly regretted having missed Maslenitsa–that celebration at the start of spring when for a whole week Russians eat nothing but pancakes. And could those really be *vatrushka* buns poking from under a tea cloth?

I was happily spooning dollops of cherry jam onto a plate when an agonising groan–someone or something in terrible pain–made me stop short. The sound seemed to be coming from the boot room. I set down my plate as quietly as possible summoning up the courage to go and investigate. At first, I thought it might be vermin burrowing for grain or a hare captured by one of the dogs. But when it came again, a low guttural tormented cry, I decided it was no animal's. I pulled a knife from the butcher's block. I'd have been happier arming myself with one of Papa's pistols or a sword taken from the display cabinet–outdated certainly but effective in warding off a drunken peasant. I felt brave, steady. I was in my own kitchen, in my own home, what was there really to fear?

The sound of breaking glass, a further wail and a cloaked figure covered in blood set me trembling with terror and call out myself as all rational thought left me. Were my earlier fears actually being realised? The monster from the fairy tale, *Vodyanoy*, as the name suggested (of water), lived in pools, and pools were something Yasnaya could happily boast. It was said that he prevented lovers from marrying. Had he come for Mama when she was skating? Might he really exist? After all, we'd grown up on Papa's story about the green stick. He'd never questioned its veracity and nor had we. But then the voice of reason cut in. Of course, Vodyanoy didn't exist! I was being utterly ridiculous. It must just be a robber. Just! Ah! I wanted to scream, to alert the household, but no sound came. Did we even have roubles in the house? I rather doubted it. We never had any money. Although, with his new-found prosperity, perhaps Repin had cash hidden somewhere. What could I possibly offer in return for my life? I didn't really want to answer that.

The figure nursed a bottle of vodka and a small silver-edged cup. This was no robber, not even the King of the Deep but Koshei himself, the very embodiment of evil! It *must* be Koshei. I shivered. Nothing evoked pure terror in me quite so much as the idea of that black goblin, so dastardly that his soul must be kept separate from his body and hidden in a needle. As the matryoshka of all folklores went, it was then placed in an egg which was hidden inside a duck, which was hidden inside a hare, which was hidden in an iron chest and buried under an oak tree on an island in the middle of the ocean!

Was it true then? My mind must be playing tricks. But the physical fear I experienced was real enough as I dropped the knife. The hooded figure looked directly at me before kicking the knife away from us both. Perspiration was dripping down my back, my thumping heart was agony. My fingers felt along the range behind me alighting on a pan of simmering milk. My only weapon. I turned briefly, lifting the heavy cast iron pot with both hands all the better to swing it. And then something about the figure made me hesitate. When it took a lurching step closer, I jumped in the air.

"*Sergei?*" I said in disbelief as the creature, stumbled, his fall broken by a kitchen chair. He sat sideways to the table; his grubby, muddy boots splayed out before him. What had happened to the dashing Imperial Guard's officer of only a few months ago? A soldier of the elite Semyonovsky regiment whose boots were rubbed down by his valet the moment he jumped from his horse? Before me was a dirty, bedraggled vagrant, whose taut muscular figure had turned to fat. Had he been court-marshalled? Thrown out of the army? His beard like our father's was sparse and untidy, his hair had grown long like a girl's.

"Sergei?" I repeated setting down the saucepan incredulous that someone could have changed so much. I picked up a cloth dipping it in water. The blood on his face had caked into irregular scabs. I flinched at the stench of body odour and alcohol that seemed to come away with every wipe of the cloth. Part of me too, was still a little afraid. This man was a stranger. My brother seemed not to recognize me either or if he did, considered it perfectly normal to be meeting in such a way after so many months apart. He looked at me trying to focus, his eyes opening and closing with the effort. His tongue flicked over his lips and teeth desperate to taste the last vestiges of drink. His head flopped onto his chest and as it did so, the once fine lawn of his shirt ripped open. A delicate ivory button turned a couple of rounds before becoming embedded in the grouting. My brother's hairy belly was now fully exposed. I felt mine do its own turn with revulsion. Once again, I picked up my plate, hoping that the rumble of gentle snores meant he had fallen asleep and I could enjoy my breakfast in peace. A loud belch made me realise that I'd been premature in my thinking.

"Tanyushka!" said my brother miserably. "Bones of the saints, Tanyushka!"

"Bones of the saints, yourself, Sergei."

And then, without warning he flung himself in my arms, holding onto me as though it were I, not my mother who'd nearly drowned. I released his arms as gently as I could pushing him back in his chair. I set the plate of pastries I'd arranged for myself in front of him. He pushed it back to me. For a while we played a game–the plate sliding back and forth–until eventually he crammed a whole vatrushka bun in his mouth. Picking out raisins, he consumed another. As if a spell had been broken, he could not stop eating. Or drinking. He gulped down jugs of sbiten. Olga's version of spiced honey water was particularly dark in hue.

"Oh Tanya," he said mournfully as his eyes filled with tears and he began to sob into his hands–hands I noted that were also filthy. There was mud under the nails and blood from whatever recent mishap had befallen him.

"It *was* you, wasn't it?" I said coolly when I thought he'd sobered up enough, just enough for me to find out.

"What?" Sergei looked bewildered. "Was me what?"

"You wrote that letter. To Mama."

And when he started to protest and then slump so that his head hit the table with a thump, I continued mercilessly. "There was I thinking that it must have come from Arkady or Papa, or even one of his mad acolytes, but no, it was from *you*."

I fixed him with a stare, pulling his hair roughly.

Here is the head of John the Baptist…

"I want to know what you said. What did you write that could possibly have destroyed our mother like that? To have made her want to take her own life?"

Sergei pulled away from me. He was still bleeding from open cuts. I didn't care where the blood came from. I was out for my own.

209

"What?" I demanded. "Say it."

"I-" Sergei ran his hands over his face, his belly, his hair. If I didn't know him better, I'd have thought he'd become addicted to morphine. His was a wild, hunted look.

"Tell me!" I persisted. "I want to know. Then we are going to make this better."

"We- you can't," he stuttered at last. "It's too late."

"It's never too late," I said impatiently. "What did you write?"

"Bones of the saints," Sergei whispered. "It was terrible... I was angry. I didn't think."

"Yes. Understood. What did you write?"
Sergei looked around him. "Vodka?"

"Absolutely not."

My brother blinked a couple of times and then sat back in the chair, hands gripping his knees as though he were stopping himself from being sick.

"Tell me."

Sergei scratched his neck; his arms and blew his nose using the end of his grubby cravat. Staring at the wall in front of him he then seemed to fall into a sort of stupor. I kicked him with my toe.

"Wake up!" I said none too gently.

"I'm tired," he mumbled into his hands. "I just want sleep..."

"You can sleep later. Tell me."

My brother slumped even further forward, so that this time, I really did think he had fallen asleep. And then just as I was wondering what to do, and whether or not I should give him another drink if it would make him talk, he roused himself.

"I told her..." again his voice faltered. He swallowed a sob.

"Go on," I said harshly.

Sergei's bloodshot eyes locked onto mine. I nodded silently, encouraging him.

'I said..." he cleared his voice and then continued at speed. "I said, that if she went ahead, that if she divorced Papa to marry Arkady, then I would never speak to her again. Never mind how society treated her! It was nothing to how the family would. I would make sure of that. I also made it clear that I didn't want her in my life. That she was to stay away. That she would never see her grandchildren that–"

I held up my hand. "Stop!" I said and this time, going to the sideboard I poured us both a shot of vodka.

"So, let me understand this. Mama who has loved you unconditionally, who has taken your side against Papa, not only in your affair with Kitty, but in countless other affairs, is rewarded like that?"

"She's a vain creature!" said Sergei fiercely. "She's so selfish! Always thinking of her clothes, ribbons, flowers!"

I touched the cloth of his expensive coat. "And you don't?"

"Yes, but I can! I don't have children!"

I glared at him so that his hasty 'well, not yet,' was muffled. I didn't ask him if his child had been born.

"And?"

"Her head is full of…"

"Of?"

"Oh, I don't know!" My brother's voice rose in exasperation. "Having her hair curled! Trying on clothes! She spent a whole day fantasizing about a leather belt."

I looked at him astonished. "How do you know that?"

Sergei had the grace to look sheepish. "I read her diary."

"Go to the bath house!" I said in disgust searching my limited repertoire of worst insults. "Sergei," I said after a while when I felt calm again. "You really are an…*ass*. What does it matter if Mama cares about her appearance? Looking lovely, is what we all appreciate about her. It doesn't *preclude* her loving us. It never interfered with looking after us. Besides, she cared for us better *with* her preoccupation than Papa did without!"

"I do…love her," he muttered.

"Maybe, but have you ever stopped to think about what she actually does?" My voice cracked because I knew *exactly* how hard it was to look after a family! I plucked at his coat in a gesture that, had he been sober, might have reminded him of our father when we first arrived in Khamovniki. "While you spend, or *spent* time at your tailor, Mama would be busy copying Papa's novels…and then–no you *will* listen!" And to focus his attention, I pulled his hair again in exactly the way he had mine when I was little. "Think about when she first arrived here! Yasnaya was barely furnished, uncarpeted and populated with mice!"

"There are still mice," muttered Sergei.

I rolled my eyes but continued, undeterred. "You can't deny that Mama has made the house and gardens beautiful. You *know* how guests are always welcome, how they flock to her. Of course, they are curious about Papa, but it's Mama who ensures they are looked after and entertained. Do you think those tables spread on the verandah with sweets and fruit and tea appear as if by magic? A house doesn't run itself, Sergei! And Mama takes care of every aspect. She does all the mending, cutting and sewing–not just making our clothes, but Papa's too and all the estate bedlinen. She teaches the village children. And then after a long day cataloguing Papa's books, negotiating with publishers, doing the estate accounts, when she can hardly keep her eyes open, she spends the night proof reading! If she has any spare time she then gardens, paints, takes wonderful photographs, plays the piano, or skates–" I stopped but if I'd triggered any further remorse, Sergei seemed oblivious.

"Well, with that impressive list, I wonder she had any time for a love affair," said Sergei acidly.

"You know why," I said. I was suddenly exhausted. What more was there to say? Too much and too little…There was an explanation of sorts. That Papa was demonic. Undoubtedly a genius but also a domestic monster that like a child, needed to be fed, washed and clothed–needed to have, have everything sacrificed for him and then when all that had been done, when beauty, youth and freedom had been devoured by his genius, the reality remained that it still wouldn't be enough. Because a monster's appetite is insatiable.

It didn't take a Baba Yaga or a Vodyanoy or a Schuka to explain that. Our very own chimera was here amongst us, living with us all. I knew that there had never been a word of thanks or understanding for the fact that Mama's own creative and spiritual life had atrophied in the process of serving his. In the wake of his greatly admired, acclaimed, and very public fame, she had shrivelled. I wondered how a man who had created his Anna Karenina with such love, who understood every fibre in her makeup, who even at her death, treats her with delicacy (that famous analogy of a candle being snuffed out), could have shown our mother so little sympathy, could never have taken the trouble to understand her. And then there was the final straw–when Papa renounced all physical contact in the name of universal love…No, I didn't blame her one little bit.

"I do love her," said Sergei again, helping himself to more vodka.

"You love her in your way, but your love is conditional." Was he even listening? He seemed preoccupied with a hole in his boot. Let him drink if he wanted to! I was tired of taking care of people. Perhaps Mama had been too. A niggling thought occurred to me. Would Repin be like this one day? I frowned. A sudden gust had blown through the kitchen. I shivered. "There's a door open somewhere."

"Hadn't noticed," grimaced my brother, huddling into his coat all the same. "Let the old babyshka get it."

I shot him a disparaging look. He was having trouble focusing. He raised his head in my direction, but his glance seemed to bounce off my face and land somewhere behind my shoulder.

"Don't go anywhere," I said pressing his shoulder hard so that he grimaced. "We are going to make this right. Or rather you are. You are going to think of a way to make our mother forgive herself."

21

It wasn't just an open door that drew me to the front of the house. The clatter of horses' hooves on the cobblestones was enough to wake the good people of Tula. Voices rose loudly from the courtyard. But something made me hesitate from rushing to see what the commotion was about. A warning instinct, a gut-twisting hand of apprehension stopped me in my tracks so that I hung back, shrinking against the copious folds of a velvet curtain, a dividing wall between hall and corridor. I could see and hear everything while remaining completely hidden. I almost broke cover though when Olga appeared, a beloved, eccentric figure robed in her usual eclectic travelling garb of vibrant shawls and turban. She carried a lantern moving slowly like a giant bug. Behind her came the cloaked figure of Chekov, ever neat and dapper. And finally, holding himself as erect as a Cossack and sporting a luxurious dressing gown, complete with sable collar, was Repin.

Chekov set down his bag on the hall table while Repin helped him off with his cloak. Olga vanished in the direction of the kitchen returning with a tray heaped with buns and hot sbiten. If she had seen Sergei, she made no comment, and I was only happy we'd not eaten too many of her pastries. Repin added a bottle of vodka to their refreshments which they drank standing up. There was much muttering–references to my mother and the 'situation.' Chekov finished his drink in a swift, efficient movement that momentarily hid his face. He rolled up his sleeves and reached for his bag. Leaning towards Repin he muttered something inaudible and the two men moved towards the servants' staircase.

And just like that, all fight in me dissipated at the sight of Chekov with his doctor's hat on rather than his writer's. All harsh thoughts left me as swallows from thatched rooves. It was one thing to consider Mama as a fictitious character such as Anna Karenina, but quite another to know that she was really quite ill. There was a further unsettling revelation: Repin in clothes I would never have associated with him. He also appeared to have assumed an authority in our household that I resented. I was relieved yes, but it was a mantle that should have fallen to Sergei (ideally to our father) but not to a man who professed to despise everything we stood for, a man to whom I wasn't even engaged. A man who had become a stranger.

Slipping into the small dining room, I closed the door behind me allowing the familiar contours of the house and the comforting shapes of covered easels to calm me. I opened the shutters as quietly as I could to let in the still, damp air. Mauve light seeped onto the floor elongating the uneven rectangles of canvas, softening the drums of paint and angular brushes. Everything about the room was soothing- a tug of memory, a call to work. After months of inactivity, work was what I needed most. At last, like a long-lost friend, I felt the return of that inescapable compulsion to paint. As the faintest of ideas began coursing through my fingers so did adrenaline rush through my body. What was it that Goethe had said? 'Whatever you can or dream you can, begin it...'

Pushing away all thoughts of Repin and even my mother, I pulled out a fresh roll of canvas thrilling to the touch of jute. As if a layer of my subconscious had been scraped away, I allowed my psyche free reign. I found myself sketching a figure on a bed. I didn't want the figure to be obviously male or female, the face was to be shrouded and cloudy–phantasmal even. There would be an open window a positive note to counterbalance the penumbra. I stood back to examine my work. It was better than anything I had done in months. Repin or no, I thought to myself, from now on, I would paint what I wanted and how I wanted, in the medium I wanted. I paused to open the shutters even further.

He was certainly wrong about one thing... 'looking on darkness which the blind do see...' A painter needed light, an unobstructed view and *then* his imagination, not the other way round. It might suit Repin to paint from memory, to scrabble together transubstantiating shapes but I needed to see. My attention was diverted from the window in my painting to so much outdoor colour: the view of green hills, the bright skirts of the peasant girls as they dipped between the apple trees, an aqua sky quickly turning to cobalt with the rising sun. I threw off my dressing gown, exultant at my newfound inspiration and in so doing snared the edge of Repin's picture. I reached behind me but not quickly enough to prevent the dust sheet from slithering to the floor.

I half turned to retrieve the cloth, preoccupied with mixing just the right shade of dusty pink, when I caught sight of Repin's so-called 'commission.' Paint brush poised, I stared, momentarily dumbfounded. Here was no 'Volga Bargers' intent on heralding social change, no expression of whatever secret stoicism he believed the Russian people held in their suffering hearts. Here was no message of any description other than to expose the duplicity of the artist himself. I stood back so as to better appreciate the portrait (all gigantic ten feet of it) as objectively as possible. It did quite simply take my breath away.

The portrait was majestic in its affectation, commanding, awe-inspiring and grandiose–in short, everything one might expect of its subject. Repin had excelled himself, of that I had no doubt. If a photograph had been taken of the sitter, then the picture could not have born more of a likeness. I wanted to stroke the velvety softness of his blue uniform, the ivory kid gloves and sculpt beneath my fingers, the hollow spaces beneath the cheek bones. One small step in those magnificent leather boots would see him escape the putty brace of the picture frame to stand beside me.

I don't know how long I studied the portrait, scrutinising the smooth sections of background light, the dark shadows filling dead spaces. And all the while, subconsciously, I compared Repin's technique to my own. For the first time however, I was not intimidated by his talent. On the contrary, I recognized the clever tricks employed to achieve depth and perspective. I also understood just what was required to bring a face to life; to introduce fluidity to the human form, to make it appear supple rather than stiff. I was troubled rather by what the picture said about Repin.

But while I struggled to make sense of my erstwhile lover, everything else was suddenly much clearer. I could no longer romanticise or hide from the truth. In understanding the portrait, I had at last understood the adult world in all its starkness, its tragedy and its helplessness. My mother had fallen in love with someone other than my father, was going to have had a child with someone other than my father, and in her perceived rejection by him had chosen to end its life. Repin, for whatever reason, had done what he had always promised himself and his acolytes that he would never do, bartered his soul for a baser conviction. But where did that leave him? Where did all this leave me?

As my physical world settled once more into focus, as the spring air carried the scent of gardenia from the English garden into the dusky room and the spindly birch trees made every attempt to scratch a now brilliant sky, I realized that I did not love these fragile beings around me any less for seeing their flaws. I only wished they had been able to credit me with a maturity to fully embrace them. I realized too that over the past months I had been waiting to be rescued, for someone else to take control of the Moscow house and now of Yasnaya, when all along that had been my right, more than that, my duty. I too had been sleepwalking, unable or unwilling to see things as they really were. There was no reason for Repin to shoulder a responsibility that should be mine. I replaced the dust sheet.

Some hours later, as I was cleaning my brushes and tidying up my paints, Repin burst through the door, still in his night clothes. He seemed thunderstruck, not just to find me painting, but to see me at all. Instinctively, his hand went to his dishevelled hair and he shot furtive looks at the canvas which stood directly in front of me but which, as far as he could tell, I'd not yet seen. Inwardly, I smiled at his consternation.

"Sbiten? There's probably some in the kitchen," I said pleasantly knowing full well that there was.

217

"No. I mean I've had some," he said. "I thought you'd still be sleeping."

I smiled making a gesture to my painting to excuse my wakefulness. "How is my mother? What does Chekov think?"

Repin looked up startled.

"I know he's here," I said candidly. "Olga too. I can't tell you how relieved I am."

"Tanya–"

"Can he help her? Is it the morphine? Too much, too little? Is she an addict now?" I rattled off the questions hardly drawing breath. Repin ran his hands not only through his hair but over his entire face and protruding neck. As though he were taking off one mask and replacing it with another.

"Don't look so surprised," I said coolly. "Mama has always taken morphine at night to help her sleep. The fashionable ladies of Petersburg do you know. Sometimes she doesn't wake up as alert as she ought to though. Is that what's happened this time?"

"It's not so simple." Once again, Repin shot anxious looks in the direction of his picture caught between two potentially explosive conversations.

"Oh?" I settled myself on the fender seat, balancing a slipper on the end of my foot. My hair was wantonly loose, not in its usual braid. I felt wanton, liberated, enjoying the wafts of sweetly scented air that cut through the more putrid smells of paint. From time to time, I too looked in the direction of his painting but gave nothing away.

Repin stood rooted to the spot. "Your mother has had…a fever."

"A fever?"

"Well, all right, maybe more than a fever."

"More than a fever?" I raised an eyebrow.

"It's depression, actually. But don't worry, if there's a man, never mind a doctor, who understands human nature, it's Chekov."

"He certainly does that," I said thinking of the many conversations we'd had about him in the family. "He also writes about it all afterwards. As you know. Ruthlessly."

Repin sighed. "I agree it's a risk, but he's also honest. He compromises on nothing if it will help improve conditions and the causes he cares about."

"The *cause* he cares about is Chekov."

"I don't think that's fair." Repin's tone was sharp. "His is a starker reality than the one your father, if you'll excuse me, describes. His is a Russia of icons and cockroaches."

"You quote *Trotsky*?" I said hotly feeling myself colour. How quickly we'd moved from my mother to politics!

It was Repin's turn to colour. "Just to emphasize a point," he said hastily. "Chekov writes from his experience as a doctor and that has made him unshockable."

I made an impatient gesture to suggest that if I knew about Trotsky, I certainly knew about Chekov. I knew that he had been involved with our first ever national census and I was also aware that during the cholera epidemic he had given up writing to work as a doctor. This had irrefutably altered the romantic impression of the peasant that so many artists had attempted to portray; Repin included. Chekov was appalled, not only by the squalid, impoverished conditions in which the poorest peasants lived, but by what was revealed about their character. He considered them to be mistrustful and crude. More fundamentally, questions arose as to Russia's viability as a peasant land. Chekov saw the peasant population producing little other than children and his prediction for the future was bleak. It was in complete contrast to my father's.

"His writing certainly has a...social context," I said mildly. "I can't imagine him ever..."

"Ever what?"

I hesitated briefly, enjoying the hiatus that existed between us at that moment, before the argument, explanation, misunderstanding and breach of trust that would surely follow. I pressed my fingers under my thighs and stopped swinging my legs. I searched Repin's face. No longer a teacher's, perhaps no longer my lover's, and certainly not a friend's. I examined it for some remnant of affection, of tenderness, of familiarity and saw what I

219

imagined to be, only apprehension and caginess. I couldn't tell what he saw in mine. I stood up and went over to his picture. I pulled away the cloth.

"I can't imagine Chekov ever portraying our Czar in such a *romantic* light."

There was an interminable silence. Colour gradually seeped away from the very top of Repin's high forehead, his cheeks, and finally his lips. I watched in fascination as it even appeared to drain from his neck and the rather protruding Adam's apple I had never noticed before. Nothing seemed to move. For a moment, even the breeze appeared to stop, the trees to sway, the carriage clock to tick. There was nothing but a roar of silence and a thousand unuttered cries between us.

"I don't deny it's pretty," I said at last. "It's very French, very European, very..."

"Impressionistic is the word I believe you're looking for," said Repin his tone hollow.

I appraised him coolly. "That's it, exactly."

"It's a new movement. I'm quite taken with it."

"*Ça se voit.*"

Repin looked up sharply, irritated by my use of French. "And what exactly do you mean by that?"

"I mean, " I said calmly. "It's not particularly utilitarian or thought provoking–the very opposite in fact. Unless of course you feel that a ten-foot portrait of our autocratic, some might say *tyrannical* Czar is something worth contemplating." I leant forwards as if examining it more closely. "Y–yes... perhaps it is..."

"Oh, bones of the saints Tanya!" Repin exploded. "Enough of this! You don't know what you're talking about. You're only a child."

I shot him a withering look. "Hardly. And I understand perfectly. You needed the money. You were commissioned to paint this...this *thing*. I did wonder when some of our photographs went missing from the drawing room but then knowing your politics as I thought I did..." I let my voice linger. "I told myself it was impossible, that you would never do it."

"Well, you were wrong."

"Evidently."

Repin spread his hands wide then drew the sable fur collar closer round his neck hunching his shoulders.

"I didn't plan this."

"One never does…"

"It was in Petersburg when I escorted your mother…" I raised an eyebrow and he let go of his collar. "Oh, it wasn't like that!" he said impatiently.

"No?"

"No. I bumped into her in the English Club exactly as I told you. She had been granted an audience to plead your father's case…over *The Kreutzer Sonata*."

"Yes, I know," I said curtly. "That subject has rather been done to death, wouldn't you agree?"

"She pleaded with me, to escort her," continued Repin ignoring me. "She said she'd do much better with a man on her arm. I asked her if Arkady wasn't better suited to the task and she said she hadn't been in contact with him. She seemed so distressed at even the mention of his name that I couldn't refuse her."

"Maybe, I should have tried tears," I muttered under my breath but if Repin heard me he ignore me.

"It was while I was there with her, that I was recognized… That's how it happened. I can't deny that I was flattered."

I tilted my head. "There was a time when you were impervious to the aristocracy and all it represented," I said archly. "*Especially* its flattering ways."

"Yes, well …that's before it offered me twenty-one thousand roubles for painting something pretty."

I gasped. "Twenty-one *thousand*?"

Repin nodded glumly.

"Bones of the saints, Repin!" I said with renewed respect. "Bravo! I'd have done the same."

Repin took a step towards me. "You would?" He thrust his hands in his pockets. "I was so worried you wouldn't understand. I know that I have represented a certain philosophy in painting, but I think it would be fair to

221

say that it has lately become a burden." He looked up, a frown creasing his forehead, the white at his temples catching the light. I wondered if I had been wrong about him after all. He looked worn and haunted. I went back to sit on the fender seat. I patted the worn leather. He hesitated longer than I would have liked before coming to sit beside me. We didn't touch, were strangely polite and chaste.

He gestured to the Czar's portrait. "It was done for money, I don't deny but I want to turn to purer, more artistic themes. I don't want to paint the anonymous face in the crowd. Not anymore." Repin's voice rose passionately. "I want to paint great characters, big subjects, known people." I tried not to look in the direction of my canvas which was to be exactly the opposite: a faceless, sexless body on an indistinct, unmade bed.

"So, you thought you'd start with our Czar?"

Repin made a face. "Not 'our'," he said. "He's not important. What is, is that I've fallen in love with the Impressionists. I want to go to Paris and study. I need to undo that critical side of my work that is stopping me from progressing. It used to eat me up. Now I just want to paint whatever comes, whatever takes my fancy."

I felt a pounding in my ears. "I see, hence the money."

Repin nodded.

"Well, I hope it works out for you," I said tears behind my words. I couldn't understand the conflicting emotions that washed over me. Moments before I had been unmoved by his presence, relieved even that the sight of him no longer made my stomach shoot to my knees and now the thought that I might lose him blinded me with grief.

"It's time to leave, Kotchka," he said quietly. "It may be hard to see, now that the beautiful spring is here but Russia is changing." There was a heady scent of narcissi as he looked above my head to the open window, the woodland and vast areas of juniper and oak. "This won't last. It can't. Russia is becoming more isolated, inward facing. The West has never understood us, and they don't now. We must leave before it's too late."

I felt an insane surge of optimism and I wasn't sure if it was at the idea of fleeing my troublesome family or the thought of being with Repin. "'We'?" I whispered.

"Of course, 'we,'" he said puzzled. "You didn't think I'd go on my own?"

I blinked back tears, my turn now to look away.

"Oh Kotchka, Kotchka," said Repin gently. "I'm sorry." I felt his fingertips cover my cheek bone, smooth my jaw line, my eyebrows and then, where his fingers had been his lips replaced them. "Everything was so clear to me, I never thought for a minute that it might not be the case for you too." He reached for me then, at last, as if he finally wanted me. "I just assumed...there was so much to sort out ...your mother...the secrecy of her... 'illness,' this portrait. Tell me Tanya, was I–was I wrong to hope?"

I smothered a sob, burrowing my face in the soft, tickly fur of his lapel.

"Was I?" he said fiercely and this time his hands moved to my waist, pulling me urgently, feeling my shoulders, taking me by my wrists to stand me before him while he buried his face in my belly.

"No," I said hoarsely. "No, you weren't wrong."

22

The spring months continued to unfurl with the smoothness of those same verdant lawns that appeared under ancient oaks. Hyacinth and syringa burst into blossom as did the banks of flowers of every colour and scent, terraces smothered in lilies and roses and fruit trees: apple, pear, apricot and cherry. In our little paradise we were cut off from outside events, strikes and arrests, people marching with white flags in Tula which we did not see and only heard about. Elsewhere there had been outbreaks of violence: peasants (not ours) rioting in the countryside, the assassination of government officials in Kharkov. There had been demonstrations by students at the university in St. Petersburg which led to its closure. There was talk of war with Japan. But as far as we were concerned it was just that.

We did not rush back to Moscow; in fact, we did not return at all. Each of us in our own way used every second to recover, to recoup our strength. It now seemed irrelevant that our father had once promised he would take us home to Yasnaya Polyana; we had got here all by ourselves. Repin's portrait of the Czar was transported with great pomp to St. Petersburg to be hung in the Winter Palace. Just in time as it turned out, as there was now a new czar. And with him came new quarrels, new unrest. This new emperor dismissed representative government as a 'senseless dream.'

Our dreams were more tangible. Although Repin (along with fourteen others) had founded The Wanderers to create works that were not only beautiful but wise and educational, it would now seem that my lover wished to paint pictures that were only beautiful. French-style portraits and fetching port scenes were produced where it was difficult to detect any criticism of social inequality. On the contrary, they lauded conspicuous consumption.

When we were alone, he spoke of the new life we would make together in Paris or Rome or even America. He wasn't sure where. What he was certain of though, was that we had one last summer left in Russia and that by the autumn we would have left. I had no such dilemma. I finished my portrait of Arkady taking care that Mama should not come upon it by chance. I covered it more carefully than Repin had protected his picture of the Czar, taking pains to tape up the ends at night, examining it carefully when I unwrapped it in the morning. I wasn't sure what I would do with it. I realised that it would be insensitive to give it to my mother now. I had no way of finding Arkady and wasn't certain that it was a gift he would appreciate either. And so, I kept it as a token, a reminder of what had been in our home, a catalyst for such monumental change.

The easy pace of life and a degree of normality returned to Yasnaya under Olga Feodova's steadying hand. Once again, the kitchen was the hub of all activity with a continual flow of baked pies and stewed fruit being prepared in anticipation of a winter that Repin and I would not see. She lined the kitchen dressers with oversized jars brimming with poached peaches, berries and apricots. Once again, wonderful smells drifted up as far as the attic and Masha and I ate everything put in front of us. And more. The faintest memory of cold soup and stale bread was enough to make us ask for second helpings even though our waists seemed to be expanding before our very eyes. Repin said he might not love me if I grew any plumper. Even our mother began to eat again after weeks of turning her face away from the scrumptious concoctions that Olga lovingly prepared and which ended up being consumed by Masha and me waiting like dogs outside her room to pounce on the untouched trays.

Eventually, Mama emerged from her tomb-like bedroom, wan and frail but dressed and eager to have us believe that she was well again. But from time to time, I would catch her staring out of the window oblivious of the beauty of the rolling green hills, the poplars swaying in the warm breeze carrying the scent of lilac and whitethorn. Oblivious too of the smooth, newly mowed lawns bordering the English garden and the neat hedges that edged the parterres with knots of lavender and white peonies. Unseeing, she could stare for hours, her lovely face turned in profile while tears slid unbidden down her thin cheeks.

And all the while, there was no direct news from our father. It wasn't necessary. The press had more than enough to say on his behalf. At times, it felt as though he were merely living in another part of the house for the barrage of information that came our way. What wasn't though were the proceeds from *Resurrection*–those were going directly to the Dukhobors–that group of Russian dissenters (or 'folk Protestants' as Mama dubbed them) to whom Papa had become inordinately attached. To whom he wanted to bestow his worldly goods.

But all that paled in comparison with the pages of commentary devoted to his latest tussle with the establishment. Astonishingly, after a ten-year ban, Nicholas II gave his permission for *The Power of Darkness* to be performed–a performance, for which critics agreed, its audience would require 'nerves of steel.' I had always hoped for Mama's sake, that the play might be banned indefinitely. In the meantime, I did everything in my power to keep the newspapers from her. I was pretty confident too that I had succeeded until one afternoon, emerging from a siesta, Mama announced that she had begun writing a play of her own. 'Called?' I asked somewhat apprehensively hoping it was a fairy tale to be enacted for Sergei's child when he was older. Hoping that the fact that she was writing at all meant that she had put everything behind her. That it wasn't that she felt renewed pressure to earn a living when Papa was so glibly giving everything away. 'Called,' she said darkly, *'Who is to Blame*? It's in answer to *The Kreutzer Sonata*.'

Well, as it turned out, *The Kreutzer Sonata* was indeed child's play in comparison to Papa's latest work. And a play about a child it turned out to be although nothing whatsoever to do with fairy tales. It wasn't in the slightest bit comforting to learn that, as with *Anna Karenina*, Papa had been inspired by real-life events. Not suicide this time, but the murder of a baby inconveniently born to a girl engaged to be married.

Repin tried to persuade me that the real message of the play was that people lose their humanity when forced to live in poverty and ignorance and that Papa was extremely brave to have written about the hardships of living in Imperial Russia without a kopek. He would know of course, having been born in penury, the memory of being hungry all too recent. I wondered when exactly Repin had found my father so sympathetic. His play struck me as simply revolting. Not surprisingly, the church thought so too, and our father was promptly excommunicated. Or rather, as the many statements Papa released to the press made clear, it was *he* who was renouncing the church, not the other way round. In fact, he went further by stating that in his will he expressly forbade any member of the church from visiting when he lay dying.

And there was Repin. Despite earlier doubts, and reservations as to his politics, I felt a joyful, confidence in, and a resurgence of love for my one-time teacher. And to feed our love, one morning, I wandered into the kitchen to bring him something delicious to have with his coffee.

"It won't work," grumbled Olga Feodova. Her back was to me, but she dropped a pan on the table from such a height that I not only jumped at the sound, but to avoid its sticky contents from spilling over me. Taking a corner of the voluminous shawl that draped to her knees, she used it to wipe the table, her face and then her hands.

"Why ever not?" I wasn't sure what surprised me more, the ferocity of her tone or her lack of hygiene. "You don't like him? Is that what you're trying to say?" Despite appearing not to care, I valued Olga's opinion very much and it had never occurred to me that she wouldn't love Repin as much as I did.

There was an aggressive shrug which now sent the fringe of her shawl into a custard she was boiling on the range. Sucking her teeth, she moved the pan away from the heat.

"Olga Feodova?" My stomach clenched. "You don't like him?"

"He's Ukrainian." Bang. Bang.

Having left the custard to cool, she began preparing a dish that involved pulverizing juniper berries and black pepper. With every twist of the hand, the veins in her wrist deepened in colour until they were as purple as the berries. Pepper in Russian derived from the word 'feathery' but there was nothing light about her touch as the mixture flew around the kitchen. More seemed to be landing on her feet than in the bowl.

"I am well aware," I said pleasantly. "He was born in the Kharkiev region. His father was a Cossack."

"Cossack!" she spat. "Maybe you mean peasant!"

I held her gaze. I didn't like to remind her of the condition to which she herself was born. Nor more besides. Olga may not have been able to read but she could see and if nothing else, Repin's reputation as a painter had been made by championing the plight of the peasant. Not only that, he and others like him encouraged ordinary people to revel in their beautiful countryside, to enjoy it and be proud. The Wanderers had then made these paintings available to all. Even Olga could have viewed art previously available to only a handful of nobles at the Imperial Court. I felt my cheeks redden with indignation.

"Repin's father was a Cossack and then he sold horses. We've been through this." Several times!

"Even worse. Gypsy," she snorted. "Always peasant."

"Olga Feodova," I said stiffly feeling that this might be our first real quarrel. "Ilya's father gave twenty-seven *years* to the military. His mother was a teacher. If he's a peasant, then we all are. Besides, Repin says it is the peasant that is judging now. So, it follows that he or she be represented."

Olga snorted. Alarmed, I handed her my own handkerchief which she ignored, happily wiping her nose with the same shawl that had already seen such action.

"Do you think my life has changed? With all the big words?" She looked at me pointedly. I knew she meant my father. "Or pictures?" With which she obviously meant Ilya. "What has either done for me? How exactly am *I* represented?"

Well, you are a free woman for one thing, I wanted to say. Your life *has* changed. You are at liberty to go. And you haven't been listening. For a time, yours was the *only* face The Wanderers painted.

"You work very hard, Olga Feodova," I said sincerely. "You have saved this family on more than one occasion. We could not do without you."

"I do it for your mother," she said momentarily appeased. But then she grimaced. Her eyes grew smaller, as she scratched her head with a floury hand so that her grey hair turned white and the bands of material flapping round her head looked like a metropolitan's headdress. "No one else."

I was quiet as I always was when reminded of my mother and only a little miffed that Olga didn't hold our mother's children in equal regard.

I took a pot of coffee from the range. The food of love would have to wait. And as much as I was salivating at the aroma of apple and cinnamon, I didn't want to antagonize Olga further by asking to cut into a freshly baked loaf.

"What is it that you don't like exactly?" I persisted, my back to the kitchen door. "You don't like his pictures? Is that it? They were much darker before, I agree, but The Wanderers are painting with a lighter palette, more muted. And Repin himself…"

"Repin what?"

"Repin is going…in a different direction," I finished lamely.

Olga made a face. "The only direction he should be going is away. Far away." She cupped her hands together to make the silhouette of a bird in the way she used to when we were children.

"Very funny, Olga Feodova. I still don't understand why you're so pessimistic."

"Not pessimistic. Just honest. It will never work," she repeated.

"So, you keep saying."

Olga bent down to take a smetannik from the oven. It was a layer cake made with persimmons and baked in a deep pan. It was one of my favourites. She stood up breathless with the exertion. "It's very simple my clever Tatyana Tolstaya," she said assessing her baking. "It will never work because your blood is blue, and his is red."

*

While Repin painted his pretty, French-inspired scenes, seemingly having given up on travelling any distance at all with his paintings (despite being a member of The Association of Travelling Artists), I returned to my love of portraiture, painting whatever face, either remembered or otherwise, was presented to me. I kept a vivid record of all our visitors, provided I found their features memorable enough. I painted Chekov, Rachmaninoff and Rimsky-Korsakov. I painted Masha (many times), my mother, the dressmaker, Verochka the footman, and the eight peasants who were digging the garden of the lower pond.

And in the morning, and at the end of the day, there was always Repin 'presenting his shadow to my sightless view…' Once our work for the day was completed, we would saunter through the French doors of the small dining room to the terraced lawns of the gardens below. Lying in the tall grass, our bodies touching, we would talk of our future. And our departure.

One evening, the park around us suddenly came to life with glow worms twinkling in the tall grass. Repin reached out and holding two of them against my ears, smiled, "You see, Kotchka, I always promised you, emerald ear-rings!"

Only I couldn't see how they sparkled in the evening light with a brightness no emerald truly possessed. He was distracted by the shadows he said that danced on my jaw line. He mused at how difficult it would be to capture such translucency in painting. Except that I knew he already had. I took his hand and held it against my cheek and when he kissed me, it was as tender as it was deep and long. I wondered how I could ever have doubted his love and thought it was only that I had spent so many months alone in the Moscow house, with no one really to talk to.

"When will we leave?" I asked him then.

"Soon, Tanyushka, soon," he said his lips flicking from my forehead to the tip of my nose. "Look, who's impatient now?" he added smiling.

It was true. I had altered from wanting to leave alone (in my moments of impatience with him), to being eager to start afresh, together. And while I was much enjoying my painting, I knew too that I needed a different impetus. We were both stagnating. I didn't feel that Repin's new passion for the Impressionist movement was sufficiently challenging, while I was indulging a talent that came easily to me. If I wasn't careful, however, it might be the summit of my achievement.

"Do you think my mother could have been happy with Arkady?" I asked as his lips moved down my neck and his fingers began to unbutton my muslin blouse. "I mean in the way we are?"

Repin shrugged against my skin. "I thought they were," he said. "I don't know what happened between them."

"A misunderstanding?"

"Perhaps." His lips were more insistent, but I was transfixed by the clouds chasing each other along an expanse of sky as wide as the Steppes.

"They seemed so happy that night, do you remember when he came to dinner and my mother wore the Russian headdress and Masha and her cat were drunk on champagne?"

It all seemed such a long time ago. *I* had thought them happy. I had been confused by their intimacy, aware that somehow my mother no longer loved my father but the ebullience of her love for Arkady was promising, enveloping us all in its joyfulness. The glow worms, not Repin, tickled my ear lobe.

"Yes, I remember," said Repin his voice muffled against my stomacher.

"Maybe it was the baby…"

"Tanya!" He sat up exasperated running a hand through his hair, his heels digging into the grass.

"Well, it must have seemed like a romantic idea but when it came to it–why, what is it?"

He was shaking his head in bemusement. "Tanya, Tanya," said Repin.

"You don't think they were in love at all?" I sat up propping myself on one elbow feeling my 'ear-ring' drop to my shoulder.

"I don't frankly care one way or another."

"Repin!"

"Look, when a man wants to make love to his girl it's off putting–correction–it's *extremely* off putting to see her staring at the sky and chattering on ignoring him!"

"But the sky's so beautiful!"

"Yes, but it will be here later and tomorrow and the day after."

"But not quite like it is just now and–"

"Tanya!"

"Repin."

I sat up turning away from him and he in turn, frustrated, ran a hand through his hair and groped for a cigarette. As part of his Gallic craze, he had given up his pipe. It had suddenly occurred to me while staring at the wonderful sky with its bundles of diaphanous, billowing clouds that the problem I was suddenly facing and one that pride had stopped me from identifying earlier, was boredom. Almost gone was the memory of those cold, hunger filled days in the house at Khamovniki or the straightforward tedium of keeping my mother occupied when she had finally decided to get better. Gone too was the challenge of engaging Repin or re-engaging Repin and holding his attention and now that I had, and did, the hours, the days and the weeks ahead seemed devoid of genuine purpose. I fiddled with the braid that hung down one shoulder. I had threaded it with blades of grass and wildflowers.

"Repin," I said again tentatively, voicing what had been, I realized then, a growing rumble of suppressed desire over the past months. "What if we had a child?"

Repin, inhaling on his hastily rolled cigarette, was studying a glow worm as it inched its way along his waistcoat.

"Why do you always call me Repin? Not Ilya?" he said. "It makes me feel very old."

I smiled happily. "You were my teacher before becoming my lover. It's become a habit."

But Repin wasn't interested in my answer. "See how the fine lines splay out towards the light," he was saying, completely absorbed by the ongoing challenge of recreating such sinuous strokes on canvas. "Look, it's as fine as an El Greco lace cuff or a priest's vestments. Vermeer at a push but I've not yet seen the Impressionists do this."

"*Repin!*"

"I think your mama is finally over her loss," he said carefully cupping the glow worm in both hands, his cigarette dangling from the corner of his mouth.

"I wasn't talking about my mother," I said tersely. "I said, what if *we* had our own child?"

Repin spat out the cigarette, or rather the cigarette was propelled from his mouth onto the dry, summer-drenched grass so that small sparks spluttered, threatening to singe my bare toes. Repin swore and jumped up stamping out the flames and then hopping up and down cursing in discomfort.

"It was only an idea," I said crossly drawing my knees up to my chin, the familiar, sinking feeling chasing away the closeness and harmony with which our afternoon had begun.

"It's more than an idea," replied Repin when he could speak again.

"Don't you want children then? I mean *ever*?"

"Certainly," said Repin flicking ash from his trouser leg. He sat down carefully beside me on a cool patch of grass and stared ahead of him. "When I meet the right person, I'll marry them in a heartbeat."

There was a moment's silence, a stunned silence on my part. "I thought you had," I said quietly, hardly above a whisper.

Repin in the process of flexing a leg caught my expression. "Oh, I didn't mean–" he said quickly.

"What did you mean then, exactly? You said 'when.'" I heard the tightness in my voice as if from a great distance, as if the hurt that shot through it belonged to someone else.

"I have, of course," he said hastily. "It's just that we haven't known each other so very long. We have to be absolutely certain it's what we want. I mean obviously we're happy. " Once again, he caught my expression. "But children, although a joy are also problematic. And then there's my income. I don't earn a great deal. Oh, I admit that recently things have been much better, but I work on commission as you know and my jobs come in fits and starts. I have commitments to The Wanderers. More importantly, we haven't left the country yet." He made a feeble attempt at humour. "You might run off with a dashing young Frenchman the minute we arrive in Paris. You may decide that I'm too old after all."

Nice little speech.

"Too old for what?"

"You know what I mean."

"I don't actually."

Repin tried again. "You've seen that not all stories have happy endings."

I began putting on my shoes. "It depends on where you stop the story though, doesn't it?"

Repin made a small grimace. "It does but certainly with your mother–"

"Do *not* bring her into this!" I said, the corners of my eyes smarting with unwanted tears. It was my turn to be irritated. Nothing he said now could make up for that automatic response. 'When I meet the right person...'

"You said when..."

"Yes, but...Look, I wouldn't be talking about moving to Rome or Paris if I didn't want to be with you..."

"Be with me, yes," I said bitterly unable to bite back the words. "Marry me, no."

Repin turned to me at last. "Is that what you want?" he said smoothly, his look devoid of any affection.

My heart was pounding, and the palms of my hands were suddenly clammy. I wiped them on the grass. I felt myself colouring. Now that we were talking about it, I wasn't at all sure. I had thought I was. What I knew as he talked was what I *didn't* want and that was to be proposed to, if that's what might happen, in this way. I wanted to be wanted for me. Above all others...I didn't want to stumble into something we might regret. I was doubtful only because he was.

"I don't know."

"Well, then."

He tried to take my hand, but my fingers were unyielding. My heart, my thoughts were as limp as my limbs and I was suddenly cold in the warm sunshine. He had said 'when.' There was no going back from that. There was no re-writing his initial response. I was not the one. Slowly I finished buttoning my shoes and removed the glow worms from my ears. I wasn't sure if it was the light or not, but they no longer seemed to shine as brightly. Repin released his grip.

"Oh, don't be like that!" he said crossly. "Don't be angry."

"I'm not," I said stiffly.

"You are."

Not.

I looked at him, trying *not* to remember how gullible I'd been, how my heart had flipped at the slightest compliment or endearment. How tender moments had made me feel close. Had any of it meant *anything*? I considered the lazy eye, the high cheekbones, the way he sometimes turned his head, owl-like when aroused or captivated. I knew every inflection of his voice, every shading of his face and unseeing as I had been during that very first lesson, I could have painted his portrait quite accurately. And accurately too, there would have been a dimension to this picture that would not have been there before. The lips would show just a hint of weakness, the eyes shifting ever so slightly, shying from the light, from the truth. I clenched my jaw, clamping out the hurt.

"Don't worry," I said coolly. "I don't want children either. I just needed to know."

Repin breathed an obvious sigh of relief.

"I thought so," he said happily. "You'll see, Tanya. We'll have a wonderful time when we get to Europe. A child would only slow us down. There's so much to see and do and learn. And you're so young! So... so...gifted!"

I allowed an insincere smile to flicker on my lips. My precious talent...was becoming a curse.

"Besides," he added as if it had only just occurred to him. "You're so young, you can have a child whenever you choose. You can afford to wait."

But I wanted one then. That was the truth of it. From one day to the next, I had been overcome with a visceral desire, a longing for something of my own. I wanted to start again, with Repin and with a child. Or at least that's what I *had* wanted when he hung the glow worm earrings from my earlobes. Why was it that we seemed to see-saw from one searing emotion to the other? Was it that we cared too much? Or too little?

Repin had begun to walk on ahead of me, his heavy feet pounding the delicate grassland. For the first time I noticed how he barely lifted his feet when he walked, as if he were wearing mules. There were hundreds of small things that were beginning to irritate me about him. I noticed for example, how the charm that I had thought natural and ingenious was contrived and rehearsed. His voice could soften and modulate at will, depending on his audience.

I glared at his retreating back, hating myself for wanting him so much. I felt the glow worms in the pocket of my dress sheltering in the warm corners of linen flex. Could I really follow Repin to Europe and did I love him enough to live with him if there was to be no promise of marriage? What was I prepared to give up to be with him? Once, I'd been prepared to give up everything. Could I really walk out of this house and never look back? Why did he make me so bad-tempered?

23

In the end, as they so often are, all doubts and questions were settled by events that had been quietly gathering momentum all the while Repin and I made plans to go away. It wasn't just he and I who had been busy though. Mama published a collection of illustrated poems. There were delicate watercolours of herbs in the most delicious hues of pink and purple, primroses in the palest yellow and leaves in every shade of green. She revealed a plant life at Yasnaya that I had no idea existed. Nor had I any idea that she could paint so beautifully. Encouraged by its positive reception, she was now working on a novel called *Groans*. It's sub-title, *A Tired Woman* made me wonder however, if she wasn't regressing in terms of her recuperation.

Following in Papa's footsteps, Sergei didn't marry the mother of his child but a would-be opera singer (a much worse outcome it turned out in our parents' eyes) and had gone to live with her Vladivostok. And Masha, quiet mouse-like Masha who I had thought was spending her time playing the piano and looking for morels, suddenly announced that she wanted to go back to Moscow. To be with our father no less. How was it that we failed to see that she was growing up? How could *I* have missed it? She, who had been my second shadow when she was little. But then there was so much that was just there under the surface, that had escaped me, or perhaps I had simply chosen to ignore.

For now, as I traipsed behind Repin to the house, I was so absorbed by my thoughts that I hadn't noticed a peasant from Tula waiting patiently in the hall. But Olga Feodova had. In between trying to prevent Mama from strolling to the lake (for obvious reasons), she tried to shoo the poor man away. It was a brave man indeed who could stand up to Olga Feodova as she pounced on him half dragging him from the porch.

"Like uncut dogs!" The man covered his ears to ward of the blows that rained down on him. "I'm just the messenger! Why is it that it's always the messenger who is to blame?"

"Olga Feodova," intervened Repin alarmed at the ferocity with which the poor man was being attacked. "What on earth are you doing? Can't you see he's from the Post?"

Olga grunted, snatching an envelope from the unfortunate man's hand before kicking him in the backside.

"Thank you," said Repin smoothly. When he realised that the letter was in fact addressed to him, he ripped it open with an elaborate gesture.

Olga's expression changed in response to Repin's groan as the telegram slipped from his fingers. I bent down to pick it up and on straightening, caught a glint in Olga's eye, a look that seemed to say, 'don't say I didn't warn you!'

Repin had gone white, a muscle clenching in his cheek.

"Who is Konstantin?" I said puzzled. Repin snatched the telegram from me but not before I had scanned the few lines. It would appear that a certain Konstantin Yaklovich had been killed by marauders on the estate of one Natasha Repina. "And who is Natasha?" It sounded terrible, a brutal home invasion, but what did it have to do with Repin? Unless... "Is Natasha your...sister-in-law?" I asked wanting to appear intelligent, insightful and then adjusting my tone to reflect the gravity of the situation added, "I'm so sorry my dear. I don't understand the violence that is happening in the countryside. Is it because, is it because of the...*pogroms*?"

At Easter, Jews had been massacred in Kishinev and there had been a mutiny on the battleship Potemkin. I knew that my voice had risen in panic. Something about all this wasn't right. Not by a long shot but I couldn't quite put my finger on it. I cast out blindly for ideas.

"Is it the *Czar*?"

Papa's *I cannot be Silent* had just been published, a plea to the Czar personally to intervene and end the violence.

Just as quickly it was banned, of course, though I knew it had circulated anyway.

Somewhere, out of the corner of my eye, I was aware of my mother sinking onto a low chair, making herself as small as possible. Once again, she appeared to be looking for that favourite spot of hers in the middle distance. She had taken off her sun hat though, which must have been some comfort to Olga Feodova. Repin continued to change colour faster than the impending sunset and Olga Feodova, for once had gone very quiet.

"No," said Repin hardly above a murmur.

"No?"

I looked again at the telegram. It had been sent from Gaspra, West of Yalta in the Crimea.

"No, what?"

"No, Natasha is not my sister-in-law," said Repin.

Well, that was a relief...I had envisioned Repin having to leave us to fly to the bosom of his family.

"Well, whoever she is, I'm still sorry for your loss."

My mother said something about vodka which was surprising. What was not, was that Olga Feodova ignored the instruction, stubbornly refusing to move. Even Masha thought it best to drop the subject of leaving and went to hunker down at Mama's feet.

"Well, start with Konstantin," I said shakily because at that moment I think I must have known and was playing for time. "Who is he, may God rest his soul?"

Olga Feodova crossed herself elaborately, her eyes having disappeared completely in the back of her head.

"Konstantin was my brother-in-law," said Repin his voice breaking. "I was very fond of him. He was a good friend. A fellow Populist–" Olga's eyes flew open at this. Repin had just confirmed her worst fears about the student revolutionaries who had wanted to link their lives with those of the peasants. Instead of being embraced by them, they were regarded with suspicion and reported to the authorities. Or worse. Clearly.

"It must have been–" My pleasantry had been automatic, without thought but now the words would not come, were stifled just as my brain tried to process the unwelcome news, to protect and cushion my heart. Olga Feodova and my mother faded from my peripheral vision and only Repin and I were left face to face. Intimate strangers nothing more.

"I don't understand. Do you have a sister? Was Konnie..." I giggled at the nickname that slipped out. And then gasped at what I'd said. After all the poor man was dead...

"Oh, for God's sake," said Masha from behind Mama's skirts. "Even I know this! Natasha is Ilya's *wife*."

"Common-law," corrected Repin.

I looked from my sister to Ilya. "How," I said through my teeth, enunciating every vowel. "How. Can. That. Be?"

Masha rolled her eyes. Olga's bored into mine. From being tiny currants embedded in her face, they were now huge orbs glistening with emotion. It was as if they could speak and were saying, 'See! See! See!'

With glee, glee, glee.

"Well, I have a *legitimate* wife called Vera. Natasha is my–"

My knees began to buckle, and it was only with the greatest effort that I stopped myself collapsing. *Vera*! Who on earth was Vera? It was bad enough hearing about *Natasha*! It wasn't possible. How could this revered artist have not one but *two* wives? It just couldn't be. My heart did a tumble while my mind flung an astringent gauze over my emotions. Were all men like this? Like my father and Sergei? Was there never to be any hope for women who truly loved? I took a deep breath.

"So, Ilya," I said coldly. The use of his forename startled Repin I knew, but I wanted to remind him of the tenderness we had once shared. "Let me understand this correctly. Are you saying that you have more than one?"

Repin ran a hand through his hair, hair that I noticed for the first time was thinning dramatically. He looked much older all of a sudden and far less attractive. An old man. More importantly, someone else's husband.

"Well, only one wife from whom I am not divorced. Look, surely you knew?" he said. "I mean it's no secret. Everyone knows about her, them and..." He shook his head and then looked at me squarely, unflinchingly. "With all due respect, Tanya, it's not as if *I* am not known. I have a certain fame."

Olga gave a loud snort and taking a flask of vodka from her apron pocket handed it to my mother who, to my astonishment, didn't flinch before putting it to her lips. In fact, the exchange bore all the hallmarks of an established ritual between them. I hesitated not at all before snatching the flask from them both.

Bones of the saints. Blin. Like uncut dogs. After a rain on Thursday. He was right of course. How could I *not* have known? How? Except that in my defence, due to an absence of domestic staff at the house at Khamovniki, that usual conduit of gossip and unreliable information had been denied me. The papers were rightly concerned with the general political unrest during a year Repin called one 'of disaster and shame.' When soldiers fired into a crowd of demonstrators in front of the Winter Palace, his fury had been palpable. It was also true that his fame had been growing at an incredible rate. He was perhaps the best-known painter in the country, certainly the first European to attain fame depicting Russian themes. He was as famous as my father. It was as if, like my father, he had taken personal responsibility for the injustices of the common people and for the future of our country.

But. And there was the 'but'. There was the awful realization that really, in that context I had meant nothing. That he hadn't intended anything in what he'd promised about a future together, a life together, least of all painting together. My heart was a shattered stone, my thoughts black in a tunnel of pain. Coagulating blood blocked my eardrums. I listened but didn't hear, I heard but could not listen.

"I thought you knew. Right from the start..." His words became scrambled, making no sense at all. I heard snippets of 'common-law wife', and 'children' (there appeared to be several of all ages and by different women–no wonder he wasn't keen on anymore!) and being free and loving in the moment, *for* the moment. And while love was love, and very pleasant of course, he was only ever really motivated by his art, the pursuit of new techniques that would give his work depth and fullness. My father and him both.

"So, I must go to her…"

The alcohol–probably Olga's own special recipe–ripped through by belly. My entire body felt on fire.

Of course, you must.

Though as I well knew, it wasn't a case of simply 'going'. Reaching the Crimea from Yasnaya, involved a carriage ride to Tula, a train-ride southeast to Kursk and Kharkov and finally on to (although by no means journey's end) Sevastopol. From there, a boat ferried passengers to the Black Sea and Gaspra.

Gaspra? It was then that there was some clarity in the fog of disbelief. Gaspra? Sometimes written Haspra. The very name sounded like a sigh…an expression of longing…Yes. I remembered now. Sea and mountains were the backdrop to a palace surrounded by lawns and a park. In fact, Papa had stayed there once when he was recovering from malaria. At first, he'd been appalled by the opulence, writing to Mama about pink marble staircases and tinkling fountains. A period of convalescence that had extended from six weeks to half a year. It was luxury on a scale he said he'd never before experienced. But clearly, even good socialists like Ilya and my father were not immune to feather mattresses. And the quilting that came with.

"Countess Panina," I said pensively, almost dreamily. "Is Natasha's given name."

Ilya started. "You know her then?"

If Ilya and my father were famous for their artistic endeavours, Countess Natasha Panina was famed throughout Russia for her fabulous wealth and philanthropy. Her husband, who was much older than her, was rumoured to be homosexual. Which probably explained things from her perspective. I looked at Repin as the world around me shook itself down, fragments of emotion, dissected memories

242

settling into place. Panina was Repin's wife? Certainly not common. There was nothing common about this countess-comrade, later first woman Minister for Education before being arrested. It beggared belief. I was doubly jealous. How could I, a mere girl, compete with a woman of her stature?

I sank onto a window seat. The truth, painful as it was to accept, was that I was never in the running. There was never any competition.

"Yes, you must go," I said faintly. And with those words there was stillness, a sweet teardrop of calm. For what else was there to say? Anger and shock had dissolved and, in their wake, came tranquillity.

Had I always known, deep down, that my story and Repin's would have a clear but separate ending? I think I must have. We were never really in tune at the same time. Either his painting was going well and mine was not or the other way round. Either he loved me (after a fashion) and I did not. And when I did, when I was ready to commit...

Repin, distracted, mentally already halfway to Yalta, glanced at me only briefly before bounding up the stairs to pack his things.

There was total silence, no chiming grandfather clock to mark the moment, no tinkling piano, no scratch behind the walls from some errant creature. No serfs in the fields, no protests from the gate, no Olga Feodova who had crept away, the desire to gloat having completely vanished.

Just my beating heart in its agony.

*

"Come here, darling child," said my mother after a very long time. After I'd stopped crying, after thinking myself resilient, after giving vent to uncontrollable rage and throwing an Imperial Porcelain dish, after the door had closed, and long long after the horses' hooves held in the echo of memory, had trip-trapped down the drive.

I had forgotten she was still in her chair.

243

In the twilight, I saw her not as she had become but as she was when I was very small, when she was still young herself and lovely. She held out her arms and I went to her, the only place that I wanted to be.

24

And so it was, that even greater events overtook us, submerging our turbulent domestic drama in a sea of oblivion. The revolution that rumbled in the distance across pleasant valleys and along the Voronka river, that took hold of peoples connecting Moscow to Kiev, to the Caucasus and Crimea, found its way to our very gates. Closer still. It wasn't only Natasha's brother who was killed by marauders, but countless others even before revolution and civil war really took hold. And with it, everything changed. The life that we knew; that tranquil slow-paced sometimes monotonous life, was gone forever. The memory of servants waiting at table in tailcoats seemed as fantastical as what followed. It seemed incredible to remember a time when we gathered on the verandah to enjoy tea from the enormous samovar, to eat cherries and then to sew or read. All to talk and while away the time, the ebb and flow of cordiality and courtesy as predictable as the Tyrolean clock we had left behind.

Not much later, it would be my little sister Masha, not Repin, who would go to America. There, she would carry on Papa's teachings and devote the rest of her life to Tolstoyan causes. In an even quirkier twist of fate, she would go on to set up the Tolstoy Foundation with the help of no other than Natasha Panina. And I would never see either of them again. But there were many others who would stay behind. Arkady for all his sophistication turned out to be a true Russian at heart, unable when the moment presented itself to leave the country he loved. Mama saw him once at the railway station in St. Petersburg. In much the same way Vronsky first sees Anna Karenina, Mama glimpsed Arkady in a cloud of steam and through a railway carriage going the other way. He did not see her.

Papa and Mama enjoyed a final pas de deux, if you can call it that. Papa returned to Yasnaya only to leave again, to finally attempt to live the life whose enticing mirage had taunted him for so long. But he didn't get very far and died of pneumonia in a waiting room at Astapovo railway station. It struck me as supremely ironic, that the momentous occasions of our lives whether real or fictitious, should take place among locomotives.

Astonishingly, given the atrocities carried out elsewhere, the Bolsheviks in honouring Papa's memory, permitted Mama to continue living on the estate. She was left the house in Papa's will and her beloved orchard, but the land and fields and cottages were all transferred to the peasants.

Repin did travel to Paris but he went alone before joining Natasha in Geneva. He also visited the Tyrol. I wonder if he bought a clock. And then to my surprise, I learned that he had acquired land in a village called Kuokkala where he built his own estate. Eccentric it was too, by all accounts. This strange house had a pyramidal lantern roof, a multi-coloured Egyptian-style music kiosk and an avenue of trees. I like to think fashioned on our very own at Yasnaya Polyana. In the great duchy of Russia, the Finnish village (later re-named Repina) was only an hour's train journey from St. Petersburg.

From memory and saved sketches, Repin painted more portraits of Papa than any other painter. Ranging from formal oils, to watercolours of Papa reading under a tree, they are all unquestionably Lev Tolstoy. My favourite is the one where he is barefoot, hands hooked through his belt, a book in the pocket of his peasant's smock. Like him, Repin became a vegetarian. Later, he published his impressions of the great man. In turn, my father said that Repin's life was devoted to 'approaching the light to which we all aspire.' Critics, looking for signposts to better understand his art, often concluded that his (like my father's) was a constant search for truth. That he was influenced by the dramatic conflicts of the age.

If that was the case, I wondered why he bothered to leave. Hadn't we already provided enough drama to last a lifetime? When the revolution broke out, Finland declared its independence. When its border closed with Russia, Repin remained in Kuokkala though he did not refrain from voicing his dismay at the bloodshed, using his brush to express his deep sentiments.

And Repin and I? Well, we were never together in the end, not in the conventional sense anyway. But if you look closely, I am everywhere and always with him in every painting he ever painted. Mine is the face of the young child in the drawing of a Red Army soldier stealing bread. It is the young girl on a tree branch in 'Dragonfly', the older woman in 'Celebration of the New Constitution'.

And I like to think that it is he and I in 'What Freedom,' a man and a woman together, arms outstretched to the heavens, joyous and free.

Printed in Great Britain
by Amazon

10391689R00142